For Debby
Christmas Season, 1995

Numbers in the Dark

and Other Stories

The Baron in the Trees
Cosmicomics
Difficult Loves
If on a Winter's Night a Traveler
Invisible Cities
Italian Folktales
Marcovaldo
Mr. Palomar
The Nonexistent Knight & the Cloven Viscount
The Road to San Giovanni
Six Memos for the Next Millennium
Under the Jaguar Sun
The Uses of Literature
The Castle of Crossed Destinies
t zero
The Watcher and Other Stories

Numbers in the Dark

and Other Stories

Italo Calvino

Translated from the Italian
by Tim Parks

PANTHEON BOOKS

NEW YORK

All rights reserved under International and Pan-American
Copyright Conventions. Published in the United States by Pantheon Books,
a division of Random House, Inc., New York. Originally published in Italy
as *Primal che tu dica "Pronto"* by Arnoldo Mondadori Editore, Milan, in 1993.
Copyright © 1993 by Palomar S.r.l.e., Arnoldo Mondadori S.p.A., Milano.
This translation first published by Jonathan Cape, London.

Library of Congress Cataloging-in-Publication Data

Calvino, Italo.
[Primal che tu dica "Pronto". English]
Numbers in the dark: and other stories / Italo Calvino;
translated from the Italian by Tim Parks.
p. cm.
ISBN 0-679-44205-7
1. Parks, Tim. II. Title.
PQ4809.A45P713 1995
853'.914—dc20 95-24359 CIP

Manufactured in the United States of America

First American Edition

246897531

Contents

TALES AND DIALOGUES 1968–1984

Preface

Italo Calvino began writing in his teens: short stories, fables, poetry and plays. The theatre was his first vocation and perhaps the one that he spent most time on. There are many surviving works from this period which have never been published. Calvino's extraordinary capacity for self-criticism and self-referential analysis soon led him to give up the theatre. In a letter to his friend Eugenio Scalfari written in 1945 he announces laconically, 'I've switched to stories.' Written in capitals and covering a whole page the news must have been important indeed.

From then on there was never a period when Calvino was not writing. He wrote every day, wherever he was and in whatever circumstances, at a table or on his knee, in planes or hotel rooms. It is not surprising therefore that he should have left such a huge amount of work, including innumerable stories and fables. In addition to those he brought together in various collections, there are many which only appeared in newspapers and magazines, while others remained unpublished.

The texts collected in this volume – unpublished and otherwise – are just some of those written between 1943 – when the author was still in his teens – and 1984.

Some pieces were initially planned as novels but later became stories, a process that was not unusual with Calvino, who reworked a number of sections from an unpublished novel, *The White Schooner*, for his *Collected Stories* of 1958.

1

Other pieces in this present volume came in response to specific requests: 'Glaciation', for example might never have been written if a Japanese distillery producing, amongst other things, a whisky which is extremely successful in the Far East, had not decided to celebrate their fiftieth anniversary by commissioning stories from some well-known European writers. There was only one condition: that an alcoholic drink of some kind should be mentioned in the text. 'Glaciation' first appeared in Japanese before being published in Italian. Another story with a curious history is 'The Burning of the Abominable House'. There had been a somewhat vague request from IBM: how far was it possible to write a story using the computer? This was in 1973 in Paris when it wasn't easy to gain access to data processing equipment. Undaunted, Calvino gave the project a great deal of his time, carrying out all the operations the computer was supposed to do himself. The story was finally published in the Italian edition of *Playboy*. Calvino didn't really feel this was a problem, though he had originally planned for it to be published in *Oulipo* as an example of *ars combinatoria* and a challenge to his own mathematical abilities.

As far as the stories that open this collection are concerned, almost all previously unpublished and very short – Calvino referred to them as *raccontini*, little stories – it may be useful to know that in a note found amongst his juvenilia and dated 1943, he wrote: 'One writes fables in periods of oppression. When a man cannot give clear form to his thinking, he expresses it in fables. These little stories correspond to a young man's political and social experiences during the death throes of Fascism.' When the times were right, he added – with the end of the war and Fascism, that is – the fable would no longer be necessary and the writer would be able to move on to other things. But the titles and dates of many of the pieces in this collection and of other works not included here suggest that despite these youthful reflections, Calvino did in fact continue to write fables for many years thereafter.

Also included in this volume are one or two pieces, such as 'Water Calling' which, while neither stories nor fables in the strict sense of those words, are now very difficult to find elsewhere and definitely worth the reader's attention.

In other cases, texts that may seem unconnected to the main body of his work are part of projects that Calvino had clearly developed in his mind but did not have time to finish.

Esther Calvino

Fables and Stories

1943-1958

The Man Who Shouted Teresa

I stepped off the pavement, walked backwards a few paces looking up, and, from the middle of the street, brought my hands to my mouth to make a megaphone and shouted towards the top stories of the block: 'Teresa!'

My shadow took fright at the moon and huddled between my feet.

Someone walked by. Again I shouted: 'Teresa!' The man came up to me and said: 'If you don't shout louder she won't hear you. Let's both try. So: count to three, on three we shout together.' And he said: 'One, two, three.' And we both yelled, 'Tereeeesaaa!'

A small group of friends passing by on their way back from the theatre or the café saw us calling out. They said: 'Come on, we'll give you a shout too.' And they joined us in the middle of the street and the first man said one two three and then everybody together shouted, 'Te-reee-saaa!'

Somebody else came by and joined us; a quarter of an hour later there were a whole bunch of us, twenty almost. And every now and then somebody new came along.

Organizing ourselves to give a good shout, all at the same time, wasn't easy. There was always someone who began before three or who went on too long, but in the end we were managing something fairly efficient. We agreed that the 'Te' should be shouted low and long, the 're' high and long, the 'sa' low and short. It sounded great. Just a squabble every now and then when someone was out.

7

We were beginning to get it right, when somebody, who, if his voice was anything to go by, must have had a very freckly face, asked: 'But are you sure she's at home?'

'No,' I said.

'That's bad,' another said. 'Forgotten your key, have you?'

'Actually,' I said, 'I have my key.'

'So,' they asked, 'why don't you go on up?'

'Oh, but I don't live here,' I answered. 'I live on the other side of town.'

'Well then, excuse my curiosity,' the one with the freckly voice asked carefully, 'but who does live here?'

'I really wouldn't know,' I said.

People were a bit upset about this.

'So could you please explain,' somebody with a very toothy voice asked, 'why you are standing down here calling out Teresa?'

'As far as I'm concerned,' I said, 'we can call another name, or try somewhere else. It's no big deal.'

The others were a bit annoyed.

'I hope you weren't playing a trick on us?' the freckly one asked suspiciously.

'What?' I said, resentfully, and I turned to the others for confirmation of my good faith. The others said nothing, indicating they hadn't picked up the insinuation.

There was a moment's embarrassment.

'Look,' someone said good-naturedly, 'why don't we call Teresa one last time, then we'll go home.'

So we did it again. 'One two three Teresa!' but it didn't come out very well. Then people headed off home, some one way, some the other.

I'd already turned into the square, when I thought I heard a voice still calling: 'Tee-reee-sa!'

Someone must have stayed on to shout. Someone stubborn.

The Flash

It happened one day, at a crossroads, in the middle of a crowd, people coming and going.

I stopped, blinked: I understood nothing. Nothing, nothing about anything: I didn't understand the reasons for things or for people, it was all senseless, absurd. And I started to laugh.

What I found strange at the time was that I'd never realized before. That up until then I had accepted everything: traffic lights, cars, posters, uniforms, monuments, things completely detached from any sense of the world, accepted them as if there were some necessity, some chain of cause and effect that bound them together.

Then the laugh died in my throat, I blushed, ashamed. I waved to get people's attention and 'Stop a second!' I shouted, 'there's something wrong! Everything's wrong! We're doing the absurdest things! This can't be the right way! Where will it end?'

People stopped around me, sized me up, curious. I stood there in the middle of them, waving my arms, desperate to explain myself, to have them share the flash of insight that had suddenly enlightened me: and I said nothing. I said nothing because the moment I'd raised my arms and opened my mouth, my great revelation had been as it were swallowed up again and the words had come out any old how, on impulse.

'So?' people asked, 'what do you mean? Everything's in its place. All is as it should be. Everything is a result of something else. Everything fits in with everything else. We can't see anything absurd or wrong!'

And I stood there, lost, because as I saw it now everything had fallen into place again and everything seemed natural, traffic lights, monuments, uniforms, towerblocks, tramlines, beggars, processions; yet this didn't calm me down, it tormented me.

'I'm sorry,' I answered. 'Perhaps it was me that was wrong. It seemed that way. But everything's fine. I'm sorry,' and I made off amid their angry glares.

Yet, even now, every time (often) that I find I don't understand something, then, instinctively, I'm filled with the hope that perhaps this will be my moment again, perhaps once again I shall understand nothing, I shall grasp that other knowledge, found and lost in an instant.

Making Do

There was a town where everything was forbidden.

Now, since the only thing that wasn't forbidden was the game tip-cat, the town's subjects used to assemble on meadows behind the town and spend the day there playing tip-cat.

And as the laws forbidding things had been introduced one at a time and always with good reason, no one found any cause for complaint or had any trouble getting used to them.

Years passed. One day the constables saw that there was no longer any reason why everything should be forbidden and they sent messengers to inform their subjects that they could do whatever they wanted.

The messengers went to those places where the subjects were wont to assemble.

'Hear ye, hear ye,' they announced, 'nothing is forbidden any more.'

The people went on playing tip-cat.

'Understand?' the messengers insisted. 'You are free to do what you want.'

'Good,' replied the subjects. 'We're playing tip-cat.'

The messengers busily reminded them of the many wonderful and useful occupations they had once engaged in and could now engage in once again. But the subjects wouldn't listen and just went on playing, stroke after stroke, without even stopping for a breather.

Seeing that their efforts were in vain, the messengers went to tell the constables.

'Easy,' the constables said. 'Let's forbid the game of tip-cat.'

That was when the people rebelled and killed the lot of them.

Then without wasting time, they got back to playing tip-cat.

Dry River

Well, I was back in the dry river again. For some time I had been residing in a country that wasn't my own where, rather than gradually becoming more familiar, things increasingly appeared to be veiled by unsuspected differences: in their shapes, in their colours and in their reciprocal harmonies. The hills surrounding me now were unlike those I had learnt to know, with delicately rounded declivities, and the fields too and the vineyards followed those soft declivities and the steep terraces likewise, trailing off into gentle slopes. The colours were all new, like the hues of an unknown rainbow. The trees, few and far between, were as if suspended, like small clouds, and almost transparent.

Then I became aware of the air, of how it became concrete as I looked, how it filled my hands as I thrust them into it. And I saw a self that couldn't be reconciled with the world around, rugged and stony as I was inside and with gashes of colour of a vividness that was almost dark, like shouts or laughter. And however hard I tried to put words between myself and the world, I couldn't find any that were suitable to clothe things anew; because all my words were hard and freshly hewn: and saying them was like laying down so many stones.

Again, if some drowsy memory were to form in my mind, it would be of things learnt, not experienced: fantasy landscapes perhaps, seen in the backdrop of old paintings, or perhaps the words of old poets improperly understood.

In this fluid atmosphere I lived, as it were, swimming and felt my rough edges gradually smoothed and myself dissolved, absorbed into it.

But to find myself again, all I had to do was go down to the old dry river.

What prompted me – it was summer – was a desire for water, a religious desire, for ritual perhaps. Climbing down through the vineyards that evening, I prepared myself for a sacred bath and the word water, already synonymous with happiness for me, expanded in my mind like the name now of a goddess, now of a lover.

The temple I found on the valley bottom behind a pale bank of shrubs. It was a great river of white stones, full of silence.

The only remaining trace of water was a stream trickling almost stealthily, to one side. Sometimes the scantness of the flow between big rocks blocking the way and banks of reeds, took me back among well-known streams and conjured memories of narrower harsher valleys.

It was this: and perhaps too the feel of the stones beneath my feet – the time-worn stones of the valley bottom, their backs encrusted with a veil of congealed waterweed – or the being forced to move in jumps, from one rock to another, or perhaps it was just a noise the pebbles made, slithering down the slope.

The fact is that the gap between myself and this land narrowed and composed itself: a sort of brotherhood, a metaphysical kinship bound me to those broken stones, fecund only of shy but tremendously stubborn lichens. And in the old dry river I recognized one of my fathers, ancient, naked.

So, we went along the dry river. He who walked beside me was a companion in fortune, a native of these places, the darkness of whose skin and shaggy hair falling thickly down his back together with the plumpness of the lips and the flat nose, conferred upon him a grotesque appearance as of a tribal leader, Congolese perhaps, or perhaps from the South Seas. This fellow had a proud strapping look about him which showed both in his face, albeit bespectacled, and likewise in his gait, impeded though it was by the clumsy slovenly state of the impromptu bathers we were. Despite being chaste as a quaker in his life, his conversation upon meeting him was like a satyr's. His accent was as breathy and steamy as any I had ever been given to understand: he spoke with his mouth eternally open or full of air, emitting, in a constant and sulphurous outburst, hurricanes of extraordinary insults.

Thus we two climbed up the dry river looking for somewhere where the trickle broadened and we might wash our bodies, filthy and tired as they were.

Now, as we walked along the great womb, it turned in a loop and the background took on a new richness of detail. On high white rocks, an adventure for the eye, sat two, three, perhaps four young ladies in their bathing costumes. Red and yellow costumes — blue too most likely, but this I don't remember: my eyes were in need only of red and yellow — and bathing caps, as though on a fashionable beach.

It was like a cock's crow.

A green thread of water ran nearby and came up to their heels; they crouched down in it to bathe.

We stopped, torn between the pleasure of the sight, the pangs of regret it aroused, and the shame at our now ugly and oafish selves. Then we went on towards them while they considered us without interest and we hazarded a remark or two, trying them out the way you do, the wittiest and the most banal we could manage. My sulphurous companion joined in the game without enthusiasm but with a sort of timid reserve.

In any event, a short while later, tired of the meal we were making of it and the lack of response, we set off walking again, giving free rein to more pleasant exchanges. And the memory, still present to the mind's eye, not so much of their bodies as of their red and yellow costumes was sufficient consolation.

Sometimes a branch of the stream, never deep, would widen to cover the whole river bed; and we, the banks being high and

15

impossible to climb, would cross with our feet in the water. We were wearing light shoes, of canvas and rubber, and the water streamed through them: and when we were back on the dry ground our feet squelched inside at every step, wheezing and splashing.

It grew dark. The white shingle came alive with black spots that leapt: tadpoles.

They must have only just sprouted legs, tiny and tailed as they were, and it was as if they hadn't yet come to terms with this new facility which kept sending them flying up in the air. There was one on every stone, but not for long, since the one would jump and another would take his place. And because their jumps were simultaneous and because while pressing on along the great river one saw nothing but the swarming of that amphibious multitude, advancing like a boundless army, I was struck by a sense of awe, almost as if this black and white symphony, this cartoon sad as a Chinese drawing, were fearfully conjuring the idea of the infinite.

We stopped by a pool of water that seemed to offer sufficient space for us to immerse our entire bodies; even to swim a stroke or two. I went in barefoot, bareskinned: the water was weedy and putrid from the slow decay of river plants. The bottom was slimy and swampy: when you touched it, it sent turbid clouds up to the surface.

But it was water; and it was good.

My companion went down into the water with his shoes and stockings, leaving his spectacles on the bank. Then, not fully aware of the religious aspect of the ceremony, he started soaping himself.

Thus we embarked on that joyful treat washing is when it is rare and hard to come by. The pool, which we could scarcely both fit in, bubbled over with foam and roaring, as though we were elephants bathing.

On the riverbanks there were willows and shrubs and houses with waterwheels; and so unreal were they, in contrast to the concreteness of this water and these stones, that with the grey of evening filtering through they took on the air of a faded arras.

My companion was washing his feet, now, in strange manner: without taking off his shoes but soaping the stockings and shoes on his feet.

Then we dried ourselves and dressed. When I picked up a sock a tadpole jumped out.

Laid on the bank, my companion's glasses must have been thoroughly splashed. And – as he put them on – so gay must the muddle of that world have seemed to him, coloured as it was by the last gleams of the sunset, seen through a pair of wet lenses, that he started to laugh, and to laugh, without letting up and when I asked him why he said: 'It's such a hell of a mess!'

And, neat and tidy now, a warm weariness in our bones to replace the dull tiredness of earlier on, we said farewell to our new river friend and set off along a little track that followed the bank, reasoning upon our own affairs and upon when we would return, and keeping our ears open, alert to the distant sounding of a bugle.

Conscience

Came a war and a guy called Luigi asked if he could go, as a volunteer.

Everyone was full of praise. Luigi went to the place where they were handing out the rifles, took one and said: 'Now I'm going to go and kill a guy called Alberto.'

They asked him who Alberto was.

'An enemy,' he answered, 'an enemy of mine.'

They explained to him that he was supposed to be killing enemies of a certain type, not whoever he felt like.

'So?' said Luigi. 'You think I'm dumb? This Alberto is precisely that type, one of them. When I heard you were going to war against that lot, I thought: I'll go too, that way I can kill Alberto. That's why I came. I know that Alberto: he's a crook. He betrayed me, for next to nothing he made me make a fool of myself with a woman. It's an old story. If you don't believe me, I'll tell you the whole thing.'

They said fine, it was okay.

'Right then,' said Luigi, 'tell me where Alberto is and I'll go there and I'll fight.'

They said they didn't know.

'Doesn't matter,' Luigi said. 'I'll find someone to tell me. Sooner or later I'll catch up with him.'

They said he couldn't do that, he had to go and fight where they sent him, and kill whoever happened to be there. They didn't know anything about this Alberto.

18

'You see,' Luigi insisted, 'I really will have to tell you the story. Because that guy is a real crook and you're doing the right thing going to fight against him.'

But the others didn't want to know.

Luigi couldn't see reason: 'Sorry, it may be all the same to you if I kill one enemy or another, but I'd be upset if I killed someone who had nothing to do with Alberto.'

The others lost their patience. One of them gave him a good talking to and explained what war was all about and how you couldn't go and kill the particular enemy you wanted to.

Luigi shrugged. 'If that's how it is,' he said, 'you can count me out.'

'You're in and you're staying in,' they shouted.

'Forward march, one-two, one-two!' And they sent him off to war.

Luigi wasn't happy. He'd kill people, offhand, just to see if he might get Alberto, or one of his family. They gave him a medal for every enemy he killed, but he wasn't happy. 'If I don't kill Alberto,' he thought, 'I'll have killed a load of people for nothing.' And he felt bad.

Meantime they were giving him one medal after another, silver, gold, everything.

Luigi thought: 'Kill some today, kill some tomorrow, there'll be less of them, that crook's turn is bound to come.'

But the enemy surrendered before Luigi could find Alberto. He felt bad he'd killed so many people for nothing, and since they were at peace now he put all his medals in a bag and went around enemy country giving them away to the wives and children of the dead.

Going around like this, he ran into Alberto.

'Good,' he said, 'better late than never,' and he killed him.

That was when they arrested him, tried him for murder and hanged him. At the trial he said over and over that he had done it to settle his conscience, but nobody listened to him.

Solidarity

I stopped to watch them.

They were working, at night, in a secluded street, doing something with the shutter of a shop.

It was a heavy shutter: they were using an iron bar for a lever, but the shutter wouldn't budge.

I was walking around, going nowhere in particular, on my own. I got hold of the bar to give them a hand. They made room for me.

We weren't pulling together. I said, 'Hey up!' The one on my right dug his elbow into me and said low: 'Shut up! Are you crazy! Do you want them to hear us?'

I shook my head as if to say it had just slipped out.

It took us a while and we were sweating but in the end we levered the shutter up high enough for someone to get under. We looked at each other, pleased. Then we went in. I was given a sack to hold. The others brought stuff over and put it in.

'As long as those skunky police don't turn up!' they were saying.

'Right,' I said. 'They really are skunks!' 'Shut up. Can't you hear footsteps?' they said every few minutes. I listened hard, a bit frightened. 'No, no, it's not them!' I said.

'Those guys always turn up when you least expect it!' one of them said.

I shook my head. 'Kill 'em all, that's what,' I answered.

Then they told me to go out for a bit, as far as the corner, to see if anyone was coming. I went.

Outside, at the corner, there were others hugging the wall, hidden in the doorways, coming towards me.

I joined in.

'Noises from down there, near those shops,' said the one next to me.

I took a look.

'Get your head down, idiot, they'll see us and get away again,' he hissed.

'I was looking,' I explained, and crouched down by the wall.

'If we can circle round without them realizing,' another said, 'we'll have them trapped. There aren't that many.'

We moved in bursts, on tiptoe, holding our breaths: every few seconds we exchanged glances with bright eyes.

'They won't get away now,' I said.

'At last we're going to catch them red-handed,' someone said.

'About time,' I said.

'Filthy bastards, breaking into shops like that!' the other said.

'Bastards, bastards!' I repeated, angrily.

They sent me a little way ahead, to take a look. I was back inside the shop.

'They won't get us now,' one was saying as he slung a sack over his shoulder.

'Quick,' someone else said. 'Let's go out through the back! That way we'll escape from right under their noses.'

We all had triumphant smiles on our lips.

'They're going to feel really sore,' I said. And we sneaked into the back of the shop.

'We've fooled the idiots again!' they said. But then a voice said: 'Stop, who's there,' and the lights went on. We crouched down behind something, pale, grasping each other's hands. The others came into the backroom, didn't see us, turned round. We shot out and ran like crazy. 'We've done it!' we shouted. I tripped a couple of times and got left behind. I found myself with the others running after them.

'Come on,' they said, 'we're catching up.'

And everybody raced through the narrow streets, chasing them. 'Run this way, cut through there,' we said and the others weren't far ahead now, so that we were shouting: 'Come on, they won't get away.'

I managed to catch up with one of them. He said: 'Well done, you got away. Come on, this way, we'll lose them.' And I went along with him. After a while I found myself alone, in an alley. Someone came running round a corner and said: 'Come on, this way, I saw them. They can't have got far.' I ran after him a while.

Then I stopped, in a sweat. There was no one left, I couldn't hear any more shouting. I stood with my hands in my pockets and started to walk, on my own, going nowhere in particular.

The Black Sheep

There was a country where they were all thieves.

At night everybody would leave home with skeleton keys and shaded lanterns and go and burgle a neighbour's house. They'd get back at dawn, loaded, to find their own house had been robbed.

So everybody lived happily together, nobody lost out, since each stole from the other, and that other from another again, and so on and on until you got to a last person who stole from the first. Trade in the country inevitably involved cheating on the parts both of buyer and seller. The government was a criminal organization that stole from its subjects, and the subjects for their part were only interested in defrauding the government. Thus life went on smoothly, nobody was rich and nobody was poor.

One day, how we don't know, it so happened that an honest man came to live in the place. At night, instead of going out with his sack and his lantern, he stayed home to smoke and read novels.

The thieves came, saw the light on and didn't go in.

This went on for a while: then they were obliged to explain to him that even if he wanted to live without doing anything, it was no reason to stop others from doing things. Every night he spent at home meant a family would have nothing to eat the following day.

The honest man could hardly object to such reasoning. He took to going out in the evening and coming back the following

23

morning like they did, but he didn't steal. He was honest, there was nothing you could do about it. He went as far as the bridge and watched the water flow by beneath. When he got home he found he had been robbed.

In less than a week the honest man found himself penniless, he had nothing to eat and his house was empty. But this was hardly a problem, since it was his own fault; no, the problem was that his behaviour upset everything else. Because he let the others steal everything he had without stealing anything from anybody; so there was always someone who got home at dawn to find their house untouched: the house he should have robbed. In any event after a while the ones who weren't being robbed found themselves richer than the others and didn't want to steal any more. To make matters worse, the ones who came to steal from the honest man's house found it was always empty; so they became poor.

Meanwhile, the ones who had become rich got into the honest man's habit of going to the bridge at night to watch the water flow by beneath. This increased the confusion because it meant lots of others became rich and lots of others became poor.

Now, the rich people saw that if they went to the bridge every night they'd soon be poor. And they thought: 'Let's pay some of the poor to go and rob for us.' They made contracts, fixed salaries, percentages: they were still thieves of course, and they still tried to swindle each other. But, as tends to happen, the rich got richer and richer and the poor got poorer and poorer.

Some of the rich people got so rich that they didn't need to steal or have others steal for them so as to stay rich. But if they stopped stealing they would get poor because the poor stole from them. So they paid the very poorest of the poor to defend their property from the other poor, and that meant setting up a police force and building prisons.

So it was that only a few years after the appearance of the honest man, people no longer spoke of robbing and being

24

robbed, but only of the rich and the poor; but they were still all thieves.

The only honest man had been the one at the beginning, and he died in very short order, of hunger.

Good for Nothing

Already high, the sun shone obliquely into the street, lit it con-
fusedly, projecting shadows from the roofs on to the walls of
houses opposite, kindling fancy shop windows in dazzling
gleams, popping out from unsuspected cracks to strike the faces
of people bustling past each other on the crowded pavements.

I first saw the man with the light-coloured eyes at a crossroads, standing or walking, I can't rightly recall: he was getting
nearer and nearer to me, that's for sure, so either I was walking
towards him or vice versa. He was tall and thin, wore a light-
coloured raincoat, and carried a tightly rolled umbrella hanging
neatly from one arm. On his head he had a felt hat, once again
light-coloured and with a wide round brim; immediately beneath
were the eyes, large, cold, liquid, with a strange flicker at the
corners. Thin as he was, with close-cropped hair, it was hard to
tell how old he might be. In one hand he held a book, closed,
but with a finger inside, as if to keep his place.

Immediately, I had the impression that his eyes were upon
me, motionless eyes that took me in from head to toe, that didn't
spare my back either, nor my insides. I looked away at once, but
every few steps as I walked, I felt the urge to dart a glance at him,
and each time I would find him nearer, and looking at me. In the
end he was standing in front of me, an almost lipless mouth on
the point of creasing into a smile. The man pulled a finger from
his pocket, slowly, and used it to point downwards to my feet; it
was then that he spoke, with a thin, rather humble voice.

'I beg your pardon,' he said, 'your shoelace is undone.'

It was true. Trodden and bedraggled, the two ends of the lace dangled at the sides of my shoe. I blushed a little, mumbled a 'Thank you', bent down.

Stopping in the street to tie up a shoe is annoying: especially when you stop as I did in the middle of the pavement, without a step or wall to put my foot on, kneeling on the ground, with people knocking against me. The man with the light-coloured eyes muttered a vague goodbye and went off at once.

But it was destiny that I should meet him again: not a quarter of an hour had passed before once again I found him standing in front of me, looking in a shop window. As soon as I saw him I was seized by an inexplicable urge to turn round and retreat, or better still to pass by as quick as I could, while he was intent on the window, in the hope he wouldn't notice. But no: already it was too late, the stranger had turned, had seen me, was looking at me, had something else he wanted to say to me. I stopped in front of him, afraid. The stranger had an even humbler tone.

'Look,' he said, 'it's undone again.'

I wanted to vanish into thin air. Without answering, I bent down to tie the lace with angry diligence. My ears were singing and I somehow felt the people passing by and knocking against me were the same people as had knocked against me and noticed me the first time, and that they were muttering ironic remarks to themselves.

But the shoe was tied good and tight now and I was walking along with a light sure step. Indeed, with a sort of unconscious pride, I was even hoping I'd run into the stranger again now, to recover my reputation as it were.

Yet no sooner had I taken a turn around the square to find myself a few yards away from him again, on the same pavement, than quite suddenly the pride that had been urging me on was replaced by dismay. For as he looked at me the stranger had an expression of regret on his face, and he came towards me gently shaking his head, as one pained by some natural fact beyond human control.

As I stepped forward, I squinted with apprehension at the guilty shoe; it was still as tightly tied as before. Yet to my dismay the stranger went on shaking his head for a while, then said:

'Now the other is undone.'

I felt the way you do in nightmares when you want to scrub the whole thing out, to wake up. I forced a grimace of rebellion, biting a lip as though to hold back a curse, then started yanking frantically at my laces again, crouched down in the middle of the street. I stood up, cheeks flushed beneath my eyes, and walked off head down, wanting nothing better than to escape the gaze of the crowd.

But the day's torture wasn't over yet: as I toiled home, hurrying, I could feel the loops of the bow slowly slipping over one another, the knot getting looser and looser, the laces very gradually coming undone. At first I slowed down, as though a little care would be enough to sustain the tangle's uncertain equilibrium. But I was still far from home and already the tips of the laces were trailing on the pavement, flopping this way and that. Then my walking became breathless, I was fleeing, as though from a wild terror: the terror that I would yet again come upon that man's inexorable gaze.

It was a small compact town where one went endlessly up and down the same few streets. Walking round it, you'd meet the same faces three or even four times in half an hour. Now I was marching across it as though in a nightmare, torn between the shame of being seen about with my shoelace yet again untied, and the shame of being seen bending down yet again to tie it. Eyes seemed to thicken and throng around me, like branches in a wood. I dived into the first doorway I found, to hide.

But at the back of the porch, in the half-light, hands resting on the handle of his tightly rolled umbrella, stood the man with the light-coloured eyes, and it was as though he were waiting for me.

At first I gaped in amazement, then hazarded something like a smile and pointed to my untied shoe, to stop him.

The stranger nodded with that sadly understanding expression he had.

'That's right,' he said, 'they're both undone.'

If nothing else the doorway was a quieter place to do up a shoelace, and, with a step to rest my foot on, more comfortable too, though standing behind and above me I had the man with the light-coloured eyes watching, missing not one move of my fingers, and I sensed his gaze in amongst them, muddling them up. But after all I'd been through, it didn't bother me any more now; I was even whistling as I tied those damned knots for the *n*th time, but tying them better now, being relaxed.

All would have been well had the man kept quiet, had he not started first to clear his throat, a little uncertainly, then to say all in a rush, with decision:

'I beg your pardon, but you still haven't learnt how to tie your laces.'

I turned to him, red in the face, still crouching down. I ran my tongue between my lips.

'You know,' I said, 'I'm hopeless at tying knots. You wouldn't believe it. As a child I never wanted to make the effort to learn. I take my shoes off and put them on again without untying them. I use a bootjack. I'm hopeless at knots, I get muddled. You wouldn't believe it.'

Then the stranger said something odd, the last thing you would have thought he might want to say.

'So,' he said, 'how will you teach your children, if you have any, to tie their shoes?'

But the strangest part was that I thought this over a moment and then answered, as if I'd already considered the question before and settled it and stored the answer away, somehow expecting that sooner or later someone would ask me.

'My children,' I said, 'will learn from others how to tie their shoes.'

29

Ever more absurd, the stranger came back:

'And if, for example, the great flood should come and the whole of humanity were to perish and you were the one chosen, you and your children, to continue the human race. How would you manage, have you ever thought about that? How would you teach them their knots? Because if you don't, heaven knows how many centuries might go by before humanity manages to tie a knot, to invent it over again!'

I couldn't make head or tail of this now, the knot or the conversation.

'But,' I tried to object, 'why should I of all people be the chosen one, as you put it, why me when I don't even know how to tie a knot?'

The man with the light-coloured eyes was against the light on the threshold of the door: there was something frighteningly angelic in his expression.

'Why me?' he said. 'That's how all men answer. And all men have a knot on their shoes, something they don't know how to do; an inability that binds them to others. Society depends on this asymmetry between people these days: a dovetailing of skills and incompetence. But the Flood? If the Flood came and one needed a Noah? Not so much a just man as a man able to bring along the few things it would take to start again. You see, you don't know to tie your shoes, somebody else doesn't know how to plane wood, someone else again has never read Tolstoy, someone else doesn't know how to sow grain and so on. I've been looking for him for years, and, believe me, it's hard, really hard; it seems people have to hold each other by the hand like the blind man and the lame who can't go anywhere without each other, but argue just the same. It means if the Flood comes we'll all die together.'

So saying he turned and disappeared in the street. I never saw him again and I still wonder whether he wasn't some strange maniac or an angel, for years roving the earth in vain in search of a second Noah.

Like a Flight of Ducks

He woke to the sound of gunfire and jumped down from the plank-bed; in the stampede someone opened the cell doors, his own included. A blond, bearded man appeared, waving a gun; he said: 'Come on, hurry up and get out, you're free.' Natale was glad, though without understanding; he remembered he was naked, in just his T-shirt; he pushed his legs into a pair of military trousers, his only other clothing, cursing because they wouldn't go in.

That was when the man with the stick came in, a good six feet tall; he had one cross eye and with nostrils flared he muttered, 'Where are they? Where are they?' Natale saw the stick when it was already high above his head, coming down on him. It was like a flock of ducks exploding in his brain; a flash of red burned deep in his skull. He fell in a pool of cottonwool, numb to the world.

One of the militiamen who had been in league with them from the beginning, shouted: 'What have you done? He was a prisoner!' Immediately people were fussing round the man on the ground whose head was bleeding. The man with the stick was at a loss: 'How was I to know? With those Fascist trousers he was wearing!'

Now they had to hurry, the Fascist reinforcements might arrive any moment. The thing was to get the machine-guns, the magazines, the bombs, burn the rest, especially the documents; every couple of minutes someone went to say a word to the

31

hostages: 'We're going, are you coming?' But they were in a frenzy: the general was wandering round the cell in his nightshirt. 'I'll get dressed now,' he said. The pharmacist with the anarchist's neckscarf was asking the priest for advice. But the lawyer, a woman, was up and ready.

Then they had to keep an eye on the militiamen they'd taken prisoner, two old men in plus-fours who kept getting in the way talking about their families and children, and the sergeant silent in the corner, his face thick with yellow veins.

In the end the general began to say that they were there as hostages, that they were sure to be freed soon, whereas it was hard to say how things would turn out if they went with the partisan. The lawyer, around thirty and well-endowed, would have liked to join the partisans, but the priest and the pharmacist agreed with the general and they all stayed.

The clock was striking two in the morning when the partisans headed off for the mountains, some one way, some the other, taking the two guards who'd helped them get in, a few boys freed from the cells and the three Fascist prisoners shoved along with machine-guns in their backs. The tall man with the stick wrapped the wounded man's head in a towel and carried him on his back.

They had just slipped out when they heard shooting from the other side of town. It was that idiot Gek, in the middle of the piazza, firing bursts into the air so that the Fascists would run there first and waste time.

At the camp the only disinfectant was sulphonamide cream for leg rashes: to fill the hole Natale had in his head would have taken the whole tube. In the morning two men were sent down for medicine to a doctor evacuated from the town.

Word got around, people were pleased at the night attack on the militiamen's barracks; during the day the partisans had managed to get enough supplies to give him disinfectant douches on his skull and make him a turban of gauze, plasters and bandages. But with eyes closed and mouth open, Natale was still dead to the world, and they couldn't tell if he was groaning or snoring. Then, around that point in his skull still so atrociously alive, colours and sensations gradually began to form, but each time it was a wrench right inside his head, a flight of ducks in his eyes, so that he ground his teeth and muttered something in groans. The next day, Paulin, who was cook, nurse and gravedigger, gave them the good news: 'He's getting better! He cursed!'

After the curses came hunger; he began to pour whole mess tins of minestrone into his belly as if he were drinking it, spilling it all over himself. Then he smiled, with a round blissful animal face, in the midst of bandages and plasters, mumbling something, God knew what.

'What language does he speak?' the others asked, watching him. 'Where is he from?'

'Ask him yourselves,' answered his old prison-mates and the ex-guards. 'Hey, you, where are you from?' Natale half opened his eyes to think, but then let out a groan and went back to grunting things the others couldn't understand.

'Has he gone crazy,' asked the blond man, who was in charge, 'or was he already?' The others weren't sure. 'He certainly got a big crack on the head,' they said. 'If he wasn't crazy before, he is now.'

With his round, flat, black, bottom-of-the-pan face, Natale had been on the move ever since they'd called him up many years before. Unable to read or write, he hadn't heard from home at all. They'd sent him off on leave a few times, but he got on the wrong train and ended up in Turin. After September 8th he'd found himself in the Todt and had gone on wandering around half naked with his mess tin tied to his belt. Then they had put him inside. All of a sudden they came to set him free and hit him over the head with a stick. For him this was perfectly logical, like everything else in his life.

For him the world was a mix of yellows and greens, of noises and shouts, the urge to eat and the urge to sleep. A good world, full of good things, even if you couldn't understand it at all, even if trying to understand it brought on that sharp pain deep inside his skull, that flight of ducks in the brain, the stick that cracked down on his head.

The partisans in the blond man's band were supposed to carry out raids on the town; they lived in the first pine woods above the suburbs, in an area that was all small villas where middle-class families used to spend their summers in the good old days. Given that the area was now under their control, the partisans had come out from their caves and huts and set up camp in a few Fascist leaders' villas, infesting their mattresses with fleas and installing machine-guns on their dressers. There were some bottles in the villas, some stored food, gramophones. Blondie was a tough boy, ruthless with the enemy, despotic with his friends, but he tried to keep his men happy when he could. They threw a few parties, some girls came up.

Natale was happy to be with them. The plasters and bandages had come off now; all that was left of his wound was a big bruise in the middle of his shaggy hair, a bewilderment which he didn't feel came from himself but from all the things around him. The partisans played all kinds of jokes on him but he didn't get angry, he shouted curses in his incomprehensible dialect and that was that. Or he would start wrestling with someone, even with Blondie: he always got the worst of it but was happy just the same.

One evening the partisans decided to play a joke on him: they would get him off with one of the girls and see what happened. They chose Margherita, a tubby girl, soft and fleshy, white and pink. She was game and they began to work on Natale, to put the idea in his head that Margherita was in love with him. But Natale was wary; he wasn't used to this. They all started drinking together and got her to sit next to him, to get him excited. Seeing her making eyes at him, feeling her leg press against his under the table, Natale felt more lost than ever. They left the two alone, watching them from behind the door. He laughed, in a daze. The girl pushed it a bit, provoking him. But then Natale realized that her laugh was false; she was batting her eyelashes. He forgot the stick, the ducks, the bruise: he grabbed her and threw her on the bed. He understood everything perfectly now: he understood what the woman beneath him wanted, white and pink and soft, he understood that it wasn't a game, he understood why it wasn't a game, but something theirs, his and hers, like eating and drinking.

All of a sudden the girl's already bright eyes blinked and turned hard and angry, her arms fought him off, she wriggled to be out from under him, shouting: 'Help, he's on top of me.' The others came in laughing, shouting, and tossed water over him. Then everything went back to how it had been before, that coloured pain right at the bottom of his skull; Margherita smoothing the blouse over her breasts, bursting into strained laughter, Margherita who, already bright-eyed, wet-mouthed, had started shouting and calling the others, he couldn't understand why. And, with all the partisans round him shooting their guns in the air and laughing so hard they rolled about on their beds, Natale burst into tears like a child.

One morning the Germans all woke at once: they came packed in trucks and beat the area bush by bush. Woken by the gunfire, Blondie was too late getting out and went down under a burst of machine-gun bullets in the middle of the meadow. Natale survived by crouching in a bush, sticking his head in the ground every time a bullet whistled by. After Blondie's death, the band broke up: some died, some were caught, some betrayed others and changed sides, some went on wandering about the area surviving one search after another, some joined the brigades up in the mountains.

Natale joined the brigades. Life was tougher in the mountains: Natale's job was to walk from one valley to the next, loaded like a mule, to take turns on watch and on fatigue duty; it was like being a soldier again, a hundred times worse and a hundred times better. And the partisans who laughed at him and mocked him were like the soldiers who'd laughed and mocked him in the army, yet different too, in a way he would surely have understood had it not been for that flurry of ducks in his skull.

He came to understand it all when he found himself with the Germans just beneath him climbing the road to the Goletta and firing their flamethrowers into the bushes. Stretched out on the ground, he started to fire shot after shot and he understood why he was doing it. He understood that those men down there were the militiamen who had arrested him because his papers weren't in order, they were the Todt guards marking down his hours, they were the orderly who made him clean the latrines, they were all these things at once but they were also the farmer who made him sweat the week long before he was called up, they were the boys who had tripped him on the pavement the time he went into town for the fair, and they were his father too, the time he'd shown him the back of his hand. They were even Margherita, Margherita who was on the point of going with him, then had turned against him, not exactly Margherita but whatever it was that had made Margherita turn against him: this thought was even more difficult than the others, but at that moment he understood. Then he thought about why those men down there were firing at him, shouting at him, falling under his shots. And he understood that they were men like him beaten by their fathers as children, set to work by farmers, mocked by orderlies, and now they were taking it out on him; it was crazy of them to take it out on him, he had nothing to do with it, and that was why he was firing at them, but if they had all been on his side he wouldn't have been firing at them but at others, he wasn't sure who, and Margherita would have gone with him. But how his enemies came to be these people and those, good and bad, like him and against him; why he was here, in the right, they there, in the wrong, this Natale could not understand: it was the flight of ducks; that's what it was, no more, no less.

Just a few days before the end of the war, the English decided to drop things by parachute. The partisans walked to Piedmont, they marched for two days and lit fires at night in the middle of the fields. The English dropped overcoats with gold buttons, but it was already spring, and bundles of old Italian rifles from the first African war. The partisans picked them up and pranced wildly round the fire like so many Negroes. Natale danced and shouted amongst them, and was happy.

Love Far from Home

Occasionally a train sets off along the seafront and on that train there's me, leaving. Because I don't want to stay in my sleepy, cabbage-patch village, puzzling out the licence plates of out-of-town cars like a kid down from the mountains sitting on the wall of a bridge. I'm off, bye bye village.

In the world, beyond my village, there are other towns, some on the sea, others, why I don't know, lost in the depths of the lowlands, on the banks of railways that arrive, how I don't know, after breathless journeys through endless stretches of countryside. Every so often I get off in one of these towns and I always have the look of the first-time traveller, pockets stuffed with newspapers, eyes smarting with dust.

At night in my new bed I turn off the light and listen to the trams, then think of my room in my village, so distant in the night it seems impossible that two places so far apart could exist at the same moment. And, where I'm not sure, I fall asleep.

In the morning, outside the window, there's so much to explore: if it's Genoa, streets that go up and down and houses above and below and a rush of wind between them; if it's Turin, straight streets that never end, looking out over the railings of the balconies, with a double row of trees fading away beyond into white skies; if it's Milan, houses that turn their backs on you in fields of fog. There must be other towns, other things to explore: one day I'll go and see.

But in every town the room is always the same, it seems the

landladies must send the furniture on from town to town as soon as they know I'm coming. Even my shaving kit on the marble dresser top looks as if I'd found it there when I arrived rather than putting it there myself, it has such an air of inevitability, doesn't seem mine at all. I could live years in one of these rooms after other years in other and absolutely similar rooms, without ever managing to feel it was mine or make my mark on it. Because my suitcase is always ready for the next journey, and no town in Italy is the right town, no town has work to offer, no town would be good enough even if you did find work because there's always another and better town where you hope to go to work one day. So I put my stuff in the drawers exactly how it was in my suitcase, ready to be packed again.

Days and weeks go by and a girl begins to come to the room. I could say it was always the same girl because at first there's no difference between one girl and the next, they're strangers and you communicate with them following a prescribed ritual. You have to spend a bit of time and do a lot of things with this girl for you both to understand the whys and wherefores; and then begins the season of enormous discoveries, the real, perhaps the only exciting season of love. Then, spending still more time and doing still more things with this girl, you realize that the other girls were like this too, that I too am like this, we all are, and everything she does is boring, as if repeated in a thousand mirrors. Bye bye, girlfriend.

The first time a girl comes to see me, let's say it's Mariamirella, I hardly do anything all afternoon: I go on with a book I'm reading, then realize that for the last twenty pages I've been looking at the letters as though they were pictures; I write, but really I'm doodling all over the white paper and all the doodles together become the sketch of an elephant, I shade it in and in the end it turns into a mammoth. Then I lose my temper with the mammoth and tear it up: why a mammoth every time, you baby!

I tear up the mammoth, the bell rings: Mariamirella. I run to open the door before the landlady can appear at the barred toilet window and start shouting; Mariamirella would be frightened off.

One day the landlady will die, strangled by thieves: it's written down, there's nothing anyone can do about it. She thinks she can save herself by not going to open the door when they ring, not asking: 'Whoozzat callin'?' from the barred toilet window, but it's a pointless precaution, the typesetters have already prepared the headline — Landlady Adelaide Braghetti Strangled by Unknown Killers — and are waiting for confirmation to lay out the page.

Mariamirella is there in the half-light, with her sailor's beret and pompom and her heart-shaped mouth. I open the door and she's already prepared a whole speech to make as soon as she's in, it doesn't matter what she actually says, only that we talk without a break as I lead her down the dark corridor to my room.

It ought to be a long speech, so as not to get stuck in the middle of my room without having anything left to say. The room offers no prompts, hopeless in its squalor: the metal bedstead, titles of unknown books in the little bookcase.

'Come and look out of the window, Mariamirella.'

The window is a French window with a waist-high railing but no balcony; you have to go up two steps to it and it feels as if we were climbing and climbing. Outside, a reddish sea of tiles. We look at the roofs stretching off all around as far as the eye can see, the stumpy chimneys suddenly puffing rags of smoke, the ridiculous balustrades on cornices where no one can ever look out, the low walls enclosing empty spaces on top of tumbledown houses. I put a hand on her shoulder, a hand that hardly feels like mine, swollen almost, as if we were touching each other through a layer of water.

'Seen enough?'

'Yes.'

'Down then.'

We go down and close the window. We're underwater, we fumble with vague sensations. The mammoth roams about the room, ancient human fear.

'So?'

I've taken off her sailor's beret and tossed it on the bed.

'No. I'm off now anyway.'

She puts it back on her head, I grab it and throw it up in the air, flying, now we're running after each other, playing with gritted teeth, love, this is love one for another, a scratching biting longing one for another, punching too, on the shoulders, then a weary weary kiss: love.

Now we're smoking sitting face to face: the cigarettes are huge between our fingers, like things held underwater, big sunken anchors. Why aren't we happy?

'What's the matter?' asks Mariamirella.

'The mammoth,' I tell her.

'What's that?' she asks.

'A symbol,' I tell her.

'What of?' she says.

'I don't know what of,' I tell her. 'A symbol.'

'Look,' I tell her, 'one evening I was sitting on a river bank with a girl.'

'Called?'

'The river was called the Po, and the girl Enrica. Why?'

'Oh nothing: I like to know who you've been with.'

'Okay, so we were sitting on the grassy river bank. It was autumn, in the evening, the banks were dark already and coming down the river was the shadow of two men rowing standing up. In town the lights were going on and we were sitting on the bank the other side of the river, and we were full of what they call love, that rough discovering and seeking of each other, that sharp taste of one another, you know, love. And I was full of sadness and solitude, that evening on the bank of rivers and their black shadows, the sadness and solitude of new loves, the sadness and nostalgia of old loves, the sadness and desperation of future

41

loves. Don Juan, sad hero, ancient burden, he was full of sadness and solitude and nothing else.'

'Is it the same with me too?' Mariamirella asks.

'What if you spoke a bit, now, if you said what you know?'

I started to shout with rage; sometimes when you speak you hear what might be an echo, it drives you crazy.

'What do you expect me to say? All this stuff . . . you men . . . I don't understand.'

That's how it is: everything women have been told about love has been wrong. They've been told all sorts of things, but all wrong. And their experiences, all imprecise. And yet, they trust the things they're told, not the experiences. That's why they're so wrong-headed.

'I'd like, you see, us girls,' she says. 'Men: things you read, things they whisper in your ear from when you're a little girl. You learn that *that* is more important than anything else, the aim of everything else. Then, you see, I realized that you never get to *that*, really to *that*. It's not more important than everything else. I wish it didn't exist at all, any of it, that you didn't have to think about it. Yet you're always expecting it. Maybe you have to become a mother to get to the real sense of everything. Or a prostitute.'

There: it's great. We all have our secret explanations. You only have to reveal your secret explanation and she's not a stranger any more. We lie cuddled up together like two big dogs, or river gods.

'You see,' Mariamirella says, 'maybe I'm afraid of you. But I don't know where to hide. There's nothing on the horizon, only you. You're the bear and the cave. That's why I'm cuddled up in your arms now, so that you can protect me from my fear of you.'

And yet, it's easier for women. Life flows in them, a great river, in them, the perpetuators, nature is sure and mysterious, in them. Once there was the Great Matriarchy, the history of peoples flowed as simply as that of plants. Then the conceit of the drones: a rebellion, and we had civilization. That's what I think, but I don't believe it.

'Once I found I couldn't make it with a girl,' I tell her, 'on a meadow in the mountains. The mountain was called Mount Bignone and the girl Angela Pia. A big meadow, amongst the bushes, I remember, and a cricket jumping on every leaf. That trilling of crickets, so high, no escape. She couldn't really understand why I got up then and said that the last cable car was about to leave. Because it was a place you got to by cable car: and going over the pylons you felt yourself go empty inside and she said: "It's like when you kiss me." That was quite a relief, I remember.'

'You shouldn't tell me this sort of thing,' Mariamirella says. 'There'd be no more bear nor cave either. All I'd be left with was fear, all around.'

'You see, Mariamirella,' I tell her, 'we mustn't separate things from thoughts. The curse of our generation has been just that: not being able to do what we thought. Or not being able to think what we did. I'll give you an example: years ago (I'd changed my age on my identity card because I wasn't old enough), I went to a woman in a brothel. The brothel was at 15, via Calandra and the woman was called Derna.'

'What?'

'Derna. We had the empire then and the only novelty was that the women in the brothels were called Derna, Adua, Harrar, Dessiè.'

'Dessiè?'

'Even Dessiè, as I recall. You want me to call you Dessiè from now on?'

'No.'

'Well, to go back to that time, with this Derna. I was young and she was big and hairy. I ran away. I paid what I had to pay and ran away: down the stairs I had the impression everybody came out of their rooms to look at me and laugh. But that's not important: the thing is that as soon as I was home that woman became a thought, something mental, and I wasn't afraid of her any more. I began to want her, want her terribly ... That's the point: for us things thought are different from the things themselves.'

43

'Right,' says Mariamirella, 'I've already thought of everything possible, I've lived hundreds of lives with my thoughts. Of marrying, of having lots of children, of having abortions, of marrying someone rich, of marrying someone poor, of becoming a high society lady, of becoming a prostitute, a dancer, a nun, a roast-chestnut seller, a star, an MP, an ambulance driver, a sportswoman. Hundreds of lives with all their details. And they all ended happily. But in real life none of those things I think ever happens. So every time I find myself imagining things, I get scared and try to stop the thoughts, because if I dream something it will never come true.'

She's a nice girl, Mariamirella; by nice girl I mean she understands the difficult things I say and immediately makes them easy. I'd like to give her a kiss, but then I think that if I kissed her I'd think of kissing the thought of her and she'd think of being kissed by the thought of me, so I do nothing about it.

'Our generation must reconquer the things themselves, Mariamirella,' I say. 'Think and do things at the same time. Not do things without thinking them through. We have to put an end to this difference between the things we think and the things themselves. Then we'll be happy.'

'Why is it like this?' she asks me.

'Well, it's not like this for everybody,' I tell her. 'When I was a boy I lived in a big villa, with balustrades high as if flying over the sea. And I spent my days behind those balustrades, I was a loner as a child, and for me everything was a strange symbol, the spacing of the dates hanging from the tufts on the stalks, the crooked arms of the cactuses, the strange patterns in the gravel of the paths. Then there were the grown-ups, whose job it was to deal with things, real things. All I had to do was discover new symbols, new meanings. I've stayed that way my whole life, I still live in a castle of meanings, not things, I still depend on the others, the "grown-ups", the ones who handle things. But there are people who've worked at lathes ever since they were children. At a tool that makes things. That can have no other meaning than the things it makes. When I see a machine I look at it as if it were a magic castle, I imagine tiny men turning amongst the cogs. A lathe. God knows what a lathe is. Do you know what a lathe is, Mariamirella?'

'A lathe, I'm not sure, right now,' she says.

'They must be really important, lathes. They should teach everybody to use them, instead of teaching you to use a rifle, a rifle is just another symbolic thing, with no real purpose.'

'I'm not interested in lathes,' she says.

'See, it's easier for you: you've got your sewing machines to save you, your needles and whatnot, gas rings, typewriters even. You've only got a few myths to escape from; everything's a symbol for me. But what is definite is, we've got to reconquer things.'

I'm caressing her, very softly.

'So, am I a thing?' she asks.

'Ugh,' I say.

I've found a small dimple on one shoulder, above the armpit, soft, with no bone beneath, like the dimples in cheeks. I speak with my lips on the dimple.

'Shoulder like cheek,' I say. It's incomprehensible.

'What?' she asks. But she doesn't care in the least what I say to her.

'Race like June,' I say, still in the dimple. She doesn't understand what I'm doing, but she likes it and laughs. She's a nice girl.

'Sea like arrival,' I say, then take my mouth from her dimple and put my ear there to listen to the echo. All I hear is her breathing and, buried far away, her heart.

'Heart like train,' I say.

There: now Mariamirella isn't the Mariamirella in my mind, plus a real Mariamirella: she's Mariamirella! And what we're doing now isn't something mental plus something real: the flight above the roofs, and the house swaying high like the palm trees at the window of my house in the village, a great wind has taken our top floor and is carrying it across the skies and the red ranks of rooftiles.

45

On the shore by my village, the sea has noticed me and is welcoming me like a big dog. The sea – gigantic friend with small white hands that scratch the shingle – all at once it sweeps over the buttress of the breakwaters, rears its white belly and leaps over the mountains, here it comes bounding along cheerfully like a huge dog with the white paws of the undertow. The crickets fall silent, all the lowlands are flooded, fields and vineyards, till just one peasant raises his fork and shouts: the sea disappears, as though drunk by the land. Bye bye, sea.

Going out, Mariamirella and I start running as fast as we can down the stairs, before the landlady appears at the barred window and tries to understand everything, looking us in the eyes.

Wind in a City

Something, but I couldn't understand what. People walking along level streets as if they were going uphill or down, lips and nostrils twitching like gills, then houses and doors in flight and the street corners sharper than usual. It was the wind: later on I realized.

Turin is a windless city. The streets are canals of motionless air fading into infinity like screaming sirens: motionless air, glassy with frost or soft with haze, stirred only by the trams skimming by on their rails. For months I forget there is such a thing as wind; all that's left is a vague need.

But all it takes is for a gust rising from the bottom of a street one day, rising and coming to meet me, and I remember my windblown village beside the sea, the houses ranged above and below each other, and the wind in the middle going up and down, and streets of steps and cobbles, and slashes of blue windy sky above the alleyways. And home with the shutters banging, the palm trees groaning at the windows, and my father's voice shouting on the hilltop.

I'm like that, a wind man, who needs friction and headway when he's walking, needs suddenly to shout and bite the air when he's speaking. When the wind lifts in town, spreading from suburb to suburb in tongues of colourless flame, the town opens up before me like a book, it's as though I could recognize everybody I see, I feel like yelling, 'Hey there!' to the girls, the cyclists, like shouting out what I'm thinking, waving my hands.

I can't stay in when there's wind. I live in a rented room on the fifth floor; beneath my window the trams roll in the narrow street day and night, as if rattling headlong across my room; night-time, trams far away shriek like owls. The landlady's daughter is a secretary, fat and hysterical: one day she smashed a plate of peas in the passageway and shut herself in her room screaming.

The toilet looks out on the courtyard; it's at the end of a narrow corridor, a cave almost, its walls damp and green and mouldy: maybe stalactites will form. Beyond the bars on the window the courtyard is one of those Turin courtyards trapped under layers of decay with iron balcony railings you can't lean on without getting rust all over you. One above the other, the protruding cages of the toilets make a sort of tower: toilets with mould-soft walls, marshy at the bottom.

And I think of my own house high above the sea amid the palm trees, my own house so different from all other houses. And the first difference that comes to mind is the number of toilets it had, toilets of every variety: in bathrooms gleaming with white tiles, in gloomy cubby-holes, Turkish toilets, ancient water-closets with blue friezes fabling round the bowls.

Remembering all this I was wandering round the city smelling the wind. When I go and run into a girl I know: Ada Ida.

'I'm happy: the wind!' I tell her.

'It gets on my nerves,' she answers. 'Walk with me a bit: just till there.'

Ada Ida is one of those girls who run into you and immediately start telling you their life stories and what they think about things, even though they hardly know you: girls with no secrets, except for things that are secrets to them too; and even for those secrets they'll find words, everyday words that sprout effortlessly, as if their thoughts budded ready-clothed in a tissue of words.

'The wind gets on my nerves,' she says. 'I shut myself in the house and kick off my shoes and wander round the rooms barefoot. Then I get a bottle of whisky an American friend gave me and drink. I've never managed to get drunk on my own. There's

48

a point where I burst into tears and stop. I've been wandering about for a week not knowing what to do with myself.'

I don't know how she does it, Ada Ida, how any of them do it, all those men and women who manage to be intimate with everybody, who find something to say to everybody, who get involved in other people's affairs and let them get involved in theirs. I say: 'I'm in a room on the fifth floor with the trams like owls at night. The toilet is green with mould, with moss and stalactites, and a winter fog like over a marsh. I think up to a point people's characters depend on the toilets they have to shut themselves up in every day. You get home from the office and you find the toilet green with mould, marshy: so you smash a plate of peas in the passage and you shut yourself in your room and scream.'

I haven't been very clear, this isn't really how I had thought of it, Ada Ida certainly won't understand, but before my thoughts can turn into spoken words they have to go through an empty space and they come out false.

'I do more cleaning in the toilet than anywhere else in the house,' she says, 'every day I wash the floor; I polish everything. Every week I put a clean curtain on the window, white, with embroidery, and every year I have the walls repainted. I feel if I stopped cleaning the toilet one day it would be a bad sign, and I'd let myself go more and more till I was desperate. It's a small dark toilet, but I keep it like a church. I wonder what kind of toilet the managing director of Fiat has. Come on, walk with me a bit, till the tram.'

The great thing about Ada Ida is that she accepts everything you say, nothing surprises her, any subject you bring up, she'll go on with it, as if it had been her idea in the first place. And she wants me to walk with her as far as the tram.

'Okay, I'll come,' I tell her. 'So, the managing director of Fiat had them build him a toilet that was a big lounge with columns and drapes and carpets, aquariums in the walls. And big mirrors all round reflecting his body a thousand times. And the john had arms and a back to lean on and it was high as a throne; it even had a canopy over it. And the chain for flushing played a really delightful carillon. But the managing director of Fiat couldn't move his bowels. He felt intimidated by all those carpets and aquariums. The mirrors reflected his body a thousand times while he sat on that john, high as a throne. And the managing director of Fiat felt nostalgic for the toilet in his childhood home, with sawdust on the floor and sheets of newspaper skewered on a nail. And so he died: intestinal infection after months without moving his bowels.'

'So he died,' Ada Ida agrees. 'Just so, he died. Do you know any other stories like that? Here comes my tram. Get on with me and tell me another.'

'In the tram and then where?'

'In the tram. Do you mind?'

We get on the tram. 'I can't tell you any stories,' I say, 'because I've got this gap. There's an empty chasm between me and everybody else. I wave my arms about inside it but I can't get hold of anything, I shout into it but no one hears: it's total emptiness.'

'In those situations I sing,' says Ada Ida, 'I sing in my mind. When I'm speaking to someone and I get to a point where I realize I can't go on, as if I'd got to the edge of a river, my thoughts running away to hide, I start singing in my mind the last words spoken or said, and putting them to a tune, any old tune. And the other words that come into my mind, I mean following the same tune, are the words of my thoughts. So I say them.'

'Try it.'

'So I say them. Like the time someone bothered me in the street thinking I was one of them.'

'But you aren't singing.'

'I'm singing in my mind, then I translate. Otherwise you wouldn't understand. I did the same that time with that man. I ended up telling him that I hadn't had any candies for three years. He bought me a bag. Then I really didn't know what to say to him. I mumbled something and ran off with the bag of candy.'

'I'll never manage to say anything, speaking,' I say, 'that's why I write.'

'Do what the beggars do,' Ada Ida says, pointing to one, at a tram-stop.

Turin is as full of beggars as a holy city in India. Even beggars have their special ways, when asking for money: one tries something and all the others copy. For a while now lots of the beggars have taken to writing their life stories in huge letters on the pavement, with pieces of coloured chalk: it's a good way of getting people interested enough to read and then they feel obliged to part with some change.

'Yes,' I say, 'maybe I should write my story in chalk on the pavement and sit down beside to hear what people would say. At least we'd look each other in the eyes a bit. But maybe no one would notice and they'd walk all over it and rub it out.'

'What would you write, on the pavement, if you were a beggar?' Ada Ida asks.

'I'd write, all in block capitals: *I'm one of those who write because they can't handle speaking; sorry about this, folks. Once a paper published something I'd written. It's a paper that comes out early in the morning; the people who buy it are mainly workers on their way to the factory. That morning I was on the trams early and I saw people reading the things I had written, and I watched their faces, trying to understand what line they were up to. Everything you write there's always something you're sorry you put in, either because you're afraid of being misunderstood, or out of shame. And on the trams that morning I kept watching people's faces till they got to that bit, and then I wanted to say: "Look, maybe I didn't explain that very well, this is what I meant," but I still sat there without saying anything and blushed.*'

Meanwhile we've got off the tram and Ada Ida is waiting for another tram to come. I don't know which tram I should get now and I wait with her.

'I'd write this,' says Ada Ida, 'in blue and yellow chalk: *Ladies and Gentlemen, there are people whose greatest pleasure is to have others urinate on them. D'Annunzio was one such, they say. I believe it.*

You should remember that every day, and remember that we are all the same race, and not act so superior. And what about this: my aunt gave birth to a son with the body of a cat. You should remember that things like that happen, never forget it. And that in Turin there are people who sleep on the pavements, over warm cellar gratings. I've seen them. You should think about all these things, every evening, instead of saying your prayers. And you should keep them in mind during the day. Then your heads won't be so full of plans and hypocrisy. That's what I'd write. Keep me company on this tram too, be sweet.'

I don't know why but I went on taking trams with Ada Ida. The tram went a long way through the poor suburbs. The people on the tram were grey and wrinkly, as though all grimed with the same dust.

Ada Ida insists on passing remarks: 'Look what a nervous tic that man has. And look how much powder that old woman's put on.'

I found it all upsetting and I wanted her to stop. 'So? So?' I said. 'Everything real is rational.' But deep down I wasn't convinced.

I'm real and rational too, I thought, not accepting, thinking up plans, meaning to change everything. But to change everything you have to start from there, from the man with the nervous tic, the old woman with the powder, and not from plans. And from Ada Ida too who's still saying, 'Keep me company just till there.'

'It's our stop,' says Ada Ida, and we get off. 'Keep me company just till there, do you mind?'

'Everything real is rational, Ada Ida,' I tell her. 'Any more trams to catch?'

'No, I live round that corner.'

We were at the end of town. Iron castles rose behind factory walls; the wind waved scraps of smoke at the lighting conductors of the smokestacks. And there was a river tucked in with grass: the Dora.

I remembered a windy night by the Dora, years ago, when

I walked along biting a girl's cheek. She had long, really fine hair and it kept getting between my teeth.

'Once,' I say, 'I bit a girl's cheek, here, in the wind. And I spat out hair. It's a marvellous story.'

'Here,' Ada Ida says, 'I've arrived.'

'It's a marvellous story,' I tell her, 'but it takes a while to tell.'

'I've arrived,' says Ada Ida. 'He must be home already.'

'He who?'

'I'm with this guy who works at RIV. He's fishing mad. He's filled the flat with fishing rods and artificial flies.'

'Everything real is rational,' I say. 'It was a marvellous story. Tell me what trams I have to get to get back.'

'The twenty-two, the seventeen, the sixteen,' she says. 'Every Sunday we go to the Sangone. The other day, a trout this big.'

'Are you singing in your mind?'

'No. Why?'

'Just asking. Twenty-two, twenty-seven, thirteen.'

'Twenty-two, seventeen, sixteen. He likes to fry the fish himself. There, I can smell it. It's him frying.'

'And the oil? Are your rations enough? Twenty-six, seventeen, sixteen.'

'We do swaps with a friend. Twenty-two, seventeen.'

'Twenty-two, seventeen, fourteen?'

'No: eight, fifteen, forty-one.'

'Right: I'm so forgetful. Everything is rational. Bye, Ada Ida.'

I get home after an hour in the wind, getting all the trams wrong and arguing by numbers with the drivers. I go in and there are peas and broken bits of plate in the passage, the fat secretary has locked herself in her room, she's screaming.

The Lost Regiment

A regiment in a powerful army was supposed to be parading through the city streets. Since the crack of dawn the troops had been lined up in parade formation in the courtyard of the barracks.

The sun was already high in the sky and the shadows shortened at the feet of the scrawny saplings in the courtyard. Under their freshly polished helmets, soldiers and officials were dripping with sweat. High up on his white horse, the colonel gave a sign: the drums rolled, the whole band began to play and the barracks gate swung slowly on its hinges.

Beyond you could see the city now, under a blue sky crossed by soft clouds, the city with its chimneys shedding wisps of smoke, its balconies with their washing lines bristling with pegs, glints of sunshine reflected in dressing-table mirrors, flyscreen curtains catching the earrings of ladies with their shopping, an ice-cream cart complete with sunshade and glass box for cones, and, tugged at the end of a long string by a group of children, a kite with red paper rings for a tail which skims along the ground, then lifts in jerks and straightens against the soft clouds in the sky.

The regiment had begun to advance to the beat of the drums, with a great stamping of boots on the paving and rattling of artillery; but on seeing the city before them, so quiet and good-natured, minding its own business, the soldiers felt indiscreet somehow, intrusive, the parade suddenly seemed out of place, it struck a wrong note, people could really do without it.

One of the drummers, a certain Prè Gio Batta, pretended to proceed with the roll he'd begun but in fact only skimmed the skin of his drum. What came out was a subdued tippety-tap, but not just from him: it was general; because at exactly the same moment all the other drummers did what Prè did. Then the trumpets came out with no more than a sighed solfeggio, because nobody was putting any puff into it. Glancing about uneasily, soldiers and officials stopped with one leg in the air, then put it down very softly, and resumed their parade on tiptoe.

So without anybody having given an order, the long, very long column, proceeded on tiptoe with slow restrained movements, and a muffled, swishing shuffle. Walking beside those cannons, so incongruous here, the artillerymen were suddenly overtaken by a sense of shame: some tried to pretend indifference, walking along without ever looking at the guns, as if they were there by purest chance; others stuck as close to the guns as they could, as though to hide them, to save people from such a rude and disagreeable sight, or they put covers over them, capes, so that they wouldn't be noticed, or at least wouldn't attract attention; others again assumed an attitude of affectionate mockery towards the things, clapping their hands on the gun carriage, on the breech, pointing at them with half a smile on their lips: this to show that they had no intention of using them for lethal purposes, but just meant to give them an airing, like some grotesque gadgetry, huge and rare.

This confused feeling had even penetrated the mind of Colonel Clelio Leontuomini, who had instinctively lowered his head to his horse's, while the horse, for his part, had begun to put in a pause between each step, moving with the caution of a cart horse. But it took only a moment's reflection for colonel and horse to recover their martial gait. Having made a rapid assessment of the situation, Leontuomini gave a sharp order:

'Parade step!'

The drums rolled, then began to beat a measured rhythm. The regiment quickly regained its composure and was now tramping forward with aggressive self-confidence.

'There,' the colonel said to himself, casting a quick glance over the ranks, 'that's a real regiment on the march.'

On the pavement a few passers-by stopped to line the road, and they looked on with the air of people who would like to be interested and maybe even take pleasure in the deployment of so much energy, but are troubled by a feeling they don't really understand, a vague sense of alarm, and in any event have too many serious things on their minds to start thinking about sabres and cannons.

Sensing these eyes on them, troops and officials were again overtaken by that slight, inexplicable uneasiness. They went on marching with their rigid parade step, but they couldn't rid themselves of the idea that they were doing these good citizens a wrong. In order not to be distracted by their presence, Infantryman Marangon Remigio kept his eyes down: when you march in columns your only concerns are keeping in line and keeping in step; the detachment can take care of everything else. But hundreds and hundreds of soldiers were doing what Infantryman Marangon was doing; in fact you could say that all of them, officials, ensigns, the colonel himself, were advancing without ever raising their eyes from the ground, faithfully following the column. Proceeding at parade step, their band at their head, the regiment was thus seen to veer to one side, leave the paved road, stray into a flowerbed in the park and push on determinedly trampling down buttercups and lilacs.

The gardeners were watering the grass and what did they see? A regiment advancing on them with eyes closed, stamping their heels on the tender grass. The poor men couldn't think how to hold their hoses without directing them at the soldiers. They ended up pointing them vertically upwards, but the long jets fell back in unsuspected directions; one watered Colonel Clelio Leontuomini from head to toe as he too advanced bolt upright, his eyes closed.

Showered with water, the colonel jumped and let out a shout:

56

'Flood! Flood! Mobilize for rescue!' Then immediately he pulled himself together, regained command of the regiment and led them out of the gardens.

But he was a bit disappointed. That shout of, 'Flood! Flood!' had betrayed a secret and almost unconscious hope: that a natural disaster would suddenly occur, without killing anyone, but dangerous enough to call off the parade and give the regiment a chance to do all kinds of useful things for people: building bridges, organizing rescues. This alone would have soothed his conscience.

Having left the park, the regiment was now in a different part of town, not in the broad avenues where they were supposed to be parading, but in an area of narrow, quiet, winding lanes. The colonel decided he would cut through these streets to get to the square without wasting any more time.

An unusual excitement reigned in the area. Electricians were fixing the streetlamps with long portable ladders and lifting and lowering the telephone wires. Surveyors from the civil engineers were measuring the streets with ranging rods and spring-wind tape measures. The gasmen were using picks to open up big holes in the pavement. Schoolchildren were walking along in line. Bricklayers were tossing along bricks to each other, shouting: 'Hey up, hey up!' Cyclists went by with stepladders on their shoulders, whistling hard. And at every window a maid was standing on the sill washing the panes and wringing out wet cloths into big buckets.

Thus the regiment had to proceed with its parade down those winding streets, pushing their way through a tangle of telephone wires, tape measures, stepladders, holes in the road, and well-endowed schoolgirls, and at the same time catching bricks in flight – 'Hey up! hey up!' – and avoiding the wet cloths and buckets that excited maids dropped crashing down from the fourth floor.

Colonel Clelio Leontuomini had to admit he was lost. He leaned down from his horse toward a passer-by and asked:

'Excuse me, but do you know the shortest way to the main square?'

The passer-by, a small fellow with glasses, stood for a moment in thought:

'It's complicated; but if you let me show you the way I'll take you through a courtyard into another street and you'll save at least a quarter of an hour.'

'Will the whole regiment be able to get through this courtyard?' the colonel asked.

The man shot them a glance and made a hesitant gesture:

'We-ell! We can try?' and he led them through a big door.

Lined up behind the rusty railings of the balconies, all the families in the building leaned out to look at the regiment trying to get into their courtyard with their horses and artillery.

'Where's the door we go out through?' the colonel asked the small fellow.

'Door?' the man asked. 'Perhaps I wasn't very clear. You have to climb to the top floor, from there you get through to the stairs in the next building and their door goes through to the other street.'

The colonel wanted to stay on his horse even up those narrow stairs, but after two landings he decided to leave the animal tied to the banister and proceed on foot. The cannons too, they decided, would have to be left in the courtyard where a cobbler promised he would keep an eye on them. The soldiers went up in single file and at every landing doors opened and children shouted:

'Mummy! Come and look. The soldiers are going by! The regiment is on parade!'

On the fifth floor, to get from this staircase to another secondary one that led to the attic, they had to walk outside along the balcony. Every window gave on bare rooms with lots of pallet beds where whole families full of children lived.

'Come in, come in,' said the dads and mums to the soldiers. 'Rest a while, you must be tired! Come through here, it's shorter! But leave your rifles outside; there are kids here, you understand . . .'

So the regiment broke up along the passageways and corridors. And in the confusion, the small fellow who knew the way could no longer be found.

Came the evening and still companies and platoons were wandering through stairways and balconies. At the top, perched on the roof coping, was Colonel Leontuomini. He could see the city spread beneath him, spacious and sharp, with its chequerboard of streets and big empty piazza. Beside him, on their hands and knees on the tiles, were a squadron of men, armed with coloured flags, flare pistols and drapes with flashes of colour.

'Transmit,' said the colonel. 'Quick, transmit: Area impracticable . . . Unable to proceed . . . Awaiting orders . . .'

Enemy Eyes

Pietro was walking along that morning, when he became aware that something was bothering him. He'd had the feeling for a while, without really being aware of it: the feeling that someone was behind him, someone was watching him, unseen.

He turned his head suddenly; he was in a street a little off the beaten track, with hedges by the gates and wooden fences covered with torn posters. Hardly anybody was around; Pietro was immediately annoyed that he had given way to that stupid impulse to turn round; and he went on, determined to pick up the broken thread of his thoughts.

It was an autumn morning with a little sunshine; hardly a day to make you jump for joy, but not one to tug the heartstrings either. Yet in spite of himself that uneasiness continued to weigh him down; sometimes it seemed it was concentrated on the back of his neck, on his shoulders, like eyes that never let him out of sight, like the approach of a somehow hostile presence.

To overcome his nervousness, he felt he needed people around him: he went towards a busier street, but again, at the corner, he turned and looked back. A cyclist went by, a woman crossed the road, but he couldn't find any connection between the people and things round about and the anxiety eating into him. Turning round, his eyes had met those of a man who was likewise turning his head at the same time. Both men immediately and simultaneously looked away from each other, as if each were seeking something else. Pietro thought: 'Maybe that man felt I was looking at him. Perhaps I'm not the only one suffering from an irksome sharpening of sensibility this morning; maybe it's the weather, the day, that's making us nervous.'

He was in a busy street, and with this thought in mind he started looking at people, and noticing the jerky movements they were making, hands lifting almost to the face in annoyance, brows furrowing as if overtaken by a sudden worry or an irksome memory. 'What a miserable day!' Pietro said over and over to himself, 'what a miserable day!' and at the tram-stop, tapping his foot, he realized that the others waiting were likewise tapping their feet and reading the tramlines noticeboard as if looking for something that wasn't written there.

On the tram the conductor made a mistake giving change and lost his temper; the driver rang his bell at pedestrians and bicycles with painful insistence; and the passengers tightened their fingers round the handrails like shipwrecked sailors.

Pietro recognized the physical bulk of his friend Corrado. Sitting down, he hadn't seen Pietro yet, but was looking distractedly out of the window, digging a nail into his cheek.

'Corrado!' he called from right over his head.

His friend started. 'Oh, it's you! I hadn't seen you. I was thinking.'

'You look tense,' said Pietro, and realizing that he wanted nothing better than to recognize his own state in others, he said: 'I'm pretty tense myself today.'

'Who isn't?' Corrado said, and his face had that patient, ironic smile that made everybody listen to him and trust him.

'You know how I feel?' said Pietro. 'I feel as if there were eyes staring at me.'

'What do you mean, eyes?'

'The eyes of someone I've met before, but can't remember. Cold eyes, hostile . . .'

'Eyes that hardly think you worth looking at, but that you must at all costs take seriously.'

'Yes . . . Eyes like . . .'

61

'Like Germans?' said Corrado.

'That's it, like a German's eyes.'

'Well, it's understandable,' said Corrado and he opened his paper, 'with news like this ...' He pointed to the headlines: *Kesselring Pardoned ... SS Rallies ... Americans Finance Neo-Nazis ...* 'No wonder we feel they're on our backs again ...'

'Oh, that ... You think it's that ... But why would we only feel it now? Kesselring and the SS have been around for ages, a year, even two years. Maybe they were still in gaol then, but we knew perfectly well they were there, we never forgot them ...'

'The eyes,' said Corrado. 'You said you felt as if there were eyes staring. Up to now they haven't been doing any staring: they kept their eyes down, and we weren't used to them any more ... They were the enemies of the past, we hated what they had been, not them now. But now they've found their old stare ... the way they looked at us eight years ago ... We remember, and start feeling their eyes on us again ...'

They had many memories in common, Pietro and Corrado, from the old days. And they were not, as a rule, happy ones.

Pietro's brother had died in a concentration camp. Pietro lived with his mother, in the old family home. He got back towards evening. The gate squeaked as it always had, the gravel crunched under his shoes the way it did in the days when you listened hard every time there was a sound of steps.

Where was he walking now, the German who had come that evening? Perhaps he was crossing a bridge, pacing along a canal, or a row of low houses, their lights on, in a Germany full of coal and rubble; wearing ordinary clothes now, a black coat buttoned to the chin, a green hat, glasses, and he was staring, staring at him, at Pietro.

He opened the door. 'It's you!' came his mother's voice. 'At last!'

'You knew I wouldn't be back till now,' said Pietro.

'Yes, but I couldn't wait,' she said. 'I've had my heart in my mouth all day ... I don't know why ... This news ... These generals taking over still ... saying they were right all along ...'

'You too!' Pietro said. 'You know what Corrado says? That we all feel those Germans have got their eyes on us ... That's why we're all tense ...' and he laughed as if it were only Corrado who had thought of it.

But his mother passed a hand over her face. 'Pietro, is there going to be a war? Are they coming back?'

'There,' thought Pietro, 'up until yesterday, when you heard someone talking about the danger of another war, you couldn't imagine anything specific, because the old war had their face, and nobody knew what face the new one would have. But now we know: war has got its face back: and it's theirs again.'

After dinner Pietro went out; it was raining.

'Pietro?' his mother asked.

'What?'

'Going out in this weather ...'

'So?'

'Nothing ... Don't be late ...'

'I'm not a boy any more, Mum ...'

'Right ... Bye ...'

His mother closed the door behind him and stood listening to his footsteps on the gravel, the clang of the gate. She stood listening to the rain falling. Germany was far away, far beyond the Alps. It was raining there too, perhaps. Kesselring went by in his car, spraying mud; the SS who had taken her son away was going to a rally, in a shiny black raincoat, his old soldier's raincoat. Of course it was silly to be worried tonight; likewise tomorrow night; even in a year's time perhaps. But she didn't know how long she would be free not to worry; even in wartime there were nights when you didn't have to worry, but you were already worrying about the next night.

She was alone, outside there was the noise of the rain. Across a rain-soaked Europe the eyes of old enemies pierced the night, right through to her.

'I can see their eyes,' she thought, 'but they must see ours too.' And she stood firm, staring hard into the dark.

63

A General in the Library

One day, in the illustrious nation of Panduria, a suspicion crept into the minds of top officials: that books contained opinions hostile to military prestige. In fact trials and enquiries had revealed that the tendency, now so widespread, of thinking of generals as people actually capable of making mistakes and causing catastrophes, and of wars as things that did not always amount to splendid cavalry charges towards a glorious destiny, was shared by a large number of books, ancient and modern, foreign and Pandurese.

Panduria's General Staff met together to assess the situation. But they didn't know where to begin, because none of them was particularly well-versed in matters bibliographical. A commission of enquiry was set up under General Fedina, a severe and scrupulous official. The commission was to examine all the books in the biggest library in Panduria.

The library was in an old building full of columns and staircases, the walls peeling and even crumbling here and there. Its cold rooms were crammed to bursting with books, and in parts inaccessible, with some corners only mice could explore. Weighed down by huge military expenditures, Panduria's state budget was unable to offer any assistance.

The military took over the library one rainy morning in November. The general climbed off his horse, squat, stiff, his thick neck shaven, his eyebrows frowning over pince-nez; four lanky lieutenants, chins held high and eyelids lowered, got out of a car,

each with a briefcase in his hand. Then came a squadron of
soldiers who set up camp in the old courtyard, with mules, bales
of hay, tents, cooking equipment, camp radio, and signalling flags.

Sentries were placed at the doors, together with a notice
forbidding entry, 'for the duration of large-scale manoeuvres now
under way'. This was an expedient which would allow the enquiry
to be carried out in great secret. The scholars who used to go to
the library every morning wearing heavy coats and scarves and
balaclavas so as not to freeze, had to go back home again. Puz-
zled, they asked each other: 'What's this about large-scale
manoeuvres in the library? Won't they make a mess of the place?
And the cavalry? And are they going to be shooting too?'

Of the library staff, only one little old man, Signor Crispino,
was kept so that he could explain to the officers how the books
were arranged. He was a shortish fellow, with a bald, eggish pate
and eyes like pinheads behind his spectacles.

First and foremost General Fedina was concerned with the
logistics of the operation, since his orders were that the commission was not to leave the library before having completed
their enquiry; it was a job that required concentration, and they
must not allow themselves to be distracted. Thus a supply of
provisions was procured, likewise some barrack stoves and a
store of firewood together with some collections of old and it
was generally thought uninteresting magazines. Never had the
library been so warm in the winter season. Pallet beds for the
general and his officers were set up in safe areas surrounded by
mousetraps.

Then duties were assigned. Each lieutenant was allotted a
particular branch of knowledge, a particular century of history.
The general was to oversee the sorting of the volumes and the
application of an appropriate rubber stamp depending on
whether a book had been judged suitable for officers, NCOs,
common soldiers, or should be reported to the Military Court.

And the commission began its appointed task. Every evening the camp radio transmitted General Fedina's report to HQ.

65

'So many books examined. So many seized as suspect. So many declared suitable for officers and soldiers.' Only rarely were these cold figures accompanied by something out of the ordinary: a request for a pair of glasses to correct short-sightedness for an officer who had broken his, the news that a mule had eaten a rare manuscript edition of Cicero left unattended.

But developments of far greater import were under way, about which the camp radio transmitted no news at all. Rather than thinning out, the forest of books seemed to grow ever more tangled and insidious. The officers would have lost their way had it not been for the help of Signor Crispino. Lieutenant Abrogati, for example, would jump to his feet and throw the book he was reading down on the table: 'But this is outrageous! A book about the Punic Wars that speaks well of the Carthaginians and criticizes the Romans! This must be reported at once!' (It should be said here that, rightly or wrongly, the Pandurians considered themselves descendants of the Romans.) Moving silently in soft slippers, the old librarian came up to him. 'That's nothing,' he would say, 'read what it says here, about the Romans again, you can put this in your report too, and this and this,' and he presented him with a pile of books. The lieutenant leafed nervously through them, then, getting interested, he began to read, to take notes. And he would scratch his head and mutter: 'For heaven's sake! The things you learn! Who would ever have thought!' Signor Crispino went over to Lieutenant Lucchetti who was closing a tome in rage, declaring: 'Nice stuff this is! These people have the audacity to entertain doubts as to the purity of the ideals that inspired the Crusades! Yessir, the Crusades!' And Signor Crispino said with a smile: 'Oh, but look, if you have to make a report on that subject, may I suggest a few other books that will offer more details,' and he pulled down half a shelf-full. Lieutenant Lucchetti leaned forward and got stuck in, and for a week you could hear him flicking through the pages and muttering: 'These Crusades though, very nice I must say!'

In the commission's evening report, the number of books

examined got bigger and bigger, but they no longer provided figures relative to positive and negative verdicts. General Fedina's rubber stamps lay idle. If, trying to check up on the work of one of the lieutenants, he asked, 'But why did you pass this novel? The soldiers come off better than the officers! This author has no respect for hierarchy!', the lieutenant would answer by quoting other authors and getting all muddled up in matters historical, philosophical and economic. This led to open discussions that went on for hours and hours. Moving silently in his slippers, almost invisible in his grey shirt, Signor Crispino would always join in at the right moment, offering some book which he felt contained interesting information on the subject under consideration, and which always had the effect of radically undermining General Fedina's convictions.

Meanwhile the soldiers didn't have much to do and were getting bored. One of them, Barabasso, the best educated, asked the officers for a book to read. At first they wanted to give him one of the few that had already been declared fit for the troops; but remembering the thousands of volumes still to be examined, the general was loth to think of Private Barabasso's reading hours being lost to the cause of duty; and he gave him a book yet to be examined, a novel that looked easy enough, suggested by Signor Crispino. Having read the book, Barabasso was to report to the general. Other soldiers likewise requested and were granted the same duty. Private Tommasone read aloud to a fellow soldier who couldn't read, and the man would give him his opinions. During open discussions, the soldiers began to take part along with the officers.

Not much is known about the progress of the commission's work: what happened in the library through the long winter weeks was not reported. All we know is that General Fedina's radio reports to General Staff headquarters became ever more infrequent, until finally they stopped altogether. The Chief of Staff was alarmed; he transmitted the order to wind up the enquiry as quickly as possible and present a full and detailed report.

In the library, the order found the minds of Fedina and his men prey to conflicting sentiments: on the one hand they were constantly discovering new interests to satisfy and were enjoying their reading and studies more than they would ever have imagined; on the other hand they couldn't wait to be back in the world again, to take up life again, a world and a life that seemed so much more complex now, as though renewed before their very eyes; and on yet another hand, the fact that the day was fast approaching when they would have to leave the library filled them with apprehension, for they would have to give an account of their mission, and with all the ideas that were bubbling up in their heads they had no idea how to get out of what had become a very tight corner indeed.

In the evening they would look out of the windows at the first buds on the branches glowing in the sunset, at the lights going on in the town, while one of them read some poetry out loud. Fedina wasn't with them: he had given the order that he was to be left alone at his desk to draft the final report. But every now and then the bell would ring and the others would hear him calling: 'Crispino! Crispino!' He couldn't get anywhere without the help of the old librarian, and they ended up sitting at the same desk writing the report together.

One bright morning the commission finally left the library and went to report to the Chief of Staff; and Fedina illustrated the results of the enquiry before an assembly of the General Staff. His speech was a kind of compendium of human history from its origins down to the present day, a compendium in which all those ideas considered beyond discussion by the right-minded folk of Panduria were attacked, in which the ruling classes were declared responsible for the nation's misfortunes, and the people exalted as the heroic victims of mistaken policies and unnecessary wars. It was a somewhat confused presentation including, as can happen with those who have only recently embraced new ideas, declarations that were often simplistic and contradictory. But as to the overall meaning there could be no doubt. The assembly of generals was stunned, their eyes opened wide, then they found their voices and began to shout. General Fedina was not even allowed to finish. There was talk of a court-martial, of his being reduced to the ranks. Then, afraid there might be a more serious scandal, the general and the four lieutenants were each pensioned off for health reasons, as a result of 'a serious nervous break-down suffered in the course of duty'. Dressed in civilian clothes, with heavy coats and thick sweaters so as not to freeze, they were often to be seen going into the old library where Signor Crispino would be waiting for them with his books.

The Workshop Hen

Adalberto, the security man, had a hen. He was one of a team of security men in a big factory; and he kept this hen in a little courtyard there; the chief of security had given him permission. He would have liked, with time, to have set up a whole hencoop for himself; and he had begun by buying this one hen which they had promised him was a good layer and a quiet creature who would never dare upset the severe industrial atmosphere with any loud clucking. As it turned out he could hardly complain; the hen laid at least one egg a day, and apart from some subdued gurgling might have been entirely mute. To tell the truth the chief of security had only given Adalberto permission to keep the bird in a coop, but since the courtyard, only recently annexed to the purposes of industry, abounded not only in rusty screws but likewise in worms, it had been tacitly accepted that the hen could peck around at will. So it went back and forth reserved and discreet among the workshops, was well known to the men, and, for its freedom and irresponsibility, envied.

One day the old turner, Pietro, discovered that the equally old Tommaso, in Quality Control, was coming to the factory with his pockets full of maize. Having never forgotten his peasant origins, Tommaso had immediately appreciated the productive capacity of the fowl and linking this appreciation to his desire for revenge for injustices suffered, had embarked upon a stealthy campaign to woo the security man's hen and encourage her to lay her eggs in a box of scrap on the floor by his workbench.

70

Every time he realized his friend was up to some secret trick, Pietro was annoyed, because it always came as such a surprise to him, and he at once tried to go one better. Ever since they had become prospective relatives (his son had got it into his head to marry Tommaso's daughter), they were always fighting. So he too got hold of some maize, prepared a box using metal scraps from his lathe and in the brief respite the machines he ran allowed him, tried to attract the hen. Hence this game, where what was at stake was not so much the eggs as a question of revenge, was played out more between Pietro and Tommaso than between themselves and Adalberto, who, poor chap, searched the workers as they arrived and left, rummaged in bags and pockets and knew nothing.

Pietro worked alone in a corner of the workshop set apart from the rest by a section of wall so as to form a separate room, or 'lounge', with a glass door that looked out on to a courtyard. Until a few years ago there had been two machines and two workers in this room: Pietro and another man. But one day the other man had gone off sick with a hernia, and in the meantime Pietro had had to look after both machines at once. He learned how to regulate his movements accordingly: he would push down the lever of one machine and go to pull out the piece the other had finished. The hernia case was operated, came back, but was assigned to a different team. Pietro was stuck with the two machines for good; indeed, to make it clear that this was not just forgetfulness, a time-and-motion expert was sent to assess the situation and a third machine was added: the man had calculated that between the operations for one machine then the other there were still a few seconds free. Then, in a general overhaul of productivity bonuses, to have some dubious calculation come out, Pietro was obliged to take on a fourth. At sixty and more years old he had had to learn to do four times the work in the same hours, but since his salary was still the same, his life wasn't radically transformed, if one excludes that is the development of chronic bronchitic asthma and the bad habit of falling asleep as soon as he sat down, in whatever place or company. But he was a tough old man and, what's more, full of good spirits, and he was always hoping that major changes were just round the corner.

For eight hours a day, Pietro rotated round the four machines making the same series of movements every time, movements he knew so well now he had managed to shave off every superfluous blip and adjust the rhythm of his asthma to that of his work with perfect precision. Even his eyes moved along trajectories as precise as the stars, since every machine demanded a particular sequence of glances to check that it didn't seize up and lose him his bonus.

After the first half-hour's work Pietro was already tired, the factory noises blended in his eardrums into a single background hum with the combined rhythm of his four machines pulsing above. Thrust forward by this rhythm, he worked on in a near daze until, blessed as the first sight of land to the castaway, he caught the groan of the transmission belts slowing and stopping as a result of a breakdown or for the end of his shift.

But so inexhaustible a quality is man's freedom, that even in these conditions Pietro's mind was able to weave its web from one machine to the other, to flow on unbroken as the thread from the spider's mouth, and in the midst of this geometry of steps gestures glances and reflexes he would sometimes find he was master of himself once again and calm as a country grandfather going out late in the morning to sit under the pergola and stare at the sun and whistle for his dog and keep an eye on his grandchildren swinging on a tree and watch the figs ripen day by day.

Of course, such freedom of thought could only be achieved by following a special technique that had taken time and training: all you had to do, for example, was learn how to break off your flow of thought when your hand had to move the workpiece under the lathe, then pick it up again, almost placing it on the piece as it now proceeded towards the grooving machine, and above all take advantage of the moments you had to walk, since one never thinks so well as when one walks a well-known stretch of road, even if here the road was no more than two steps: one-two, but how many things one could think of in that space: a happy old age, all Sundays in piazzas at political meetings listening hard near the loudspeakers, a job for his unemployed son, and then all at once off with a gaggle of grandchildren fishing on summer evenings, each with his rod on the walls above the river, and a bet on a cycle race to propose to his friend Tommaso, or about the collapse of the government, but something so wild as to knock the big-headedness out of him for a bit – and at the same time glance over at the transmission belt to make sure it wasn't slipping off where it always did by the wheel.

'If in ... (pull up the lever!) ... May my son marries that idiot's daughter ... (slide the piece under the lathe!) we can move out of the big room ... (and taking two steps) ... that way when the newly-weds lie in on Sunday morning they'll get the view of the mountains from the window ... (now push down that lever there!) and me and the old woman can move into the small room ... (straighten out those pieces!) ... since who cares if we can only see the gas tank from there,' and, shifting now to another line of thought, as if the idea of the gas tank near his house had brought him back to everyday reality, or perhaps because when the lathe jammed for a second it inspired a more aggressive attitude: 'Ifthelaminatesshopstartsindustrialactionoverpiecework, we can ... (careful! it's out of line!) ... join them ... (careful!) ... with our cl ... with our claim (it's gone, damn it!) ... for higher pay grades for our spe ... cia ... liz ... a ... tions ...'

Thus the movement of the machines both conditioned and drove the movement of his thoughts. And little by little, softly and stealthily, his mind adapted itself to the confines of this mechanical mesh, as the slim muscular body of the young Renaissance cavalier adapts to its armour, learns to tense and relax biceps to wake up a sleepy arm, to stretch, to rub an itchy shoulderblade against the iron backplate, to tighten buttocks, to

73

shift testicles crushed against the saddle, to twitch a big toe away from the others: in the same way Pietro's mind stretched and loosened up inside its prison of nervous tension, automatic gestures, weariness.

For there is no prison that doesn't have its chinks. So even in a system that aims to exploit every last fraction of your time, you discover that with proper organization the moment will come when the marvellous holiday of a few seconds opens up before you and you can even take three steps back and forward, or scratch your stomach, or hum something: 'Pompety pom . . .' and assuming the foreman isn't around to bother you, there'll be time, between one operation and the next, to say a couple of words to a workmate.

So it was that when the hen turned up Pietro was able to go: 'chucketty chuck chuck . . .' and to make a mental comparison of his own pirouetting between the four machines, big and flat-footed as he was, to the movements of the hen; and he began to drop his trail of maize that, leading to the scrap metal box, was supposed to lure the fowl into laying its egg for him and not for that stooge Adalberto nor for his friend and rival Tommaso.

But neither Pietro's nor Tommaso's nests impressed the hen. It seemed she laid her eggs at dawn, in Adalberto's coop, before beginning her rounds of the workshops. Both the turner and the quality controller got into the habit of grabbing hold of her and poking her abdomen as soon as they saw her. The hen, tame as a cat by nature, let them, but was always empty.

It should be said that Pietro was no longer on his own with his four machines. That is, the job of running the machines was still entirely his but it had been decided that a certain number of pieces needed a special finishing and a few days ago a worker with a file had joined him and every now and then would take a handful of pieces, carry them to a small bench set up close by and, scrape scrape grind grind, he very calmly filed them down for ten minutes. He gave Pietro no help, on the contrary he was always getting in his way and muddling him up, and it was clear that his real job had nothing to do with the filing. He was already well known in the factory, this worker, and even had a nickname: Giovannino the Stink.

He was scrawny, dark as dark, with thick curly hair, and a snub nose that pulled up his lip with it. Where they had found him nobody knew; what they did know was that the first job he'd been given in the factory, the day they took him on, was that of toilet maintenance man; but the truth was he was supposed to be there all day listening to people talk and passing things on to the management. Quite what there was to hear in the toilets that was so important no one ever really understood; it seems that there being nowhere else in the factory where one could exchange a few words without being fired on the spot, two workers from the Internal Committee, or some other diabolical union invention, had taken to swapping ideas from one cubicle to another, pretending they were there to answer nature's calling. Not that the workers' toilets in a factory are a quiet place, having as they do no doors or just a low gate affair leaving head and shoulders visible so that no one can stop for a smoke, and with the security men poking their heads in every few minutes to see that no one stays too long and check whether you're defecating or just taking it easy, but all the same, compared with the rest of the factory, the toilets are calm, even comfortable places. The fact is that these two men were eventually accused of engaging in political activity during working hours and fired; so someone must have told on them and it didn't take long to identify that someone as Giovannino the Stink as he was henceforth to be called. He was shut away in there, it was spring, and all day he heard watery noises, flushing, plopping, splashing; and he dreamed of open streams and fresh air. No one talked any more in the toilets. So they moved him. Unskilled, manipulated by the unwarranted fears of a management forever in a state of alarm, he was assigned first to one team then another, given vague and obviously pointless tasks but with secret instructions to spy on the others; and wherever he went his workmates turned their backs on him in silence, not deigning so much as a glance at the superfluous tasks he muddled over as best he could.

Now he had wound up on the heels of an old worker, deaf and alone. What was he supposed to find out? Was he too at his last assignment before being put out on the street like the victims of his spying? Giovannino the Stink racked his brains for a trail, a suspicion, a clue. The moment was propitious; the whole factory was in turmoil, the workers at boiling point, the management with their hackles up. And for a while Giovannino had been churning over an idea. Every day, around the same time, a hen would come into the workshop. And the turner Pietro would prod at it. He lured it with a few grains of maize, got close to it and put his hand right under it. What on earth could it mean? Was it a system for passing secret messages from one workshop to another? Giovannino was sure of it now. The way Pietro touched the hen it was exactly as if he were looking for something, or slipping something inside its feathers. And one day, when Pietro let go of the bird, Giovannino the Stink followed it. The hen crossed the yard, climbed on a pile of iron girders – Giovannino did a balancing act to follow – dived into a segment of piping – Giovannino crawled after it – crossed another patch of courtyard and went into Quality Control. Here there was another old man who seemed to be waiting for the hen: he was watching for it to appear at the doorway, and as soon as he saw it he dropped his hammer and screwdriver and went to meet it. The hen was on friendly terms with this man too, so much so that she let herself be picked up by the feet and, once again! prodded under the tail. By now Giovannino was sure he had struck gold. 'The message,' he thought, 'is sent every day from Pietro to this fellow here. Tomorrow, as soon as the hen leaves Pietro, I'll have it stopped and searched.'

The next day, having half-heartedly prodded the hen for the nth time and then sadly replaced it on the ground, Pietro saw Giovannino the Stink set down his file and go off almost at a run.

76

When he raised the alarm, the watchmen on duty gave chase. Surprised in the yard pecking at maggots between bolts strewn in the dust, the hen was taken to the security chief's office.

Adalberto knew nothing as yet. Given that connivance on his part could not be excluded, the operation had been conducted without his being informed. Summoned to head office, no sooner did he see the hen immobilized by two colleagues on the boss's desk than his eyes all but filled with tears. 'What has she done? What's happened? I always kept her shut in her coop!' he began to say, thinking they were blaming him for having let the bird wander about the factory.

But the accusations were far more serious, as he quickly appreciated. The security chief fired off a volley of questions. He was a retired carabiniere inspector and over the ex-carabinieri amongst his security staff he continued to exercise the hierarchical authority typical of the force. Throughout the questioning, more than his love of the hen, more than his hopes to become a chicken breeder, what was uppermost in Adalberto's mind was the fear that he would compromise himself. He came clean, he tried to justify himself for having left the hen free, but when it came to questions about the relationship between the hen and the unions, he didn't dare compromise himself by clearing the bird or excusing it. He withdrew behind a wall of 'I don't know, I've got nothing to do with it,' concerned only that he should in no way be held responsible for the affair.

The security man's good faith was accepted; but, with a lump in his throat and a pang of remorse, he was now looking at a hen that had been abandoned to its destiny.

The inspector ordered that the bird be searched. One of the agents stalled saying it made him feel sick, and after some fierce pecking another withdrew sucking a bleeding finger. In the end the inevitable experts emerged, more than happy to demonstrate their zeal. The oviduct was shown to be free of any messages inimical to the interests of the company, or indeed of any other

77

variety. Expert in the many techniques of war, the inspector insisted that they search under the bird's wings, where the Pigeon-Lover Brigade are wont to conceal their messages in special sealed cartridges. They searched; feathers, down and dirt were strewn across the desk, but nothing was found.

Nonetheless, considered too suspect and treacherous to be innocent, the hen was condemned. In the dingy courtyard two men in black uniforms held it by the claws while a third wrung its neck. The bird let out a last long heart-breaking shriek, then a lugubrious cluck, she who had been so discreet as never to dare cluck for joy. Adalberto hid his face in his hands, his harmless dream of a cackling hencoop buried stillborn. Thus does the machine of oppression ever turn against those who serve it. The owner of the company, concerned that he had to meet a delegation of workers who were protesting against firings, heard the hen's death wail in his office and sensed it boded ill.

Numbers in the Dark

The evening dark slips into streets and avenues, shades the spaces between the leaves of the trees, dots the moving tram arms with sparks, opens up in soft cones beneath the punctual streetlamps, turns on festive displays in shop windows, throwing into relief the curtained domesticity of apartments above. But on first floors and mezzanines, broad rectangles of unshaded light reveal the mysteries of a thousand city offices. The working day is over. The last letters are wound out from the drums of a line of typewriters and separated from their carbons; files full of correspondence are laid for signing on managers' desks, the typists cover their machines and head for the cloakroom, or they are already in line in the coated bustle waiting to clock out. Soon all is deserted. The windows reveal a series of empty rooms, immersed in the chalky whiteness that reverberates from fluorescent tubes on walls divided by cheerful colours into different sections, on bare polished desks, on the data-processing machines, which, the urgent patter of their straining thought now over, sleep on their feet like horses. Until all at once this geometric scenario is filled with middle-aged women, wrapped in flowery scarlet-and-green gowns, their heads tied in scarves or with 'Empire' hairstyles or a fichu, wearing skirts too short for them from which swollen legs protrude in woolly stockings, cloth-slippered feet. Accountancy's night spawns witches. Brush and broom in hand they launch themselves across those smooth surfaces, tracing out their spells.

In a square of window, a boy's freckled face, thick wave of black hair above, appears and flits away, reappears at the next window, and the next, and the next again, like a moon-fish in an aquarium. There, he's stopped in the corner of a window, and with a sudden crash a shutter rolls down, the bright rectangle of the aquarium is gone. One two three four, darkness falls on all the windows and in each the last thing you see is the moon-fish grimace of that little face.

'Paolino! Got all the shutters down, have you?'

Although he has to be up early for school in the morning, Paolino's mother takes him with her every evening so that he can help a bit and learn how to work. By this time a soft cloud of sleep is beginning to weigh down on his eyelids. Coming in from the already dark streets, these deserted, brightly lit rooms put him in a sort of daze. Even the desklamps have been left on, their green shades on long adjustable necks leaning towards the shiny desktops. Passing by, Paolino presses buttons to turn them off and ease the glare.

'What are you doing? You can't play now. Come and give us a hand! Have you got the shutters down yet?'

With a sharp tug Paolino lets the shutters fall all at once. The night outside, the haloes of the streetlamps, the softened glow of distant windows across the street, disappear; now there is nowhere but this box of light. With every rattle of a shutter, it's as if Paolino were gradually waking from his torpor: but as though in sleep when you dream of waking only to go into another and deeper dream.

'Can I do the waste-bins, Mum?'

'Good boy, yes, take the bag, off you go!'

Paolino takes the bag and goes off round the offices to empty the wastepaper bins. The bag is bigger than he is and Paolino drags it after him so that it slides across the floor. He walks slowly to make the job last as long as possible: of the whole evening this is the moment he likes best. Big rooms with lines of identical calculators and filing cabinets open before him, rooms with authoritative desks crammed with touch-button telephones and intercoms. He likes going round the offices alone, to immerse himself in those metallic ornaments, those sharp right-angles, forgetting everything else. Above all he likes getting away from the sound of his mother and Signora Dirce's chatter.

The difference between Signora Dirce and Paolino's mother is that Signora Dirce is very conscious of the fact that she is cleaning SBAV's offices, whereas it's all the same to Paolino's mother whether she is cleaning an office, a kitchen or the back of a shop.

Signora Dirce knows the names of all the departments. 'Now we'll go into Accounts, Signora Pensotti,' she says to Paolino's mother.

'Come again?' says Signora Pensotti, a small fat little woman, only recently arrived from the provinces.

Signora Dirce on the other hand is long and thin, very haughty, and wears a kind of kimono. She knows all the company's secrets, and Paolino's mother listens agape. 'You see how untidy Dr Bertolenghi is, it's incredible,' she says, 'I bet exports are bad with all this mess.'

Paolino's mother tugs her sleeve: 'Who's he when he's at home . . . ? Oh give it a rest . . . What do you care, Signora Dirce? Don't you know that if the desks aren't cleared we don't have to clean them. Just give the phone a quick wipe, to take off the worst . . .'

Signora Dirce even sticks her nose in the papers, picks up a letter, holds it close to her nose because she's short-sighted, says: 'Hey, listen to this, three hundred thousand dollars, it says here . . . You know how much three hundred thousand dollars is, Signora Pensotti?'

As Paolino sees it, the two women strike a false note, they're an affront to the composure of the office. They get on his nerves, both of them: Signora Dirce is arrogant, ridiculous when, to dust intercom keyboards or drawer handles, she sits in the manager's big chair and, wiping things with her rag, assumes the managerial expression of someone doing something important;

and his mother is still the country woman she always was, dusting calculators as if she were pushing cows round the farm.

The further Paolino gets away from them, adventuring into the deserted offices, so the further his eyes, droopy with sleep, push back that bare, linear horizon, and he likes to think of himself as an ant, an almost invisible creature crossing a smooth desert of linoleum, amid shiny mountains that fall sheer to the ground beneath a flat white sky. Then he's overawed; and to pull himself together he looks around for signs of human life, always varied and disordered. Under the glass top of a desk – a woman's it must be – there's a photograph of Marlon Brando; someone else is keeping a pot of daffodil bulbs on a windowsill; there's a magazine in a waste bin; in another a sheet of block-notes has been filled with pencil sketches of little figures; a typist's stool smells of violets; in an ashtray there are some of those small foil cups that chocolate liqueurs come in. There, he only has to latch on to these details and his awe at that geometric desert subsides, but Paolino feels almost humiliated, as if he were being a coward, because it's precisely what most strikes awe in him that he wants to and must make his own.

One room is full of machines. They're motionless now, but Paolino saw them working once, with a constant hum and thick sheets of perforated paper jerking up and down like insect wings; and a man in a white doctor's coat who was operating the machines stopped to talk to Paolino. 'There'll come the day when machines like this do all the work,' he said, 'with no need for anybody, not even me.'

Paolino had immediately run to Signora Dirce. 'Do you know what those machines make?' he had asked her, hoping to catch her out; the man in the white coat had just explained that the machines didn't produce anything, but managed all the company's business, they looked after the accounts, they knew everything that happened and that was going to happen.

'Those?' Signora Dirce had said, 'you can't even catch mice with those, I'm telling you. You want to know something? The company that markets those machines is owned by the brother-in-law of Dr Pistagna, so he got SBAV to buy them. That's what happened.'

Paolino had shrugged his shoulders: once again it was clear that Signora Dirce didn't understand anything: she didn't even realize that those machines knew the past and the future, that they would operate offices on their own one day, and the offices would be deserted and empty like now at night. Dragging the bag with the wastepaper after him, Paolino tries to imagine how it will be then, to concentrate on that idea, as far as possible from his mother and Signora Dirce, but there is always something that prevents him, a sort of jarring presence. What is it?

He is going into an office to get the wastebin when some-one shouts 'Oh!' in fright. A man and a woman staying late for overtime have seen a shock of hair bristling like a porcupine peep round the door, then the little boy with his green and red striped jersey coming in dragging a big bag behind him. Unhappily Paolino realizes that that intruding presence is no other than his own.

The office workers on the other hand seem to be in tune with the room. She is a redhead, with glasses, while the man's hair is shiny with brilliantine. He is dictating numbers to her and she is typing them out. Paolino stops to watch them. The man dictating feels the need to walk about, but the way he moves amongst the tables, always turning at right-angles, it's as if he were in a maze. He approaches the girl again, then goes away again; the numbers pour down like dry hail, the keys raise and lower the typewriter's little hammers, the man's nervous hands touch the desk calendar, the papertrays, the backs of the seats, and everything they meet is metal. At one point the girl makes a mistake, stops to rub it out against the drum, and for a moment everything takes on a softer almost caressing feel; the man repeats the number in a quieter voice, places his hand on the back of her seat, and she arches her back so it just brushes his hand, and their eyes lose that fixed glaze of concentration as they meet for a moment. But the rubbing out is over now; she begins to drum on the keys again, he to fire off the figures; they separate, all is as before.

Paolino has to go and get the wastebin; to strike an attitude he starts whistling. The two stop, raise their eyes. Paolino points at the bin. 'Go ahead, please.' Paolino goes over to it, his lips pursed as though to whistle, but without making any sound. As he goes towards the bin the two take a moment's involuntary break, and during this break they come together again, their hands brush against each other, and their eyes stop darting about and turn to meet each other. Slowly Paolino opens the mouth of his bag, lifts the bin; the young man and the girl are about to smile at each other. With a brusque twist of the hand, Paolino turns the bin upside down, then bangs on the bottom to have the paper fall in the sack; the office worker and the typist are already furiously at work again, he dictating numbers one right after the other, she bent over her typewriter, her red hair covering her face.

'Paolino! Paolino! Come and hold the steps for me!'

Paolino's mother is cleaning windows on a step-ladder. Paolino goes to hold it for her. Pushing her mop back and forth across the floor, Signora Dirce has words to say about the lack of doormats: 'What would it cost a company like this to buy a few doormats, so they don't tread mud into the offices . . . But no, who cares when it's always us has to slave, and woe betide if there isn't a shine on the floor . . .'

'Doesn't matter, we'll be waxing it Saturday, Signora Dirce, you'll see how nice it'll come up . . .' says Signora Pensotti.

'Oh, I've nothing against Dr Uggero, you know, Signora Pensotti, between you and me it's Dr Pistagna, that . . .'

Paolino doesn't listen. He's thinking of the young man and the typist in the other room. When men and women do overtime together after dinner, there's an atmosphere as if they were undergoing some kind of special trial together. They're working hard, you might say, but they put something tense, something secret into it. Paolino wouldn't know how to put it into words,

84

but it's something he saw in their eyes, and he'd like to go back and see them.

'Hey, hold on to the steps, sleepyhead! You want me to fall off, or what?'

Paolino starts to look at the graphs hanging on the walls. Up, down, up, up, down a bit, up again. What do they represent? Perhaps you could read them by whistling: a note that goes up, and up, then a low note, then a longer high note. He tries whistling the line of a graph: 'Whee, wheeeeee ...' then another, then another. A nice tune comes out. 'Stop whistling, are you stupid?' his mother shouts. 'Do you want a spanking?'

Now Paolino goes round with the bin to empty all the ashtrays. He goes back to the office with the two working overtime. He can't hear the tippety-tap of the typewriter. Have they gone? Paolino pokes his head round. The girl is standing, stretching out a hand bent at the knuckles and with brightly varnished nails towards the brylcreamed young man; he lifts an arm as if to take her by the throat. Paolino begins to whistle: what comes to his lips is the tune he invented a few moments ago. The two compose themselves. 'Oh, it's you again?' They've already got their coats on and are standing together looking at some papers for tomorrow's work. 'The ashtray!' Paolino says. But they're not interested, they put the papers down and go. At the bottom of the corridor he takes her arm.

Paolino's sorry they've gone. Now there really is nobody left: all he can hear is the hum of the polisher and his mother's voice. Paolino crosses the Board of Directors' conference room with its mahogany table, so shiny you can see your face in it, and the big leather chairs all round. He'd like to take a run up and do a fish dive on the table top, slide from one end to the other, then collapse in a chair and fall asleep. But all he does is rub a finger across, look at the damp mark it makes like the wake of a ship, then rub it off with the elbow of his sweater.

The big accounts department is divided into lots of cubicles. There's a tippety-tap coming from the bottom. There must be somebody there still, working overtime. Paolino goes from one cubicle to another, but it's like a maze where every passage is the same and the tippety-tapping always seems to be coming from a different place. In the end, in the very last cubicle, bent over an old adding machine, he finds a skinny accountant in a pullover, with a green plastic eyeshade halfway down a bald, oblong skull. To tap the keys the accountant lifts his elbows with the movement birds make when they beat their wings: he looks just like a big bird perched there, his visor like a beak. Paolino goes to empty the ashtray, but the accountant is smoking and at that very moment puts his cigarette down on the rim.

'Hi,' the accountant says.

'Good evening,' says Paolino.

'What are you doing up and about at this time?' The accountant has a long white face and dry skin, as if he never saw the sun.

'I'm emptying the ashtrays.'

'Little boys should be in bed at night.'

'I'm with my mother. We do the cleaning. We start now.'

'How late do you stay?'

'Till half-past ten, eleven. Then sometimes we do overtime, in the morning.'

'The opposite of what we do, overtime in the morning.'

'Yes, but only once or twice a week, when we do the waxing.'

'I do overtime every day. I never finish.'

'Finish what?'

'Getting the accounts right.'

'They won't come out right?'

'They never do.'

Motionless, the handle of the adding machine in his fist, his eyes on the thin strip of paper dangling almost to the ground, the accountant seems to be expecting something of the line of numbers that rises from the drum, as the smoke from the cigarette held tight between his lips likewise rises, first in a straight line in front of his right eye, till it meets his visor, takes a turn, then floats up again as far as the light bulb where it gathers in a cloud beneath the shade.

'Now, I'll say it,' thinks Paolino, and he asks: 'Excuse me, but aren't there electronic machines that do all the sums on their own?'

Irritated by the smoke, the accountant closes one eye. 'All wrong,' he says.

Putting down the cloth and the bin, Paolino leans on the accountant's desk. 'Those machines make mistakes?'

The man with the visor shakes his head. 'No, from the start. It was wrong from the start.' He gets up, his pullover is too short and his shirt puffs out all round his belt. He picks up his jacket from the back of his seat and puts it on. 'Come with me.'

Paolino and the accountant walk past the cubicles. The accountant takes big steps and Paolino has to trot to keep up. They go the whole length of the corridor; at the bottom the accountant lifts a curtain: there is a spiral staircase going down. It's dark, but the accountant knows where there's a switch and turns on a dim bulb down below. Now they go down the spiral staircase, down into the company vaults. In the vaults there's a little door closed with a chain: the accountant has the key and he opens the door. There can't be any electricity because the accountant strikes a match and immediately finds a candle and lights it. Paolino can't see very much, but he realizes he's in a tight space in a sort of little cell, and piled right up to the ceiling are stacks of notebooks, registers, dusty papers, and clearly this is where the mouldy smell is coming from.

'They're all the company's old ledgers,' says the accountant, 'in the hundred years of its existence.' Pulling himself up on to a stool, he opens a long, narrow ledger on a high bench that's angled for reading. 'See? This is the handwriting of Annibale De Canis, the company's first accountant, the most conscientious accountant there's ever been: look how he kept the registers.'

Paolino's eye runs down columns of numbers written in a fine oblong hand with little flourishes.

'You're the only person I've shown this to: the others wouldn't understand. And somebody has to see: I'm old.'

'Yes, sir,' says Paolino in a whisper.

'There never was another like Annibale De Canis,' and the man with the green visor moves the candle, to show, above a pile of registers and beside an old abacus with rickety rods, the photograph of a man with a moustache and goatee beard posing with a Pomeranian dog. 'Yet this infallible man, this genius, see here, 16 November 1884' – and the accountant turns the pages of the ledger to open it where a dried up goose-feather has been left as a bookmark – 'yes, here, a mistake, a stupid mistake of four hundred and ten lire in an addition.' At the bottom of the page the total is ringed in red pen. 'And nobody realized, only I know about it, and you're the first person I've told: keep it to yourself and don't forget! And then, even if you did go round telling people, you're only a boy and no one would believe you ... But now you know that everything's wrong. Over all these years, you know what that mistake of four hundred and ten lire has become? Billions! Billions! The calculating machines and electronic brains and whatnot can grind out numbers all they like. The mistake is right at the core, beneath all their numbers, and it's growing bigger and bigger and bigger!' They had shut up the little room now and were climbing the spiral staircase, walking back down the corridor. 'The company has grown big, huge, with thousands of shareholders, hundreds of subsidiaries, endless overseas agencies, and all of them grinding out nothing but wrong figures, there's not a grain of truth in any of their accounts. Half the city is built on these mistakes! No, not half the city, what am I saying? Half the country! And the exports and imports? All wrong, the whole world is distorted by this mistake, the only mistake in the life of Annibale De Canis, that master of book-keeping, that giant of accountancy, that genius!'

The man goes over to get his coat from a peg and puts it on. Without his green visor, his face seems even sadder and paler for a moment, then it's in the shadow again as he pulls his hat brim down over his eyes. 'And you know what I think?' he says, leaning down, voice hushed, 'I'm sure he did it on purpose!'

He stands up, thrusts his hands in his pockets. 'We two have never met, never known each other,' he mutters to Paolino.

He turns and heads for the door with a gait that wants to be upright but comes out crooked, and he's humming: '*La donna è mobile* . . .'

A telephone rings. 'Hello! Hello!' It's Signora Dirce's voice. Paolino runs over to her.

'Yes, yes, SBAV here. What's that? What's that? Where, Brazil? Fancy: they're calling from Brazil. Yes, but what do you want? I don't understand . . . Know what, Signora Pensotti? They're speaking Brazilian, do you want to hear a bit too?'

Calling at this hour, it must have been a customer from the other side of the world who'd muddled up the time difference.

Paolino's mother grabs the receiver from Signora Dirce's hand: 'There's no one here, no one, understand?' she starts shouting. 'You can call to-o-mor-ro-ow! There's only u-us here no-ow! The cleaners, understand? The cleaners!'

The Queen's Necklace

Pietro and Tommaso were always arguing.

At dawn the squeaking of their old bicycles and the sound of their voices – Pietro's hollow and nasal, Tommaso's husky and sometimes hoarse – were the only noises to be heard in the empty streets. They used to cycle together to the factory where they worked. From the other side of the shutter slats you could still feel the sleep and the darkness weighing on the rooms. The muffled ringing of alarm clocks began a sporadic dialogue from one house to the next, becoming denser in the suburbs, until finally it merged, as town merged into country, into a back and forth of cock-a-doodle-doos.

Busy as they were arguing at the tops of their voices, the two workers didn't notice this first stirring of daily sounds: anyway they were both deaf; Pietro had been a little hard of hearing for some years now, while Tommaso had a constant whistle in one ear that went back to the First World War.

'That's how things are, old friend,' Pietro, a big fellow of sixty-odd, uncertainly balanced on his wobbling machine, thundered down at Tommaso, five years his elder, but smaller and already somewhat bent. 'You've lost faith, old friend. I know myself that with the way things are today having kids means going hungry, but tomorrow you never know, you never know which side the scales might come down, tomorrow having kids could mean wealth. That's how I see things, and rightly so.'

Without taking his eyes off his friend, yellow bulbs opening

90

wide, Tommaso let out sharp cries that would suddenly turn hoarse: 'Ye-ess, ye-ess! What's got to be said to a worker starting a family is this!: bringing babies into the world you're only adding to poverty and unemployment! That's what! That's what he's got to know! I'm telling you. I've said it before and I'll say it again!'

Their discussion this morning was on the general question, does an increase in the population favour or damage the workers? Pietro was optimistic and Tommaso pessimistic. Behind this conflict of views lay the marriage planned between Pietro's son and Tommaso's daughter. Pietro was for it and Tommaso against.

'And anyway, they haven't had kids yet!' Pietro suddenly came back. 'All in good time! That's all we need! We're talking about an engagement, not about kids!'

Tommaso yelled: 'When people marry, they have kids!'

'In the country! Where you were born!' Pietro came back. He almost got his wheel caught in a tram rail. He swore.

'Wha-aat?' Tommaso shouted, pedalling ahead.

Pietro shook his head and said nothing. They went on in silence for a while.

'Then, of course,' Pietro said, winding up a train of thought out loud, 'when they come, they come!'

They had left the city behind them and were riding along a raised road between fields left fallow. There were some last patches of fog. Above a grey horizon not far away loomed the factory.

An engine droned behind them; they had just got themselves on the verge when a big smart car went by.

The road wasn't tarred, the dust the car lifted cloaked the two cyclists and from the thick cloud came Tommaso's raised voice: 'And it's in the exclusive interest o-of . . . oh, oh, oh!' The dust he'd swallowed brought on a fit of coughing and his short arm emerged from the cloud and pointed in the direction of the car, doubtless to suggest the interest of the ruling classes. Pietro, trying to speak while coughing from a red face, said: 'Uugh . . .Not

... uugh ... for ... uugh ... lo-ong,' pointing at the car with a decidedly negative gesture to express the idea that the future did not belong to the owners of custom-built automobiles.

The car was racing away when one of its doors came open. A hand thrust it wide so that it banged back and a woman in silhouette almost threw herself out. But whoever was driving braked at once; the woman jumped down, and in the thin morning mist the workers saw her run across the road. She had blonde hair, a long black dress and a cape of blue fox furs, their tails in fringes.

A man wearing an overcoat got out of the car, shouting: 'You're crazy! You're crazy!' The woman was already dashing away from the road through the bushes, and the man set off after her until they both disappeared.

Below the road were meadows with dense thickets of shrubs, and the two workers saw the woman appearing and disappearing in and out of them, her steps short and quick in the heavy dew. With one hand she held her skirt from touching the ground and she jerked her shoulders to free herself from the branches that caught at her fox tails. She even began to bend the branches so that they would spring back on the man who was chasing her, though without really hurrying and without, it seemed, too much desire to catch her. The woman ran wild in the meadows, shrieked with laughter, shook the dew on the branches down on to her hair. Until he, calm as ever, instead of following her, cut her off and took her by the elbows; and it looked as though she was wriggling to escape and biting him.

The two workers followed the chase from the raised road, though they never stopped pedalling or paying attention to where they were going. They watched silently, eyebrows raised and mouths open, with a gravity more diffident than curious. They were almost up to the stationary car, left there with its doors open, when the man in the overcoat came back, holding the woman who was forcing him to push her along and yelling almost like a child. They shut themselves in the car and set off; and again the cyclists ran into the dust.

'While we're starting our day,' choked Tommaso, 'the drunkards are ending theirs.'

'Actually,' objected his friend, stopping to look back, 'he wasn't drunk. Look how sharply he stopped.'

They studied the tyre marks. 'No, no, no...you're joking ...no, a car like that,' came back Tommaso, 'do it myself! Don't you realize that a car like that stops you dead...'

He didn't finish his sentence; looking down at the ground, their eyes had come to rest on a point just off the road. There was something sparkling on a bush. Simultaneously, softly they both exclaimed: 'Oh!'

They got down from their saddles and stood their bikes against the kerb. 'The chicken's laid an egg,' said Pietro and jumped down into the meadow with a lightness you wouldn't have expected in him. On the bush was a necklace of four strings of pearls.

The two workers stretched out their hands and, delicately, as though picking a flower, plucked the necklace from its branch. They both held it, with both hands, feeling the pearls with their fingertips, but ever so carefully, and as they did so lifted it closer and closer to their eyes.

Then, both together, as though rebelling against the awe and fascination the object inspired, they dropped their fists, but neither one of them let go of the necklace. Feeling somebody would have to say something, Pietro breathed out and commented, 'See the sort of ties that are in fashion these days...'

'It's fake!' Tommaso immediately shouted in one ear, as if he'd been bursting to say it for the last few minutes, indeed as if it had been his first thought the moment he'd set eyes on the necklace and had only been waiting for some sign of gloating from his friend to be able to hit back at him with this remark.

Pietro raised the hand that held the necklace, thus lifting Tommaso's arm too. 'What do you know?'

'I know that you'd better believe what I'm telling you: they always keep their real jewels in the safe.'

Their big, tough, wrinkled hands felt the necklace, turning their fingers between one string and the next, slipping their nails into the spaces between the pearls. The pearls filtered a soft light, like dewdrops on spiders' webs, a wintery, morning light that hardly convinces you of the existence of things.

'Real or fake . . .' Pietro said, 'I, as it happens . . .' and he was trying to provoke a hostile attitude towards whatever he was about to say.

Tommaso, who wanted to be the first to take the conversation that way, realized that Pietro had got in before him and tried to regain the upper hand by showing that he'd already been developing his own train of thought for some time.

'Oh, I pity you,' he said, with an air of irritation. 'The first thing I . . .'

It was clear that they both wanted to express the same opinion, yet were looking daggers at each other. They both shouted, in unison and as fast as they could: 'Give it back!' Pietro raising his chin with the solemnity of one uttering a verdict, Tommaso red-faced and wide-eyed as if all his energy were engaged in getting the words out before his friend.

But the gesture had excited them and aroused their pride; apparently good friends all of a sudden, they exchanged satisfied glances.

'We won't dirty our hands!' Tommaso shouted. 'Not us!'

'Right!' laughed Pietro. 'We'll give them a lesson in dignity, we will.'

'We,' Tommaso proclaimed, 'will never hoard their trash!'

'Right! We're poor,' Pietro said, 'but more gentlemen than they are!'

'And you know what else we're going to do?' Tommaso's face lit up, happy to have finally gone one better than Pietro. 'We won't accept their reward!'

They looked at the necklace again; it was still there, hanging from their hands.

'You didn't get the licence number of the car, did you?' asked Pietro.

'No, why? Did you?'

'Who would have thought?'

'So, what to do?'

'Right, a fine mess.'

Then, in unison, as if their hostility had suddenly flared up again: 'The Lost Property Office. We'll take it there.'

The fog was lifting; no longer a mere shadow, the factory turned out to be coloured a deceptive pink.

'What time do you think it is?' asked Pietro. 'I'm afraid we'll be clocking in late.'

'We'll be fined,' said Tommaso. 'The same old story: those folks live it up and we pay up!'

They had both lifted their hands together with the necklace that kept them together like handcuffed prisoners. They weighed it in their palms as if both about to say: 'Well, I'll let you look after it.' But neither of them did; each had the highest possible opinion of the other, but they were too used to arguing for either to concede a point to the other.

They must get back on their bikes again fast, and still they hadn't tackled the question: which of them was to keep the necklace before they could hand it back or in any event take a decision as to what to do? They went on standing there without saying a word, looking at the necklace as if it might somehow answer the question itself. And it did: whether in the skirmish or when it fell, the hook that held together the four strings of pearls had been damaged. A tiny twist and it snapped.

Pietro took two strings and Tommaso the other two, with the understanding that whatever was to be done with them would be agreed on together first. They gathered the precious things up, hid them away, got back on their bikes, silently, without looking at each other, and resumed their squeaky pedalling towards the factory under a sky of gathering white clouds and rising black smoke.

They'd hardly got going before a man appeared from behind a billboard at the side of the road. He was scrawny, lanky and badly dressed; he had been watching the two workers from a distance for some minutes. His name was Fiorenzo, he was unemployed, and he spent his time looking through dumps in the suburbs in search of anything usable. It's an occupational hazard of people like this that they always nurse a stubborn yearning that one day they will discover treasure. On his regular morning round of these fields, Fiorenzo had seen the car set off and the workers run down the embankment to pick something up. And immediately he realized that he had missed a rare, even a once-in-a-lifetime opportunity by less than a minute.

Tommaso was a member of the internal commission that was supposed to see Dr Starna. Deaf and stubborn he might be, with obsolete attitudes and a spirit of contradiction, but still Tommaso always managed to get elected in internal factory votes. He was one of the oldest workers in the company, everybody knew him, he was a symbol; and even though his workmates on the commission had long felt that it would be better to have a more able negotiator in his place, somebody sharper and better informed, all the same they recognized that Tommaso had the advantage of a prestige that came of tradition, and they respected him for it and would repeat the most important things said at the meeting in the ear without the whistle.

The day before, one of Tommaso's sisters who lived in the country and who sometimes came to see him had brought him a rabbit for his birthday, even though his birthday had been a month ago. A dead rabbit, of course, to be casseroled at once. It would have been nice to have kept it for Sunday lunch to have with the whole family round the table; but perhaps the rabbit would go off, so Tommaso's daughters immediately steamed it and he was carrying his share to work with him in a stick of bread.

Whatever they were having for lunch — tripe, stockfish, or omelette — Tommaso's daughters (he was a widower) would cut a big stick of bread in two and squash the food in the middle; he put the bread in his bag, hung the bag on his bike and set off in the early morning for his day's work. But though this loaf stuffed with rabbit should have been the consolation for a worrisome day, Tommaso never managed to take so much as a bite of it. Changing for the meeting and not knowing where to hide the stupid necklace, he had had the bad idea of stuffing it in the bread inside the steamed rabbit meat.

At eleven o'clock someone comes to tell Tommaso, along with Fantino, Criscuolo, Zappo, Ortica and all the others, that Dr Starna has agreed to the meeting and is waiting for them. They wash and change as fast as they can and then go up in the lift. On the fifth floor they wait and wait: comes the lunchbreak and still Dr Starna hasn't seen them. Finally the secretary, a blonde with the beautiful body and ugly face of a cycling champion, appears to tell them that the doctor can't see them for the moment, they should go back to the factory floor with the others and as soon as he's free he'll call them.

In the canteen, all their workmates were waiting with bated breath: 'So? So, what happened?' But union talk was forbidden in the canteen. 'Nothing, we're going back in the afternoon.' And already it was time to return to work: the men on the committee sat down at the zinc tables to grab a quick bite and get back, because every minute they were late would be docked from their pay. 'But what are we going to do about tomorrow?' the others asked, leaving the canteen. 'As soon as we've had the meeting, we'll tell you and we can decide what to do.'

Tommaso reached in his bag and pulled out a head of boiled cauliflower, a fork and a tiny bottle of oil. He poured a little oil on to an aluminium plate and ate the cauliflower with one hand while the other was in his jacket pocket stroking that fat sandwich full of meat and pearls that he couldn't pull out because of his workmates. And with a sudden greedy hunger for the rabbit, he cursed the pearls that were keeping him chained to a diet of cauliflower all day, and preventing him from feeling at ease with his friends, imposing a secret on him that, just at the moment, was no more than an irritation.

Suddenly, standing opposite him on the other side of the table, he saw Pietro, come to say hello before going back to work. The big man stood in front of him twisting a toothpick in his mouth and closing one eye in an exaggerated wink. Seeing him there, well fed and fancy free – or so it seemed to Tommaso – while he was swallowing forkfuls of boiled and quite insubstantial cauliflower, the older man went into such a rage that the aluminium plate started to rattle on the zinc table as though there were spirits about. Pietro shrugged his shoulders and left. By now the last workers were likewise hurrying out of the canteen, and Tommaso, greasy lips sucking on a soda bottle full of wine, dashed off too.

The workers' reaction to the Great Dane when it came into the director's waiting room – they had all turned to the door with a start thinking it was Dr Gigi Starni at last – was, on the part of some, welcoming, on the part of others, hostile. The former saw the dog as a fellow creature, a strong free thing kept prisoner here, a companion in servitude, the latter as merely a lost soul of the ruling class, a tool or accessory, a luxury. The same contrasting attitudes, in short, that workers sometimes manifest with regard to intellectuals.

Guderian's reaction to the workers, on the other hand, was one of reserve and indifference, both to those who said: 'Beauty! Come here! Give us a paw!' and those who said 'Off, scat!' With just a hint of combativeness in the way he sniffed lightly here and there and wagged his tail slowly and evenly, the dog began to do the rounds of the company: the freckled, curly-headed Ortica – the one who knew everything about everything, who was barely in the waiting room before he had his elbows planted on the table and was browsing through some ad magazines left there, and who, on seeing the dog had looked him up and down and said everything there was to be said about his breed age teeth fur – wasn't deigned so much as a glance, nor was the baby-faced Criscuolo, who, his gaze lost in the distance as he sucked on a dead cigarette, made as if to kick the animal. Fantino, who had pulled his crumpled paper from his pocket, a paper forbidden in the factory (he felt himself protected here by a sort of diplomatic immunity and so was taking advantage of the wait to read the thing, because when he got home in the evenings he immediately fell asleep) saw the dog's smoky snout with its glinting red eyes appear above one shoulder and instinctively, though he didn't often let things frighten him, folded over a page to hide the name of his paper. When he got to Tommaso, Guderian stopped, went down on his back paws and sat there with ears pricked and nose raised.

Although not the kind to start playing with pets or people, Tommaso, perhaps responding to a certain awe on finding himself in this brightly authoritative environment, felt the need to offer a few bland overtures, such as a click of the tongue, or a soft whistle, which, in his deafman's inability to control it, immediately came out as extremely shrill. In short, he tried to reassert that spontaneous trust between man and dog reminiscent of his farmboy's youth, of rustic animals, meek droopy-eared bloodhounds or hairy snarling barnyard mongrels. But the social gulf between the dogs of his past and this one, so glossy and well clipped, so much his master's creature, was immediately obvious to him, and intimidating. Sitting with his hands on his knees, he moved his head in little sideways jerks, his mouth open, as if silently barking, urging the dog to make up its mind and shove off, get lost. But Guderian sat still, at once motionless and panting, until at last he stretched out his snout towards a flap of the old man's jacket.

'You've got a friend in the management, Tommaso, and you never told us!' his friends joked.

But Tommaso went pale: he had just that moment realized it was the smell of casseroled rabbit the dog had caught.

Guderian went on the attack. He put a paw on Tommaso's chest, almost knocking him over in his chair, then licked his face, smothering it in saliva; to get rid of him the old man made as if to throw a stone, as if to shoot at a thrush, as if to jump a ditch,

99

but the dog didn't understand his mime or wasn't taken in, and wouldn't get off him; on the contrary, apparently seized by a sudden enthusiasm, he jumped up raising his front paws right above the worker's shoulders, all the time looking to push his nose in the direction of that jacket pocket.

'Off, boy, come on, off! Come on, boy, God damn!' Tommaso spoke under his breath, his eyes bloodshot, and in the middle of its demonstrations of affection the dog felt a sharp kick in one side. The animal threw itself at the man, baring its teeth at head height, then suddenly snapped at the flap of jacket and tugged. Tommaso just managed to get the bread out before the dog could rip off his pocket.

'Oh, a sandwich!' his friends said. 'Very smart, he keeps his dinner in his pocket, obvious the dogs go after him! Wish you gave us your leftovers!'

Raising his short arm as high as he could, Tommaso was trying to save the bread from the assaults of the Great Dane. 'Oh, let him have it! You'll never take it off him now! Let him have it!' his friends said.

'Pass! Pass to me! Why don't you pass?' Criscuolo was saying, clapping his hands, ready to catch the thing in flight like a basketball player.

But Tommaso didn't pass. Guderian jumped even higher than before and went to lie down in a corner with the sandwich between his teeth.

'Let him have it, Tommaso, what do you think you're going to do now? He'll bite you!' his friends said, but crouching down beside the Great Dane the old man seemed to be trying to talk to him.

'What do you want now?' his friends asked. 'To get a half-eaten sandwich back?' but at that moment the door opened and the secretary reappeared: 'Would you like to come through now?' and everybody hurried to follow her.

Tommaso got up to go after them, though he was still far from resigned to losing the necklace like this. He tried to get the dog to come in with him, then thought that having the thing appear in front of Dr Starna with the necklace in his mouth would be worse, and struggling to twist his angry face into a smile as grotesque as it was pointless, he bent down again to whisper: 'Come on, here boy, here you wretched beast!'

The door had closed again. There was no one left in the waiting room. The dog carried his prey into a secluded corner, behind an armchair. Tommaso wrung his hands, though what really upset him was not so much the loss of the necklace (hadn't he insisted throughout that it meant nothing to him?) as his having to feel guilty towards Pietro, having to tell him how it had happened, having to justify himself . . . and then the fact that he didn't know how to get out of here, that he was wasting time in a situation at once completely stupid and inexplicable to his friends . . .

'I'll snatch it off him!' he decided. 'If he bites me, I'll ask for damages.' And he got down on all fours beside the dog behind the armchair, then stretched out a hand to the animal's mouth. But the dog, being extremely well fed and trained, what's more, after his master's school of procrastination, wasn't eating the bread, but just nibbling at one side of it, nor did the animal react with that blind ferocity typical of the carnivore whose food you are trying to steal; no, he was playing with it, displaying certain decidedly feline traits that in such a bull of a beast could only amount to a serious sign of decadence.

The others in the committee hadn't noticed that Tommaso hadn't followed them. Fantino was presenting their case, and, having reached the point where he was saying: '. . . And there are men here amongst us with white hair who have given the company more than thirty years of their lives . . .' he meant to point to Tommaso, and first he pointed right, then left, and everybody realized that Tommaso wasn't there. Had he been taken ill? Criscuolo turned and tiptoed out to look for him in the waiting room. But saw no one: 'He must have felt tired, poor old guy,' he thought, 'he must have gone home. Never mind! He's deaf anyway! Could have told us though!' And he went back into the committee, never thinking to look behind the armchair.

Curled up together back there, the old man and the dog were playing; Tommaso with tears in his eyes and Guderian baring his teeth in a doggy laugh. Tommaso's obstinacy was not unfounded: he was convinced that Guderian was stupid and that it would be shameful to give up. He was right. Taking advantage of the animal's feline friendliness, he managed to knock the bread in such a way that the top part flew off, at which the dog leapt off after the half-sandwich he had lost, allowing Tommaso to hold on to the other half with the pearls and the rabbit. He grabbed the necklace, brushed off the pieces of rabbit caught between the pearls, stuffed it in his pocket and stuffed the meat in his mouth, having rapidly reflected that the dog's teeth had never got further than the edge of the sandwich and never penetrated the filling.

Then, treading on tiptoe, face purple and mouth full, the whistle singing high and fierce in his ear, he went through to Dr Starna's office and joined his friends, who all threw him sidelong questioning glances. Gigi Starna, who throughout Fantino's presentation hadn't lifted his eyes from the report spread out on his desk before him, as though concentrating on the figures there, heard a noise as if of someone eating close by. Looking up he saw an extra face in front of him, one he hadn't seen before: a wrinkled, livid face, with two yellow veiny staring eyeballs, and an expression at once furious and blind around cheeks that moved in an insistent chewing motion with an angry noise of chomping jaws. The sight so unsettled him that he lowered his eyes to his figures and didn't dare look up again, and he couldn't understand how on earth that man could have come to be eating here in his presence, and he tried to get the fellow out of his mind so as to be ready to counter Fantino's arguments cleverly and forcefully, but already he was aware that much of his confidence had gone.

Every night before going to bed, Signora Umberta anointed her face with vitaminized cucumber cream. The fact that after a night on the town she had collapsed in her bed that morning – she couldn't quite remember how – without her cucumber cream, her massages and her anti-tummy-flab exercises, without, in short, her whole daily ritual for keeping beautiful, could not but result in a troubled sleep. And it was to her neglect of these rites, and not to the amount of alcohol she had drunk that she attributed the nervousness, headache, and sour taste in the mouth that afflicted her few poor hours of sleep. Only her habit of sleeping on her back, in observation of a beautician's rule that had become a way of life, allowed the restlessness of her repose to express itself in shapes at once harmonious and – she was very much alive to the fact – always attractive to an imaginary observer, appearing as they did between the crumpled folds of her sheets.

Amid her morning bleariness and disquiet, her apprehension of having forgotten something, she was seized by a vague sense of alarm. So then, she had come home, she had tossed the foxfur gown on the armchair, she had slipped off her evening dress . . . but amongst the gaps in her memory what was bothering her was: the necklace, that necklace she should have held more precious than her own soft, smooth skin, she just couldn't remember taking it off, and still less tucking it away in the secret drawer in her toilette.

She got out of bed in a swirl of sheets, fine muslin skirts and rumpled hair, crossed the room, took a quick glance at the chest of drawers, the dresser, wherever she might have left the necklace. She looked at herself a moment in the mirror, frowning her disapproval at the haggard face she found, opened a couple of drawers, looked in the mirror again in the hope that her first impression might have been wrong, went into the bathroom and looked over the shelves, put on a bed-jacket, checked how she looked in it in the mirror over the sink, then in the big mirror beyond, opened the secret drawer, closed it again, pushed a hand through her hair, carelessly at first, then with a certain pleasure. She had lost the necklace with the four strings of pearls. She went to the telephone.

'Could I speak to the Architect ... Enrico, yes, I'm up ... Yes, I'm fine, but listen, the necklace, the pearl necklace ... I had it when we left the place, I'm sure I had it ... No, no, I can't find it now ... I don't know ... Of course I've looked everywhere ... Don't you remember?'

Enrico, late for work, dog-tired (he'd slept two hours), irritated, bored, his young draughtsman using the excuse of tidying up a project to listen in on every word, smoke from his cigarette smarting in his eyes, said: 'So, you get him to buy you another...'

In response the receiver came out with such a shriek that even the draughtsman started. 'Are you cra-a-zy! It's the one my husband had forbidden me to wear! don't you understa-a-and! It's the one that cost ... no, I can't say it on the pho-o-one! Stop being stu-u-upid! If he even found out I'd been wearing it around he'd kick me out of house. If he finds I've lost it ... he'll kill me!'

'Probably in the car,' said Enrico and in a twinkling she relaxed. 'You think so?'

'I do.'

'But do you remember if I had it? ... You remember we got out of the car somewhere ... where was that?'

'How should I know ...' said Enrico, passing a hand over his face, recalling with great weariness the moment when she had run off amongst the bushes, and they had had a bit of a tussle, and it came to him the necklace could perfectly well have fallen off there, so that already he was experiencing the tedium of having to go and look for it, to search that stretch of scrub inch by inch. He felt a prick of nausea. 'Don't worry: it's so big, it'll turn up ... Look in the car ... Can you trust the man in the garage?' (The car was hers. Likewise the garage.)

'Sure. Leone's been with us for years and years.'

'So phone him right away and tell him to look.'

'What if it's not there?'

'Phone me back. I'll go and look where we got out.'

'You're so sweet.'

'Right.'

He hung up. The necklace. He pulled a face. God only knew what a fortune it was worth. And when Umberta's husband was unable to meet his debts. Very nice. Yes, this could lead to something very nice indeed. On a sheet of paper he drew a necklace with four strings of pearls, filling it in minutely pearl by pearl. He must keep his eyes open. He turned the pearls in the drawing into eyes, each with its own iris, pupil, lashes. There was no time to lose. He must go and search those fields. Why wasn't Umberta phoning back at once? The hell it was in the car. 'You can get on with that on your own,' he said to the draughtsman. 'I've got to go out again.'

'Are you going to see the contractor? Remember those papers . . .'

'No, no, I'm going to the country. For strawberries.' And with his pencil he filled in the necklace to make a huge strawberry, complete with sepals and stalk. 'See, a strawberry.'

'Always after the women, boss,' the boy said, smirking.

'Dirty so-and-so,' said Enrico. The phone rang. 'As I thought, nothing. Keep calm. I'll go now. Did you warn the man in the garage not to say anything? To him I mean, for God's sake, to what's his name, his majesty! Good. Yes of course I remember where it was . . . I'll phone you . . . bye then, don't worry . . .' He hung up, began to whistle, pulled on his coat, went out, jumped on his scooter.

The city opened up before him like an oyster, like a halcyon sea. When you're young and on the move, and especially when you're driving fast, a town can suddenly open up before you, even a familiar place, a place that's so routine as to have become invisible. It's the thrill of adventure does it: the only youthful thrill this prematurely cynical architect retained.

Yes, going after lost necklaces was turning out to be good fun, not boring as he had at first imagined. Perhaps precisely because he cared so little about the thing. If he found it well and good, and if not, too bad: Umberta's problems were the problems of the rich, where the bigger the figure at stake the less it seems to matter.

And then what could ever really matter to Enrico? Nothing in the whole world. Yet this town he was now racing across, carefree and bold, had once been a kind of fakir's bed for him, with a shriek, a fall, a sharp nail wherever you looked: old buildings, new buildings, cheap housing projects or aristocratic apartments, derelict shells or building site scaffolding, the town had once presented itself as a maze of problems: Style, Function, Society, the Human Dimension, the Property Boom ... Now he looked with the same self-satisfied sense of historical irony on neoclassical, liberty, and twentieth century alike, while the old unhealthy slums, the new tower blocks, the efficient factories, the frescos of mould on windowless walls were all seen with the objectivity of someone observing natural phenomena. He no longer heard that shrill blast as of trumpets at Jericho which had once followed him on his city walks, proclaiming that he would punish the monstrous urban crimes of the bourgeoisie, that he would destroy and rebuild for a better society. In those days, if a workers' march with its placards and its long tail of men pushing bicycles were to fill the streets towards the police station, Enrico would join in, while above the humble crowd he had the impression there hovered, white and green in a geometric cloud, the image of that Future City he would build for them.

He'd been a revolutionary then, Enrico had, waiting for the proletariat to take over and give him the job of building the City. But the proletarian triumph was slow in coming, and then the masses didn't seem to share Enrico's obsessive passion for huge bare walls and flat roofs. So the young architect embarked on that bitter and dangerous season when the flag of every enthusiasm is lowered. His rigorous sense of style found another outlet: seaside villas, which he designed, for philistine millionaires unworthy of the honour. This too was a battle: outflanking the enemy, attacking from within. To reinforce his positions he would strive to become a fashionable architect; Enrico had to start taking the problem of 'career advancement' seriously: what was he doing still riding round on a scooter? By now the only thing he was interested in was getting hold of profitable work, of whatever kind. His designs for the City of the Future gathered dust in the corners of his studio and every now and then, while hunting about for a piece of drawing paper, he would find one of those old rolls in his hand and on the back sketch out the first outline of a roof extension.

Driving through the suburbs on his scooter that morning did not prompt Enrico to return to youthful reflections on the squalor of workers' housing projects. Instead, like a deer after fresh grass, his nose picked up the scent of potential building sites.

Indeed it was a potential site he had been meaning to go and see early that morning when he got into Umberta's car. They were coming out of a party, she was drunk and didn't want to go home. Take me to this place, take me to that. For his part Enrico had been toying with the idea for some time: and since they were driving here there and everywhere they might as well go and take a look at a place he knew; there wouldn't be anybody there at this time of day and he could get a good idea of its potential. It was a piece of property Umberta's husband owned, some land round a factory. Enrico was hoping that with her help he could get the man to give him a contract for something big. It had been on the way to the factory that Umberta had come close to jumping from the moving car. They were arguing; she was pretending to be more drunk than she was. 'And where are you taking me now?' she whined. Enrico said: 'Back to your husband. I'm fed up with you. I'm taking you to see him in his factory. Can't you see that's where we're going!' She half sang something to herself, then opened the door. He broke hard and she jumped out. Which was how she had lost the necklace. Now he had to find it. Easily said . . .

A bushy slope of abandoned land fell away beneath him. He only knew he was in the same place as this morning because the road was dusty and not often used and the tyre marks were still there where he'd braked: aside from that the whole landscape was shapeless; never had the official expression, *terrain vague*, taken on such a precise and subtly disturbing relevance in his mind. Enrico took a few steps this way and that peering between the branches of the bushes at the matted ground beneath: as soon as he set foot on the mean barren earth, insensitive to any footprint, strewn with litter, elusive and indefinable, smeared with a streaky pale light that might have been slug slime, any zest for adventure ebbed, the way a readiness to love shrinks and retreats when met by coldness, or ugliness, or apprehension. He was seized by the nausea that had been coming over him in waves ever since he woke up.

He began his search already convinced that he wouldn't find anything. Perhaps he should have settled on a rigid method first, established the area where Umberta had probably been, divided it into sectors, scoured it inch by inch. But the whole enterprise seemed so pointless and unrewarding that Enrico went on walking about at random, barely bothering to move the twigs. Looking up, he saw a man.

He had his hands in his pockets, in the middle of the field, bushes up to his knees. He must have sneaked up quietly, though where from Enrico couldn't have said. He was lanky and lean, pointy as a stork; he had an old military cap pulled down on his head with balaclava flaps dangling like bloodhound ears, and a jacket, likewise military, its shoulders in tatters. He was standing still, as if waiting for Enrico at some threshold.

The truth is he had been waiting there for quite a few hours: since even before Enrico had realized he would have to come. It was the unemployed Fiorenzo. Having got over his first flush of frustration at seeing those two workers snatch what might well be a treasure from under his nose, he had told himself that the thing to do was to stay put. The game was by no means over yet: if the necklace really was valuable then sooner or later the person who had lost it would come back to look for it; and when treasure was at stake there was always the hope you might grab a bit of it.

108

Seeing the other man standing there motionless, put the architect on the alert again. He stopped, lit a cigarette. He was beginning to take an interest in the story again. He was one of those people, Enrico, who think they have put down foundations in things and ideas, but who really have no other guiding principle in life than their shifting and intricate relationships with others; confronted with the vastness of nature, or the safe world of things, or the order of reasoned thought, they feel lost, recovering their poise only when they get wind of the manoeuvres of a potential enemy or friend; so that for all his plans the architect never actually built anything, either for others or for himself.

Having caught sight of Fiorenzo, Enrico, to get a better idea of what the fellow was up to, went on stooping and searching along a straight line that would take him nearer to the other but not actually to him. After a moment or two, the man also began to move, and in such a way that he would cross Enrico's path.

They stopped a yard or so apart. The out-of-work Fiorenzo had a gaunt, bird-like face, mottled with scraggy beard. It was he who spoke first.

'Looking for something?' he said.

Enrico raised his cigarette to his lips. Fiorenzo smoked his own breath, a small thick cloud in the cold air.

'I was looking . . .' Enrico said vaguely, making a gesture that took in the landscape. He was waiting for the other to declare himself. 'If he's found the necklace,' he thought, 'he'll try to find out how much it's worth.'

'Did you lose it here?' asked Fiorenzo.

Immediately Enrico said: 'What?'

The other waited a moment before saying: 'What you're looking for.'

'How do you know I am looking for anything?' said Enrico quickly. He had been wondering for a moment whether he should be brutally direct and intimidating, as the police were with anybody scruffily dressed, or polite and formal like urbane and egalitarian city folk; in the end he had decided the latter was

109

better suited to that mixture of pressure and readiness to negotiate which he thought should set the tone for their relationship.

The man thought a little, let out another little puff of air,
turned and made to leave.

'He thinks he's got the upper hand,' Enrico thought. 'Could
he really have found it?' There was no doubt but that the stranger
had put himself in the stronger position: it was up to Enrico to
make the next move. 'Hey!' he called and offered his pack of
cigarettes. The man turned. 'Smoke?' asked Enrico, offering the
pack, but without moving. The man came back a few steps, took
a cigarette from the pack, and as he pulled it out with his nails
snorted something that might even have been a thank-you. Enrico returned the pack to his pocket, pulled out his lighter, tried
it, then slowly lit the other man's cigarette.

'You tell me what you're looking for first,' he said, 'and then
I'll answer your question.'

'Grass,' the man said, and pointed to a basket laid by the
side of the road.

'For rabbits?'

They had climbed back up the slope. The man picked up
the basket. 'For us. To eat,' he said and began to walk along the
road. Enrico got on his scooter, started up and moved slowly
alongside the man.

'So, you come round here looking for grass every morning,
do you?' and what he wanted to say was: 'This is your territory
in a way, isn't it? Not a leaf falls here without you knowing about
it!' But Fiorenzo got in first: 'This is common land, everybody
comes.'

Clearly he had understood Enrico's game, and whether he had
found the necklace or not, he wasn't going to say. Enrico decided
to show his hand: 'This morning somebody lost something right
there,' he said, stopping the scooter. 'Did you find it?' He left a pause
then, expecting the man to ask, 'What?' Which he eventually did, but
not before having thought it over a bit: a bit too much.

'A necklace,' Enrico said, with the twisted smile of one

110

referring to something that was hardly important; and at the same time he made a gesture as though stretching something between his hands, a string, a ribbon, a child's little chain. 'It's got sentimental value for us. So you give it to me and I'll pay,' and he made to pull out his wallet.

The unemployed Fiorenzo stretched out a hand, as though to say: 'I haven't got it,' but then was careful not to say so, and with his hand still stretched out said instead: 'That'll be hard work, looking for something in the middle of all this . . . it'll take days. It's a big field. But we can start looking . . .'

Enrico leant on his handlebars again. 'I thought you'd already found it. That's too bad. Not to worry. I'm sorry for you more than me.'

The jobless man tossed away his cigarette stub. 'The name's Fiorenzo,' he said. 'We can come to some arrangement.'

'I'm an architect, Enrico Pré. I was sure we could get down to business.'

'We can come to some arrangement,' Fiorenzo repeated. 'So much every day and then so much on delivery of the missing item, whenever that is.'

Enrico almost whirled round, and even as he moved he didn't know whether he was going to grab the man by the scruff of the neck, or whether he just wanted to test his reactions again. As it turned out, Fiorenzo stopped still without making any move to defend himself, an ironic expression of defiance on his plucked-chicken face. And it seemed impossible to Enrico that the pockets of that skimpy crumpled jacket could hold four strings of pearls; if the man knew something about the necklace, God only knew where he had hidden it.

'And how long do you want to spend, combing that field,' he asked, dropping his respectful tone.

'Who says it's still in the field?' said Fiorenzo.

'If it's not in the field you've got it at home.'

'That's my home,' said the man, and pointed away from the road. 'Come with me.'

Fiorenzo's territory ended where the first scattered apartment blocks of the outskirts turned their backs on each other in foggy fields. And near the border, where the capitals of the most remote countries tend to be situated, was his house. All kinds of historic events and upheavals had combined to create it: the low brick walls, half in ruins, were part of an old army stable, later closed upon the decline of the cavalry; the Turkish toilet and an indelible piece of graffiti were the result of later use as an armoury for the training corps; a barred window was the sinister reminder that the place had been a prison during the civil war; it was to winkle out the last platoon of warriors that they had started that fire that had almost destroyed the place; the floor and the piping belonged to the period when it had been a camp first for the wounded and then for refugees; later a long winter plundering for firewood, roof tiles and bricks had once again demolished the place; until, evicted from their last abode, along came Fiorenzo and family with their beds and boards. He completed the effect by replacing half the roof with an old rolldown shutter found in the vicinity and apparently twisted in some explosion. Thus Fiorenzo, his wife Ines and their four surviving children once again had a home where they could hang pictures of relatives and family allowance slips on the walls and await the birth of their fifthborn with some hope that the child would live.

If one could hardly say that the look of the building was much improved since the day the family moved in, this was because Fiorenzo's genius in inhabiting the place was closer to that of the primitive man huddling up in a cave than the industrious castaway or pioneer who strives to recreate about him something of the civilization he has left behind. Of civilization round about him Fiorenzo had all his heart could desire, but civilization was hostile, forbidden territory to him. After losing his job and having quickly forgotten the meagre skills he had somehow once managed to acquire – those of a copper pipe polisher – his hands made sluggish in a manual job that again had not lasted very long, cut out – from one day to the next and with a whole family

112

dependent on him – from the great circular flow of money, it hadn't taken Fiorenzo long to retrace man's steps back along the course of history, until, having lost the notion that if you need something you build it or grow it or make it, he now cared for nothing but what could be gathered or hunted down.

Fiorenzo now saw the city as a world of which he could not be a part, just as the hunter does not think of becoming the forest, but only of plundering its wildlife, plucking a ripe berry, procuring shelter against the rain. So for Fiorenzo the city's wealth meant the cabbage stalks left lying on the cobbles of district markets after the stalls are taken down; the edible grasses that garnish the suburban tramlines; the public benches that could be sawn up piece by piece for firewood; the lovelorn cats that would intrude on common property at night never to return. A whole city existed for his benefit, a cast-off, second- or third-hand city, half buried, excremental, made of worn-out shoes, cigarette stubs, umbrella handles. And even way down at the level of these dust-laden riches there was still a market, with its supply and demand, its speculations, its hoarders. Fiorenzo sold empty bottles, rags and catskins, thus still managing the occasional fleeting peck at the monetary cycle. The most tiring activity, but the most profitable too, was that of the mine prospectors who would dig at the bottom of a steep bank below a factory looking for scrap iron in the industrial waste there, and sometimes in a single day they would unearth kilos and kilos of the stuff at three hundred lire a kilo. It was a city with seasons and harvests all its own: after the elections there were the layers of posters to strip from all the walls with the fierce insistent rasping of an old knife; the children helped too filling sacks of coloured scraps to be weighed by the miserly steelyard of the wastepaper dealers.

On these and other expeditions Fiorenzo was accompanied by his two eldest sons. Having grown up to this life they could imagine no other, and would run wild and voracious about the city's outskirts, akin to the mice they shared their food and games with. Ines on the other hand had developed the mentality of the lioness; she wouldn't budge from the lair where she licked their lastborn, she had lost the homely habit of tidying and cleaning, she pounced greedily on the loot that man and sons brought home, sometimes helping them to make it saleable by unstitching pieces of shoe uppers to be sold for patches to cobblers, or scraping the tobacco from the cigarette stubs; and despite their famished life, she had become fat and squat and, after her fashion, calm. The other world, of stockings and cinema, no longer called to her from hoardings whose images to her mind had completely lost their meaning, had become huge indecipherable enigmas. Day after day, when she dusted the glass of the photograph of herself wearing her bride's white veil beside Fiorenzo on their wedding day, she was no longer sure whether it was herself or her great-grandmother. Rheumatism had led to the habit of lying down all day, even when she had no pain. On her bed in broad daylight in the ramshackle house, her baby beside her, she looked up at a heavy, foggy sky and fell to singing an old tango. Thus Enrico, approaching the hovel, heard singing: he was understanding less and less.

With expert eye he took in the warped tilt of the roof, the irregular angles of the fire-mottled walls. One or two effects would not have been out of place in a seaside villa. He should bear that in mind. He remembered a paper he'd once given at a conference on urban design: It is not from the chateau that we set out upon our adventure, gentlemen, but from the shack . . .

Becalmed in the Antilles

You should have heard my Uncle Donald, who had sailed with Admiral Drake, when he started telling us one of his yarns.

'Uncle Donald, Uncle Donald!' we would shout in his ears when we caught the glint of an eye through his ever half-closed lids, 'tell us about that time you were becalmed in the Antilles!'

'What? Ah, becalmed, yes yes, truly becalmed . . .' he would begin in a feeble voice. 'We were sailing off the Antilles, advancing at a snail's pace, sea smooth as oil, all sails unfurled to catch any rare breath of wind. And all of a sudden we're only a cannon shot away from a Spanish galleon. The galleon was hove to, so we down sails as well and there, in the middle of that dead calm, we prepare to engage. We couldn't get past them, and they couldn't pass us. But the fact of the matter is that they had no intention of advancing: they were there on purpose so as not to let us pass. Whereas we, Drake's fleet, had sailed far and wide for no other purpose than to give no quarter to the Spanish fleet, to seize the Grand Armada's treasure from papist hands and deliver it into those of her Gracious Britannic Majesty, Queen Elizabeth. Still, with that galleon's cannons to deal with, our handful of culverins weren't enough to carry the day, so we were careful not to fire the first shot. Ah yes, m'boys, that was the position of the opposing forces, get it? Those damned Spanish had provisions of water, fruit from the Antilles, open supply lines back to their ports, they could stay there as long as they liked: but they were as careful not to start shooting as we were, because the way

115

things were going that little war with the English suited His Catholic Majesty's admirals down to the ground, whereas if the situation were to alter, as a result of a naval battle, whether won or lost, then the whole balance of power would go up in smoke, inevitably there would be changes, and they didn't want any changes. So the days went by, still the wind wouldn't blow and still we were here and they were there, lying off the Antilles, becalmed...

'And how did it end? Tell us, Uncle Donald!' we said, seeing the old seadog's chin already sinking on his chest as he nodded off again.

'What? Ah yes, becalmed! Weeks it went on. We could see them through our spyglasses, those mollycoddled papists, those make-believe mariners, under their tassled sunshades, handkerchiefs between scalp and wig to soak up the sweat, eating their pineapple icecreams. While we, the most able seamen of all the oceans, we whose destiny it was to conquer for Christendom all those lands that lived in darkness, we were stuck there with our hands in our pockets, fishing lines dangling over the bulwarks, chewing our tobacco. We'd been sailing the Atlantic for months, our supplies were down to the dregs and rotting too, every day the scurvy carried someone off, we dropped them into the sea in sacks while our boatswain muttered a couple of quick verses from the Bible. Over on the galleon, the enemy watched through their spyglasses, seeing every sack that plunged into the sea and making signs with their fingers as if busy counting our losses. We railed against them: they'd have to wait a long time indeed before they could count us all dead, we who had survived so many hurricanes, it would take a lot more than a becalmed sea off the Antilles to finish us off...'

'But how did you get out of it, Uncle Donald?'

'What's that you said? How get out of it? Well, that's what we were always asking ourselves, all the months we were becalmed there... Many of us, especially the eldest and the most thickly tattooed, they said that we had always been a sprint ship, good for rapid escapades, and they remembered the times when

our culverins had thinned out the masts of the most powerful
Spanish ships, punched holes in their bulwarks, jousted in brusque gybes ... For sure, when it came to rapid seamanship we
were strong indeed, but there had been wind then, the ship
moved fast ... Now, becalmed as we were, all this talk of gun-
battles and grappling hooks was just a way of passing the time
while we waited for God knows what; a rising south-westerly, a
gale, even a typhoon ... So our orders were that we shouldn't
even think about it, and the captain explained that the real naval
battle was this stopping still where we were, looking at each
other, keeping ourselves ready, going over the plans of Her
Britannic Majesty's great naval battles, and the sail-handling rulebook and the perfect helmsman's manual, and the culverin instruction book, because the rules of Admiral Drake's fleet were
still and in every detail the rules of Admiral Drake's fleet: if ever
they were to start changing those, God only knew where ...'

'And then, Uncle Donald? Hey, Uncle Donald! How did
you manage to get moving?'

'Hum ... hum ... where was I? Ah yes, woe betide us if we
didn't keep to the strictest discipline and observation of the nautical rules. On other ships in Drake's fleet there had been official
changes and even mutinies, rebellions: people were looking for
another way to sail the seas, there were simple seamen, lookouts,
and even cabin boys who had become self-styled experts and
wanted to say their piece on navigation ... Most of the officers
and quartermasters felt that this was the biggest danger of all, so
woe betide you if they got wind of any talk about a radical
rewriting of Her Majesty Queen Elizabeth's naval rulebook. No,
we had to go on cleaning up the mortars, washing down the
deck, checking that the sails were shipshape, even though they
hung limp in the windless air, and through the empty hours of
those long days, the healthiest entertainments, as the officers saw
it, were the inevitable tattoos on chest and arms glorifying our
fleet that ruled the waves. And when we talked we ended up turning a blind eye on the ones who saw no other hope than a change

117

in the weather, a hurricane perhaps that with a bit of luck would send everybody, friend and foe alike, straight to the bottom, and were tougher on to those who wanted to find a way to move the ship in its present situation ... One day a topman, a certain Slim John, whether because the sun had gone to his head or what, I don't know, began to daydream over a coffeepot. If the steam lifted the lid of the coffeepot, said this Slim John, then our ship, if constructed like a coffeepot, would like-wise be able to move, and without sails ... It was admittedly a somewhat incoherent line of thought, but perhaps if we had thought some more about it there was profit to be had there. But no: they chucked his coffeepot overboard and very nearly threw him out with it. These coffeepot fantasies, they said, were little better than papist ideas ... coffee and coffeepots were Spanish truck, not ours ... Well, I didn't understand a thing, but so long as those pots moved, with that scurvy that was still carrying people off ...'

'And so, Uncle Donald,' we cried, eyes shining with impatience, taking him by the wrists and shaking him, 'we know you got away, we know you routed the Spanish galleon, but tell us how you did it, Uncle Donald!'

'Ah yes, it wasn't that everybody saw eye to eye in the galleon either, not by a long chalk! Watching them through your eyeglass you could see that they had their people who wanted to get moving too; some wanted to fire their cannons at us and others had decided that the only way out was to join us, since a victory of Elizabeth's fleet would have given a big boost to trade, which had been falling off for some time ... But like us, they also had their officers, and the officers of the Spanish Armada didn't want anything to change, oh no. On that point the commanders on our ship and on the enemy ship, loathe each other as they might, were wholeheartedly agreed. So that with no sign of any breeze blowing up, they began to send each other messages, with flags, from one boat to the next, as if they wanted to start talks. Except they never went further than a: Good morning! Good evening! Marvellous weather, no! and so on ...'

'Uncle Donald! Uncle Donald! Don't go back to sleep, please! Tell us how Drake's ship managed to get moving!'

118

'Hey, okay, I'm not deaf you know! You have to understand, no one realized how long we would be becalmed there, off the Antilles, for years even, with the haze and humidity, the sky leaden and lowering as if a hurricane were about to break any moment. We were streaming sweat, all naked, climbing in the rigging, looking for a bit of shade under the furled sails. Everything was so still that even those of us who were most impatient for change, for something to happen, were motionless too, one at the top of the foretopmast, another on the main jib aft, another again astride a spar, perched up there leafing through atlases and nautical maps . . .'

'So then what, Uncle Donald!' We threw ourselves on our knees at his feet, begging him, hands together in supplication, then we shook his shoulders, yelling.

'Tell us how it ended, for God's sake! We can't wait to find out! Go on with your story, Uncle Donald!'

Note 1979

I have re-read 'Becalmed in the Antilles'. Perhaps this is the first time I've read the story since I wrote it. It doesn't seem dated, not only because it works as a story in its own right, quite apart from the political allegory, but also because the paradoxical contrast between bitter struggle and enforced immobility is a common condition, both in political-military and epic-narrative terms, at least as old as the *Iliad*, so that it seems only natural to refer it to one's own experience of history. As an allegory of Italian politics, when one thinks that twenty-two years have gone by and the two galleons are still there facing each other, the image becomes even more distressing. Of course these twenty-two years have been anything but becalmed as far as Italian society is concerned, on the contrary it has changed more than in the hundred years before. And the time we live in could hardly be described as 'a dead calm'. So in that sense one can't really

119

claim that the metaphor corresponds to the situation; but – slowly does it – even twenty-two years ago one had to bend the words a little to talk of being becalmed: they were years of acute social tension, of dangerous conflicts, of discrimination, of collective and individual drama. The word 'becalmed' has a certain good-natured calm to it that has nothing in common with the climate as it was then, nor with the situation today; but what it also expresses is that heavy atmosphere of dead calm weather at sea, so threatening and unnerving for sailing ships, as depicted in the novels of Conrad and Melville, from which of course my story takes its cue. Thus the success my metaphor enjoyed in Italian political journalism can be explained by the fact that it says something more than any political jargon word, as for example 'immobilism'. It is the impasse in a scenario of conflict, of irreconcilable antagonism, and then corresponding to that an immobility within the two camps engaged: the innate immobility of the 'Spanish' since immobility suits their ends and aims; while in the 'pirate' camp we have the contradiction between the vocation for the 'rapid war' with its relative ideology ('the rules of Admiral Drake's fleet') and a situation where recourse to cannonfire and grappling hooks is not only impossible but would be counterproductive, suicidal even ... I didn't offer any solutions in my story – just as I wouldn't be able to offer any now – I just mapped out a sort of catalogue of possible responses. There were the two opposing command structures, united in their desire to perpetuate the situation with the minimum amount of change (for opposite but far from unfounded reasons) first and foremost within their respective ships and then in the balance of forces outside the ships. (In this regard one can hardly deny that there have been changes, mainly in the Communist Party and on the left in general, but also amongst the Christian Democrats if only as a result of exhaustion.) Then there were the supporters, on both sides, of direct conflict, people whose policies had more to do with temperament than strategy; and the supporters, on both sides, of dialogue. (The development of these two poles corresponds to what has actually happened, the conflicting policies of achieving broad understandings and of applying revolutionary pressure each giving the illusion of activity while hardly changing the situation at all.) There is also the apocalyptic point of view ('a hurricane perhaps that with a bit of luck would send everybody to the bottom'), an allusion to the discussions on the prospect of a nuclear war, which at the time divided the Soviets, who saw it as the end of civilization, and the Chinese, who tended to play down the risks. Likewise typical of the time the story was written is the reference to technological development, which people then hoped might offer a solution (there was a great deal of talk of 'automation' as of something that would radically alter the parameters of the problem). But the invention of the steam engine I evoked has perhaps remained at the level of the pirate who plays with his coffeepot.

A few 'historical' details: I am unable to establish the exact date of the story; I remember that there was a long delay in the publication of that issue of *Città aperta*, so the story must have been written some months before when I was still in the thick of internal discussions for the renewal of the Communist Party. Among the people engaged in this debate my story was immediately praised by the supporters of revisionism, whether on the right or the left: both 'revolutionaries' and 'reformers' felt it supported their points of view; though it has to be said that the two camps were not always clearly defined then. After the issue of *Città aperta* was published, the story then appeared in *Espresso* and hence reached a very wide audience. *Avanti* wrote an editorial about it. Later an extreme left-wing pamphlet, *Azione comunista*, published a parody of the story, tying it in to particular situations and people. Maurizio Ferrara then replied to this parody with another parody, likewise personal and polemical, which was published in *Rinascita* under the pseudonym 'Little Bald'. But in the meantime, in the summer of 1957, I had resigned from the Communist Party, and 'Becalmed' was seen as a sort of message to explain that decision, which wasn't the case since the story belonged to an earlier period.

The Tribe with Its Eyes on the Sky

The nights are beautiful and missiles cross the summer sky.

Our tribe lives in huts of straw and mud. In the evening when we get back tired from gathering coconuts we sit at the entrances, some on their heels, some on a mat, the children, bellies big as footballs, playing round about, and we watch the sky. For a long time, perhaps since time began, the eyes of our tribe, these poor trachoma-inflamed eyes of ours, have been gazing at the sky: but especially since new celestial bodies began to cross the starry vault above our village: jet planes with white trails, flying saucers, rockets, and now these guided missiles, so high and fast you can't see or hear them, but in the sparkle of the Southern Cross, if you look very hard, you can pick up a sort of shiver, a tremor, at which the most expert of us say: 'There, a missile passing at twenty thousand kilometres an hour; a little slower, if I'm not mistaken, than the one that went by last Thursday.'

Now, since this missile business has been in the air, many of us have been seized by a strange euphoria. Some of the village witch-doctors, in fact, have led us to believe, by inference, that since this shooting star originates from beyond Kilimanjaro, it is the sign foreseen in the Great Prophecy, and hence the day fast approaches, as promised by the Gods, when after centuries of slavery and poverty our tribe will reign over the whole valley of the Great River, and the barren savannah will bring forth millet and maize. So – these witch-doctors appear to be insinuating – it is hardly worth us racking our brains over new ways of emerg-

122

ing from our present situation; we should trust in the Great Prophecy, rally round its only rightful interpreters, without asking to know more.

It has to be said, however, that even though we are a poor tribe of coconut gatherers, we are well informed about everything that goes on: we know what a nuclear missile is, how it works, how much it costs; we know that it won't only be the cities of the white sahibs which will be scythed down like fields of millet, that as soon as they really start to fire them these things will leave the whole of the earth's crust as spongey and cracked as a termites' nest. No one forgets for one moment that the missile is a diabolical weapon, not even the witch-doctors; on the contrary, in line with the teaching of the Gods, they are always heaping curses on it. But that doesn't change the fact that it is convenient to consider the missile in a good light too, as the shooting star of the prophecy; not letting one's mind dwell too much on it perhaps, but just leaving a little mental window open to that possibility, partly so as to let all our other worries fly out the same way.

The problem is – and we've seen this time and again – that a little while after some devilry appears in the sky above our village coming, as the prophecy foresaw, from beyond Kilimanjaro, another, worse than the first, always appears from the opposite direction, and shoots away to vanish beyond the peak of Kilimanjaro: and this is a sign of ill-omen, dashing our hopes that the Great Day is approaching. Thus, one moment in hope the next in fear, we stare up at an ever more armed and lethal sky, as once we read our destiny in the serene trajectories of the stars, the wandering comets.

The only thing people talk about in our tribe now are guided missiles, while we are still going about armed with crude axes and spears and blowpipes. Why worry? We are the last village at the edge of the jungle. Nothing is going to change here, until the Great Day of the prophets dawns.

Yet even here these are no longer the times when a white

merchant would occasionally arrive in his piragua to buy our coconuts, and sometimes he would cheat us on the price and sometimes it was us fooled him: now we have the Nicer Nut Corporation, who buy the whole harvest *en bloc*, imposing their prices on us, and we have to gather the nuts faster than before in teams that work shifts day and night to reach the targets laid down in the contract.

Nevertheless there are those among us who say that the times promised in the Great Prophecy are nearer than ever, not because of the celestial omens, but because the miracles announced by the Gods are now just so many technical problems that only we, and not the Nicer Nut Corporation, can solve. Easier said than done! Meantime, you try and touch the Nicer Nut Corporation! Seems their agents with their feet up on the tables of their offices in the docks on the Great River, glasses of whisky in their hands, are only concerned about whether this new missile mightn't be bigger than the last; in short, they don't talk about anything but missiles either. There is agreement, here, between what they say and what the witch-doctors say: it is in the power of these shooting stars that our entire destiny lies.

I too, sitting at the entrance to my hut, look up at the stars and at the rockets appearing and disappearing, I think of the explosions poisoning the fish in the sea, and of the courtesies those people who decide the explosions exchange with each other between one missile and the next. I'd like to understand more: certainly the will of the Gods is made manifest in these signs, certainly they foretell the ruin or the fortune of our tribe . . . Still, there's one idea I can't get out of my head: that a tribe that relies entirely on the will of shooting stars, whatever fortune they may bring, will always be selling off its coconuts cheap.

Nocturnal Soliloquy of a Scottish Nobleman

The candle keeps guttering because of the air wafting in through the window. But I can't allow darkness and sleep to invade the room, and I must keep the window open to survey the heath which is moonless tonight, a formless expanse of shadows. There is no light whether of torch or lantern for at least two miles, that's for sure, nor any sound other than the cry of the grouse, and the footsteps of the guard on the castle walls. A night like any other, and yet the MacDickinsons' attack could come before the day dawns. I must spend the night keeping watch and reflecting on the predicament we find ourselves in. A little while ago Dugald, the oldest and most loyal of my men, came up to my room to reveal a problem of conscience: like most of the peasants around here he is a member of the Episcopal church and his bishop has ordered all the faithful to take the MacDickinson family's side, forbidding them to bear arms for any other clan. We, the MacFergusons, belong to the Presbyterian church, but out of an old tradition of tolerance we don't make religion an issue for our people. I told Dugald I considered him free to act according to his conscience and his faith, but I couldn't help reminding him how much he and his family owed to our clan. When that rough and ready soldier left, his white whiskers were dripping tears. I still don't know what he has decided. It's no use pretending otherwise: the ancient conflict between the MacFergusons and the MacDickinsons is about to erupt in a war of religion.

Since time immemorial the highland clans have fought it out amongst themselves along the lines of good old Scottish custom: every time we get the chance we avenge the murder of our kinsmen by murdering members of rival families, while each in turn seeks to occupy and devastate the lands and castles of the others, yet this strip of Scotland has so far been spared the ferocity of a religious war. Of course everybody knows that the Episcopal church has always openly supported the MacDickinsons, and if today these poor highlands are ravaged more by the raids of the MacDickinsons than by the hail, we owe it to the fact that the Episcopal clergy have always made fair weather or foul in this land. But so long as the greatest enemy of the MacDickinsons and the Episcopal church were the MacConnollys, who being proselytes of the pernicious Methodist sect believe that peasants who don't pay their rents should be pardoned and ultimately that one should hand out one's lands and chattels to the poor, the clans hostile to the MacDickinsons all preferred to turn a blind eye. From every Episcopal pulpit ministers preached hell and damnation on the MacConnollys and whomsoever bore arms under them or even so much as served in their household, and we MacFergusons, or MacStewarts, or MacBurtons, good Presbyterian families, let the matter pass. Of course the MacConnollys were themselves partly responsible for this state of affairs. Hadn't it been they who, when their clan was far more powerful than now, recognized the Episcopal clergy's old right to a tithe upon our lands? Why did they do it? Because, as they said, it was not these things (mere formalities or little more) that were important in their religion, but other more substantial matters; or because, as we said, those damned Methodists thought they could beat the Devil at his own game and fool us all. In any event ill befell them and in very short order. We, for our part, certainly can't complain. We were allied to the MacDickinsons then and took care to increase the strength of their clan, since they were the only ones who could take on the MacConnollys and their accursed ideas with regard to oat harvest taxes. When we saw the Episcopalians leading one of MacConnolly's men into the village square with a noose round his neck and proclaiming him a creature of the Devil, we didn't turn our horses that way because it was none of our business.

And now that the MacDickinsons and their people are lording it in every village and hostelry, bullying and browbeating everybody so that no one can walk the high roads of Scotland without a kilt of their tartan, the Episcopal church chooses this moment to hurl anathema at us, the families of the upright Presbyterian faith, and to stir up our peasants and even our cooks against us. It's clear what they're after: an alliance with the Macduffs or the MacCockburns, old supporters of King James Stuart, papists or very nearly, that will bring them down from their mountain castles where they have been reduced to living like bandits among the goats.

Will it be a religious war? Really there's nobody, not even the most bigoted Episcopalian, who believes that fighting for steak-guzzling MacDickinsons capable of knocking back pints of beer even on a Sunday would amount to fighting for the faith. How do they see it, then? Perhaps they think that this is part of God's plan, like the captivity in Egypt. But Isaac's offspring were never asked to fight for the Pharaohs, even if God did choose to make them suffer so long in exile! If there is a war of religion, we MacFergusons will accept it as a test to strengthen our faith. But we know that on these shores the faithful of the rightful Church of Scotland are an elect minority, and that they may have been chosen by God – though God forbid! – for martyrdom. I have picked up my Bible again, which in the recent months of frequent enemy forays I had somewhat neglected, and now I leaf through the pages in the candlelight, though never losing sight of the moor down below where a rustle of wind has lifted, as always just before dawn. No, I'm at my wit's end; if God starts getting involved in our Scottish family quarrels – and in the event of a

127

war of religion he can hardly do otherwise – who knows where it will end; each of us has his interests and his sins, the MacDickinsons more than anybody, and the Bible is there to tell us that God's intentions are always different from those that men imagine.

Perhaps this is where we have sinned, in always refusing to think of our wars as wars of religion, in the illusion that we would thus have greater liberty to compromise when it suited us. There is too great a spirit of appeasement in this part of Scotland, not a clan that doesn't fight without its ulterior motives. We have never taken sufficiently seriously the question of whether our religion should be administered by the hierarchy of this or that church, or through the community of the faithful, or from the depths of our consciences.

There, down there, at the edge of the heath, I can see them, torches gathering. Our guards have seen them too: I can hear the whistle sounding the alarm from the top of the tower. How will the battle go? All of us perhaps are about to pay for our sins: we didn't have the courage to be ourselves. The truth is that amongst all these Presbyterians Episcopalians Methodists there's not one in this part of Scotland who believes in God: not one I say, whether noble or cleric, tenant or serf, who truly believes in that God whose name is forever on his lips. There, the clouds are paling to the east. Come on, everybody, awake! Quick, saddle me my horse!

A Beautiful March Day

The thing that most disturbs me as we wait — and we're all here now, under the Senate portico, each in his place, Metellus Cimber with the petition he has to present, Casca behind him who is to strike the first blow, Brutus down there under the statue of Pompey, and it's almost the fifth hour, he shouldn't be long now — the thing that most disturbs me is not this cold dagger hidden under my toga here, nor any tension as to how it will go, the possibility that something unforeseen could thwart our plans, it isn't the fear that someone has betrayed us, nor uncertainty as to what will happen afterwards: it's just seeing that it's a beautiful March day, a holiday like so many others, and that people are going around enjoying themselves, not giving a damn about the Republic and Caesar's powers, families heading for the country, young folks going to the chariot races, the girls wearing a kind of tunic that falls straight down, a new more cunning way of having you guess their shape. Standing here between these columns, shamming, pretending casual conversation, I feel we must look more suspicious than ever; but who would ever guess what's happening? The people passing by are a thousand miles from thinking of such things, it's a beautiful day, all is calm.

When we leap, our daggers bared, there, on the usurper of republican freedoms, our actions must be quick as lightning, deft, yet furious too. But will we be up to it? Everything has moved so slowly recently, dragged out so long, vague and slack, the Senate surrendering its rights little by little day by day, Caesar

129

always apparently on the point of putting the crown on his head, but in no hurry, the crucial hour always about to strike but always delayed, for another hope, another threat. Everybody's been bogged down in this sludge, ourselves included: why did we wait till the Ides to carry out our plan? Couldn't we have done it at the Calends of March? And now we're here, why not wait for the Calends of April? Oh, it wasn't this, it wasn't this we imagined when we dreamt of fighting tyranny, we young men educated in the republican virtues: I remember evenings when some of those here with me under this portico – Trebonius, Ligarius, Decius – were studying together, reading stories about the Greeks, picturing ourselves freeing our city from tyranny: we dreamed of dramatic tense days, under glaring skies, fervid tumults, mortal struggles, everybody on one side or the other, for freedom or for the tyrant; and we, the heroes, would have the people on our side, cheering us on, saluting our victory after the swiftest of battles. But there's none of that: perhaps future historians will tell, as always, of heaven knows what omens in stormy skies or the entrails of birds; but we know that it is a mild March, with the occasional shower of rain, yesterday evening a bit of wind that took the straw off a roof or two in the suburbs. Who would guess that we were going to kill Caesar this morning (or Caesar us, may the gods forbid)? Who would think that Rome's history was about to change (for better or worse the dagger will decide) on a lazy day like this?

What frightens me is that, daggers pointed at Caesar's breast, we too will begin to procrastinate, to weigh up the pros and the cons, to wait to hear what he has to say, to decide what to answer him, and meanwhile the dagger blades will begin to dangle slack as dogs' tongues, will melt like so much butter against Caesar's conceited breast.

But why do even we end up finding it so strange that we are here now to do our duty? All our lives haven't we been hearing people insist that the republic's freedoms are the most sacred thing there is? Wasn't the whole purpose of our civic life

130

to guard against whoever tried to usurp the powers of the Senate and the consuls? Yet now that it has come to this, everybody has begun to equivocate – the senators, the tribunes, even Pompey's friends, even the learned men we most admired, Marcus Tullius himself for example – to say that, yes, Caesar is violating republican statutes, is gaining strength from the veterans' bullying, is blathering on about the divine honours he supposedly deserves, yet all the same he is a man with a glorious past, a man with more authority than anyone else to negotiate a peace with the barbarians, the only one who can steer the republic through this crisis, and, in short, that amidst a sea of evils, Caesar is the lesser. Then, what do you expect, as far as the people are concerned Caesar is just fine, or rather they don't care, after all it's the first holiday with spring weather fine enough to bring the Roman families out into the meadows with their picnic baskets, the air is mild. Perhaps we missed our moment, we friends of Cassius and Brutus; we thought we would go down in history as the heroes of freedom, we imagined ourselves with arms raised in statuesque gestures, when in fact no gestures are possible now, our arms will freeze, hands opening in mid-air in defensive, diplomatic poses. Everything's taking longer than it should: even Caesar is late, no one wants to do anything this morning, that's the truth. The sky is so delicately veined with gossamery ribbons of cloud, and the first swallows are darting about the pines. From the narrow streets comes the clatter of wheels bouncing on the cobbles and screeching at the bends.

But what's happening at that door there? Who are those people? There, I was daydreaming and Caesar is here! There's Cimber grabbing at his toga, and Casca, Casca's already pulling out a dagger red with blood, everybody's on him, and oh, here's Brutus, he'd been standing to the side as if lost in thought, but now he's rushing forward too, and now it seems everyone's tumbling down the steps, Caesar's down that's for sure, the surge pushes me on top of him, and now I get my dagger out too, I strike, and below I can see Rome's red walls opening out in the

131

March sun, the trees, the carts hurrying unknowingly by, there's a woman's voice singing at a window, a notice announcing a circus, and withdrawing my dagger I'm overcome by a sort of vertigo, a feeling of emptiness, of being alone, not here in Rome, today, but alone forever after, in the centuries to come, the fear that people won't understand what we did here today, that they won't be able to do it again, that they will remain distant and indifferent as this beautiful calm morning in March.

Tales and Dialogues
1968-1984

World Memory

Here's why I called for you, Müller. Now that my resignation has been accepted, you are to be my successor: your appointment as director is imminent. Please don't pretend this is such a big surprise: the rumour has been doing the rounds for some time and I'm sure you will have heard it yourself. Then, there's no doubt that of the young élite in our organization, you are the most competent, the one who knows, you could say, all the secrets of our work. Or so at least it would seem. Allow me to explain: I am not speaking to you on my own initiative, I was told to do so by our superiors. There are only one or two things you don't yet know, Müller, and the time has come to fill you in. You imagine, as does everybody else for that matter, that our organization has for many years been preparing the greatest document centre ever conceived, an archive that will bring together and catalogue everything that is known about every person, animal and thing, by way of a general inventory not only of the present but of the past too, of everything that has ever been since time began, in short a general and simultaneous history of everything, or rather a catalogue of everything moment by moment. And that is indeed what we are working on and we can feel satisfied that the project is well advanced: not only have we already put the contents of the most important libraries of the world, and likewise the archives and museums and newspaper annals of every nation, on our punch cards, but also a great deal of documentation gathered *ad hoc*, person by person, place by place. And all this material is being put through a reduction process that brings it down to the essential, condensed, miniaturized minimum, a process whose limits have yet to be established; just as all existing and possible images are being filed in minute spools of microfilm, while microscopic bobbins of magnetic tape hold all sounds that have ever been and ever can be recorded. What we are planning to build is a centralized archive of human kind, and we are attempting to store it in the smallest possible space, along the lines of the individual memories in our brains.

But it's hardly worth my while repeating this to someone who won admission to our organization with a project entitled, 'The British Museum in a Nutshell'. Relatively speaking, you have only been with us a few years, but by now you are as familiar with the workings of our laboratories as I myself, who am or was the foundation's director. I would never have left this job, I assure you, if I still felt I had the energy. But since my wife's mysterious disappearance, I have sunk into a depression from which I still have not recovered. It is only right that our superiors – accepting what are anyway my own wishes – should decide to replace me. Hence it falls to me to inform you of those official secrets which have so far been kept from you.

What you are not aware of is the true purpose of our work. It has to do with the end of the world, Müller. We are working in expectation of an imminent disappearance of life on Earth. We are working so that all may not have been in vain, so that we can transmit all we know to others, even though we don't know who they are or what they know.

May I offer you a cigar? Forecasts that the Earth will not be able to support life, or at least human life, for much longer should not distress us unduly. We have all been aware for some time that the sun is halfway through its lifespan: however well things went, in four or five billion years everything would be over. That is, in a short while the problem would have presented itself anyway; what is new is that the deadline is now very much nearer, we have no time to lose, that's all. Obviously the extinction of our species is not a happy prospect, but crying about it offers only the same empty consolation as when we mourn the death of an individual. (I'm still thinking of my dear Angela, do forgive my emotion.) There are doubtless millions of planets supporting life forms similar to our own; it hardly matters whether our image lives on in them or whether it be their descendants rather than our own who carry on where we left off. What does matter is that we give them our memory, the general memory put together by the organization of which you, Müller, are about to be made director.

No need to be overawed; the scope of your work will remain as it is at present. The system for communicating our memory to other planets is being designed by another sector of the organization; we already have our work cut out, we needn't even concern ourselves whether they decide on optical or acoustic media. It may even be that it's not a question of transmitting information at all, but of putting it in a safe place, beneath the earth's crust: wandering through space the remains of our planet may one day be found and explored by extra-galactic archaeologists. Nor do we even have to worry about what code or codes will be chosen: there's a sector exclusively dedicated to looking for a way of making our stock of information intelligible whatever linguistic system the others may use. For you, now that you know, I can assure you that nothing has changed, except the responsibility that rests on your shoulders. That's what I wanted to talk over with you a little.

What will the human race be at the moment of its extinction? A certain quantity of information about itself and the world, a finite quantity, given that it will no longer be able to propagate itself and grow. For a certain time, the universe enjoyed an excellent opportunity to gather and elaborate information; and to create it, to bring forth information there where in other circumstances there would have been no one to inform and nothing to inform them about: such was life on earth, and above all human life, its memory, its inventions for communicating and remembering. Our organization can guarantee that this body of information not be lost, regardless of whether it is actually passed on to others or not. The duty of the director is to make sure that nothing is left out, because what is left out is as if it had never been. At the same time it will also be your duty to treat any element that might end up causing confusion, or obscuring more essential elements, as if it had never been – everything, that is, that rather than increasing the body of information would generate pointless clutter and clatter. What matters is the general model constituted by the whole of our information, from which further information, which we are not giving or perhaps don't have, may be deduced. In short, by not giving certain kinds of information, one is giving more than one would if one did. The final result of our work will be a model in which everything counts as information, even what isn't there. Only then will it be possible to say what really mattered out of all that has been, or rather what really was, since the final state of our archive will constitute at once that which is, has been and will be, and all else is nothing.

Of course there are moments in our work – you will have experienced them too, Müller – when one is tempted to imagine that the only things that matter are those which elude our archives, that only what passes without leaving any trace truly exists, while everything held in our records is dead detritus, the left-overs, the waste. The moment comes when a yawn, a buzzing fly, an itch seem the only treasure there is, precisely because completely unusable, occurring once and for all and then promptly forgotten, spared the monotonous destiny of being stored in the world memory. Who could rule out the possibility that the universe consists of the discontinuous network of moments that cannot be recorded, and that our organization does nothing but establish their negative image, a frame around emptiness and meaninglessness.

But the quirk of our profession is this: that as soon as we concentrate on something, we immediately want to include it in

138

our files; with the result, I confess, that I have often found myself cataloguing yawns, pimples, unhelpful associations of ideas,
little tunes I've whistled, and then hiding them amongst the mass
of more useful information. For the position of director which
you are about to be offered brings with it this privilege: the right
to put one's personal imprint on the world memory. Please understand me, Müller: I'm not talking about arbitrary liberties or
an abuse of power, but of an indispensable element in our work.
A mass of coldly objective and incontrovertible information
would run the risk of presenting a far from truthful picture, of
falsifying what is most specific in any situation. Suppose we received from another planet a message made up of pure facts,
facts of such clarity as to be merely obvious: we wouldn't pay
attention, we would hardly even notice; only a message containing something unexpressed, something doubtful and partially indecipherable, would break through the threshold of our
consciousness and demand to be received and interpreted. We
must bear this in mind: the director's task is that of giving the
whole of the data gathered and selected by our offices that slight
subjective slant, that touch of the opinionated, the rash, which it
needs in order to be true. That's what I wanted to warn you
about, before handing over: in the material gathered to date you
will notice here and there the mark of my own hand – an extremely delicate one, you understand – a sprinkling of appraisals,
of facts withheld, even lies.

Only in a superficial sense can lies be said to exclude the
truth; you will be aware that in many cases lies – the patient's lies
to the psychoanalyst, for example – are just as revealing as the
truth, if not more so; and the same will be true for those who
eventually interpret our message. What I'm telling you now,
Müller, I'm no longer telling you because instructed to do so by
our superiors, but drawing on my own personal experience,
speaking as colleague to colleague, man to man. Listen: the lie is
the real information we have to pass on. Hence I didn't wish to
deny myself a discreet use of lying where it didn't complicate the

message, but on the contrary simplified it. When it came to information about myself in particular, I felt it legitimate to indulge
in all kinds of details that are not true (I don't see how this could
bother anyone). My life with Angela, for example: I described it
as I would have liked it to be, a great love story, where Angela
and I appear as two eternal lovebirds happy in the midst of every
kind of adversity, passionate, faithful. It wasn't exactly like that,
Müller: Angela married me out of convenience and immediately
regretted it, our life was one long trail of sourness and subter-
fuge. But what does it matter what happened day by day? In the
world memory Angela's image is definitive, perfect, nothing can
taint it and I will always be the most enviable husband there ever
was.

At first all I had to do was to apply some cosmetics to the
data our everyday life provided. But there came the point when
the facts I found myself confronted with as I watched Angela day
by day (then spied on her, finally followed her) became increasingly contradictory and ambiguous, such as to justify the worst
suspicions. What was I to do, Müller? Muddy that image of
Angela at once so clear, so easy to transmit, so loved and love-
able, was I to make it incomprehensible, to darken the most
brilliant light in all our archives? I didn't hesitate, day after day I
eliminated these facts. But I was constantly afraid that some clue,
some intimation, some hint from which one might deduce what
she, what Angela did and was in this transitory life, might still be
hovering around her definitive image. I spent the days in the
laboratory, selecting, cancelling, omitting. I was jealous, Müller:
not jealous of the transitory Angela – that was a game I'd already
lost – but jealous of that information-Angela who would live as
long as the universe itself.

If the information-Angela was not to be contaminated, the
first thing that must be done was to stop the living Angela from
constantly superimposing herself on that image. It was then that
Angela disappeared and all searches for her proved vain. It would
be pointless, Müller, for me to tell you now how I managed to

140

get rid of the body piece by piece. Please, keep calm, these details are of no importance as far as our work is concerned, since in the world memory I remain that happy husband and later inconsolable widower you all know. But this didn't bring peace of mind: the information-Angela was still part of an information system where certain data might lend themselves to being interpreted – whether because of disturbances in transmission, or some malevolence on the part of the decoder – as ambiguous conjectures, insinuations, slander. I decided to destroy all references to people Angela could have had relationships with. I was sad about that, since there will now be no trace of some of our colleagues in the world memory, it will be as though they had never existed.

You imagine I'm telling you all this in order to seek your complicity, Müller. But that's not the case. I feel obliged to inform you of the extreme measures I am being forced to take to make sure that information relative to everybody who might have been my wife's lover is excluded from the archives. I am not worried about any repercussions on myself; the few years that remain for me to live are a trifle compared to the eternity I am used to measuring things against; and the person I really was has already been definitively established and consigned to the punchcards.

If there is nothing that needs correcting in the world memory, the only thing left to do is to correct reality where it doesn't agree with that memory. Just as I cancelled the existence of my wife's lover from the punchcards, so I must cancel him from the world of the living. Which is why I am now pulling out my gun and pointing it at you, Müller, why I'm squeezing the trigger, killing you.

Beheading the Heads

1

I must have arrived in the capital the day before a festival. They were building platforms in the squares, hanging up flags, ribbons, palmfronds. There was hammering everywhere.

'The national festival?' I asked the man behind the bar.

He pointed to the row of portraits behind him. 'Our heads of state,' he said. 'It's the festival of the heads of state, the leaders.'

I thought it might be the presentation of a newly elected government. 'New?' I asked.

Amid the banging of the hammers, loudspeakers being tested, the screeching of cranes lifting platforms, I was forced to keep things short if I was to be understood, and yell almost.

The man behind the bar shook his head: they weren't new, they'd been around for a while.

I asked: 'The anniversary of when they came to power?'

'Something like that,' explained a customer beside me. 'The festival comes round periodically and it's their turn.'

'Their turn for what?'

'To go on the platform.'

'What platform? I've seen so many, one at every street corner.'

'Each has his own platform. We have lots of leaders.'

'And what do they do? Speak?'

142

'No, speak, no.'

'They go on the platform, and then what?'

'What do you think they do? They wait a bit, while things are being prepared, then the ceremony is over in a couple of minutes.'

'And you?'

'We watch.'

There was a lot of coming and going in the bar. The carpenters and the workers unloading things from trucks to decorate the platforms – axes, blocks, baskets – stopped by to have a beer. Whenever I asked someone a question it was always someone else who answered.

'It's a sort of re-election, then? A confirmation of their jobs, you could say, their mandate?'

'No, no,' they corrected me, 'you don't understand? It's the end. Their time is up.'

'And so?'

'So they stop being heads, living up there: and they fall down.'

'So why do they go up on the platforms?'

'With the platforms you can see better how the head falls, the jump it makes, cleanly cut, and how it ends up in the basket.'

I was beginning to understand, but I wasn't quite sure. 'The heads' heads, you mean? The leaders'? In the baskets?'

They nodded. 'Right. The beheading. That's it. Beheading the heads.'

I'd only just arrived, I didn't know anything about it, I hadn't read anything in the papers.

'Just like that, tomorrow, all of a sudden?'

'When the day comes it comes,' they said. 'This time it falls midweek. There's a holiday. Everything's shut.'

An old man added, pontificating: 'When the fruit is ripe you gather it, and a head you behead. You wouldn't leave fruit to rot on the branches, would you?'

The carpenters had been getting on with their work: on

143

some of the platforms they were erecting the scaffolding for grim guillotines; on others they were anchoring blocks for use with axes and placing comfortable hassocks beside (one of the assistants was testing the arrangement by putting his head on the block to check that the height was right); elsewhere people were setting up things that looked like butcher's benches, with channels for the blood to run off. Waxed cloth was being stretched on the platform boards, and sponges were already in place to clean up any splashes. Everybody was working away enthusiastically; you could hear laughter and whistling.

'So you're happy? Did you hate them? Were they bad leaders?'

'No, what gave you that idea?' they exchanged looks of surprise. 'They were good. Or rather, no better and no worse than anyone else. Well, you know what they're like: heads of state, leaders, commanders . . . to get one of those jobs . . .'

'Still,' one of them said, 'I liked this lot.'

'Me too. And me,' others agreed. 'I never had anything against them.'

'So aren't you sad they're killing them?' I said.

'What can you do? If someone agrees to be a leader he knows how he'll end up. He could hardly expect to die in his bed!'

The others laughed. 'That'd be a fine thing! Someone rules, commands, then, as if nothing had happened, stops and goes back home.'

Someone said: 'Everybody would want to be leader then, I'm telling you! Even me, look, I'd be up for it, here I am!'

'Me too, me too,' lots of them said, laughing.

'Well I wouldn't,' said one man with glasses. 'Not on those terms. What would be the point?'

'Right. There'd be no point in being boss on those terms,' several of them agreed. 'It's one thing doing a job like that when you know what to expect, and quite another . . . but how could you do it otherwise?'

The man with the glasses, who must have been the best educated, explained: 'Authority over others is indivisible from the right of those others to have you climb the scaffold and do away with you, one day in the not too distant future ... What authority would a leader have without the aura of this destiny around him, if you couldn't read it in his eyes, his sense of his end, for every second of his mandate? Civil institutions depend on this dual aspect of authority; no civilization has ever used any other system.'

'And yet,' I objected, 'I could quote you cases ...'

'I mean: real civilization,' insisted the man with glasses, 'I'm not talking about barbarian interregnums, however long they may have lasted in the history of peoples.'

The pontificating old man, the one who'd talked about fruit on branches, was muttering something to himself. He exclaimed: 'The head commands so long as it's attached to the neck.'

'What do you mean?' the others asked. 'Do you mean that if for example a leader went beyond his term and, just for the sake of argument, didn't get his head cut off, he'd stay there ruling, his whole life long?'

'That's how things used to be,' the old man agreed, 'in the times before it was clear that whoever chose to be leader chose to be beheaded in the not too distant future. Those who had power hung on to it ...'

I could have interrupted at this point, quoted some examples, but no one would listen to me.

'So? What did people do?' they asked the old man.

'They had to cut their heads off willy-nilly, with brute force, against their wishes! Not on appointed days, but when they just couldn't put up with them any more. That's what used to happen before things were organized, before the leaders accepted ...'

'Oh, we'd just like to see them try not to accept!' the others said. 'Oh we'd like to see that!'

'It's not the way you think,' interrupted the man with the glasses. 'It's not true that the leaders are forced to undergo execution. Say that and you miss the real meaning of our statutes, the real relationship that binds our leaders to the rest of the people. Only heads of state can be beheaded, hence you can't wish to be a head without also wishing for the chop. Only those who feel they have this vocation can become heads of state, only those who already feel themselves beheaded the moment they take up a position of authority.'

Little by little the customers in the bar had thinned out, each going back to his work. I realized that the man with the glasses was talking exclusively to me.

'That's what power is,' he went on, 'this waiting for the end. All the authority one has is no more than advance notice of the blade hissing through the air, crashing down in a clean cut, all the applause you get is no more than the beginning of that last applause that greets your head as it rolls down the waxed surface of the scaffold.'

He took off his glasses to clean them on his handkerchief. I realized his eyes were full of tears. He paid for his beer and left.

The man behind the bar bent down to my ear. 'He's one of them,' he said. 'See?' He pulled out a pile of portrait posters from under the bar. 'Tomorrow I have to take those ones down and stick up these.' The first picture showed the man with the glasses, an ugly enlargement from a passport photo. 'He's been elected to succeed the ones on their way out. Tomorrow he'll be taking over. It's his turn, now. If you ask me it's not right to tell him the day before. You heard the way he was talking about it? Tomorrow he'll be watching the executions as if they were already his own. They're all like that, the first days; they get upset, excited, they make a big deal of it. "Vocation": what pompous words they come out with!'

'And afterwards?'

'He'll get used to it, like everybody else. They have so much to do, they don't think about it any more, until their day comes around. But then: who can see into a leader's mind. They give the impression they're not thinking about it. Another beer?'

2

Television has changed a lot of things. Once power was remote, distant figures puffed up on a platform, or portraits assuming expressions of conventional pride, symbols of an authority that could barely be related to any flesh and blood individual. Now, with television, the physical presence of politicians is something immediate and familiar to us; their faces, blown up on the screen, visit the homes of private citizens every day; quietly sunk in their armchairs, at leisure, everybody can pore over the slightest movement of the features, the irritated twitch of eyelids under spotlights, the nervous moistening of the lips between one word and the next ... In its death throes in particular, that face, so well known from the many close-ups of formal or speech-making postures on both solemn and festive occasions, betrays itself completely: it is at that moment more than any other that the simple citizen feels his leader is his, is something that will always belong to him. But even before that, in all the preceding months, every time the citizen saw the leader appear on the small screen, strutting about his duties – opening some building project, for example, or pinning medals on worthies' chests, or just climbing down the steps of aeroplanes waving an open hand – he was already searching that face for painful spasms, trying to imagine the convulsions that would precede rigor mortis, to guess from the delivery of his speeches and toasts how the death rattle would sound. It is in this that the public man's ascendance over the crowd consists: he is the man who will have a public death, the man whose death we are sure to be there for, all together, and that is why so long as he lives he will enjoy our interested, anticipatory concern. We can no longer imagine what it was like in the past, in times when public men died in private: we laugh today when we hear that they described some of their erstwhile procedures as democratic; for us democracy can only begin once we are sure that on the appointed day the television cameras will frame the death throes of our ruling classes to the last man, and then, as an epilogue to the same programme (though many will switch off their sets at this point), the investiture of the new faces who are to rule (and to live) for a similar period. We know that in other times just as today the mechanics of power were based on killings, on slaughters whether slow or sudden, but aside from rare exceptions the victims then were shadowy folk, subordinates, hard to identify; often the massacres went unreported, were officially ignored, or given specious justifications. Only this now definitive conquest, this unification of the roles of torturer and victim, in continuous rotation, has allowed us to quench every last flicker of hatred and pity in our minds. The close-ups of the mouth yawning open, of the carotid throbbing in the starched collar, of the raised hand that clutches and tears at a breast sparkling with medals, are watched by millions of viewers with the serene absorption of one observing the movement of the heavenly bodies in their recurrent cycles, a spectacle all the more reassuring the more alien we find it.

3

You don't want to kill us already, do you?

The words were pronounced by Virghilij Ossipovic with a slight trembling in his voice that contrasted with the almost bureaucratic though often harsh and polemical tone of the discussion so far and thus broke the tension in the meeting of the 'Volja i Raviopravie' movement. Virghilij was the youngest member of the Executive Committee; a thin down of hair darkened a prominent lip; locks of blond hair fell over his oblong grey eyes; those red-knuckled hands, their wrists always sticking out from shirt sleeves that were too short had not trembled when they primed the bomb beneath the Tsar's carriage.

Grass-roots activists took up all the places round the low, smoky basement room; most of them sitting on benches and stools, others crouched on the ground, others on their feet leaning against the wall, arms folded. The Executive Committee sat in the centre, eight boys bent over a table laden with paper, like a group of students intent on the final slog before the summer exams. To the repeated interruptions fired at them by the activists from all four corners of the room, they answered without turning or raising their heads. Every now and then a wave of protest or agreement swept through the meeting and – since many got to their feet and pressed forward – seemed to converge from the walls on the table, there to wash over the backs of the Executive Committee.

Liborij Serapionovic, the heavily bearded secretary, had already and on several occasions pronounced the stony maxim he often resorted to to soften irreconcilable differences: 'Where comrade parts company with comrade, there enemy joins hands with enemy', and in reply the assembly had intoned with one voice: 'The head still at the head after the victory, victorious and honoured the day after shall fall' – a ritual warning that the 'Volja i Raviopravie' activists never forgot to direct at their leaders whenever they spoke to them, and that the leaders themselves would say to each other as a form of greeting.

The movement was struggling to establish, on the ruins of autocracy and of the Duma, an egalitarian society in which power would be regulated by the periodic execution of the elected heads. The movement's strict rules, all the more necessary as the imperial police stepped up their repression, demanded that all activists obey Executive Committee decisions without argument; at the same time every text setting out the movement's theory reminded the leaders that no exercise of authority was admissible unless by those who had already renounced enjoyment of the privileges of power, those who to all intents and purposes were no longer to be considered as among the living.

The young leaders of the organization never thought of the fate that a still utopian future held for them: for the moment it was tsarist repression that unfortunately guaranteed an ever more rapid turnover in their numbers; the danger of arrest and execution was too real and immediate for the notional future of the theory to take shape in their imaginations. A youthfully ironic, disdainful attitude served to repress in their minds what was nevertheless the distinguishing element in their doctrine. The grass-roots activists knew all this, and just as they shared the risks and hardships of the committee members, so they understood their spirit; and yet they nursed an obscure awareness of their destiny as executioners, a destiny to be fulfilled not only at the expense of the *status quo*, but of the future government too, and being unable to express themselves any other way, they would flaunt an insolent attitude, which, while always expressed in the formal tones of the meeting, nevertheless weighed down on their leaders like a threat.

'So long as the enemy before us is the Tsar,' Virghilij Ossipovic had said, 'foolish is the man who would seek the Tsar in his comrade.' It was an untimely thing to say perhaps, and certainly badly received by the noisy assembly.

Virghilij felt a hand gripping his own; sitting on the floor at his feet was Evghenija Ephraïmovna, knees pulled up in her pleated skirt, hair knotted on her neck and hanging at the two sides of her face like spirals from a tawny coil. One of Evghenija's hands had found its way up Virghilij's boots to encounter the young man's fingers closed in a fist, it had skimmed the back of that fist, as though in a consolatory caress, then dug sharp nails into it scratching slowly until they drew blood. Virghilij realized that there was a precise and stubborn determination guiding the floor of the meeting today, something that had to do with them, the leaders, in person, and that would soon be revealed.

'Let none of us ever forget, comrades,' Ignatij Apollonovic, the oldest member of the Committee and with a reputation for being a peacemaker, attempted to calm the waters, 'what must not be forgotten ... in any event, it is only right that you remind us from time to time ... although,' he added, chuckling in his beard, 'when it comes to reminding us, Count Galitzin and his horses' hoofs are only too reliable ...' He was alluding to the commander of the Imperial Guard who had recently torn one of their protest marches to pieces with a cavalry charge at Maneggio Bridge.

150

A voice, it wasn't clear where from, interrupted him with: 'Idealist!' and Ignatij Apollonovic lost his way. 'Why's that?' he asked, disconcerted.

'Do you think we need do no more than keep the words of our doctrine uppermost in our minds?' said a tall lanky fellow from another part of the room, a man who had made a name for himself as one of the most militant of recent recruits. 'You know why our doctrine can't be confused with those of all the other movements?'

'Of course we know. Because it's the only doctrine which once it has achieved power cannot be corrupted by power!' grumbled a shaved head bent over papers, and that was Femja, the one the others called 'the ideologue'.

'So why wait till the day we've got power, my lovey-dovey comrades,' insisted the lanky fellow, 'to put it into practice?'

'Here, now!' the cry was raised from various parts of the room. The Marianzev sisters, known as 'the three Marias' stepped forward between the benches, chirping 'Excuse me! Excuse me!' and catching their long tresses on things. Carrying tablecloths folded over their arms, humming to themselves and pushing aside the boys, it was as if they were laying table for a snack on the veranda of their house in Izmailovo.

'What's different about our doctrine is this,' the lanky fellow went on with his sermon, 'that the only way to write it is with a sharp blade on the bodies of our beloved leaders!'

There was a mill of people and benches turning over because many in the meeting had got up and rushed forward. The ones who shoved and shouted most were the women: 'Sit down, little boys! We want to see! Mother of God, what hotheads! We can't see anything at all here!' and they thrust their schoolmistressy faces between the men's backs, short hair under peaked caps lending an air of resolution.

There was only one thing could shake Virghilij's courage, and that was female hostility, even the slightest sign of it. He had got up, sucking the blood from Evghenija's scratches on the back

151

of his hand, and he had scarcely spoken those words: 'You don't want to kill us already, do you?' when the door opened and in came a procession of people in white coats pushing trolleys laden with glittering surgical instruments. From that moment on something in the mood of the meeting changed. There was a sharp patter of voices, one hard on another. 'Of course not . . . who said anything about killing you? . . . you're our leaders . . . with how much we like you and everything . . . what would we do without you? . . . there's still a long way to go . . . we'll always be here beside you . . .' and the lanky fellow, the girls, those who a few moments before had seemed to constitute the opposition, were now falling over each other to encourage the leaders, in reassuring, almost protective tones. 'It's only a little thing, significant, yes, but not serious in itself, no no no, a bit painful, for sure, but it's so we can see you as our real leaders, our well-loved leaders, a mutilation, that's all, when it's done it's done, a little mutilation every now and then, you're not going to get mad about such a little thing, it's what marks out the leaders of our movement, what else if not that?'

Already the members of the Executive Committee had been immobilized by scores of strong arms. Laid on the table were gauze, basins with cotton wool, serrated knives. The smell of ether filled the room. The girls laid things out quickly and carefully, as if they'd all been practising their tasks for some time.

'Now the doctor will explain everything properly. Come on, Tòlja!'

Anatòl Spiridionovic, a medical degree begun and never finished, stepped forward holding red rubber-gloved hands high over an already obese stomach. He was a strange character, Tòlja, a man who perhaps to hide his shyness would put on a comic, infantile grin and come out with a string of witticisms.

'The hand . . . Ah, the little handy pandy . . . the hand is a prehensile organ . . . oh yes, very useful . . . that's why we have two of them . . . and of fingers, as a rule, we have ten . . . every finger is made up of three bone segments, or phalanges . . . or at least that's what they're called in our part of the world . . . phalanx, middle phalanx, terminal phalanx . . .'

'Stop it. You're getting on our nerves! What do you want to do, give us a lecture!' People grumbled. (In the end nobody liked this Tòlja fellow.) 'Let's get to the real thing! Come on! Let's get down to it!'

The first person they brought out was Virghilij. When he realized they were only going to amputate the first phalanx of his ring finger, he recovered his nerve and bore the pain with a pride worthy of his reputation. But some of the others screamed; it took several people to hold them down; fortunately sooner or later most of them fainted. There were different amputations for different people, but generally speaking no more than two phalanges for the more important leaders (the other phalanges would be cut off later a few at a time; one had to remember there would be many of these ceremonies over the years to come). Blood loss was greater than expected; the girls mopped up carefully.

Lined up on the tablecloth, the amputated fingers looked like small fish, throats pierced by the hook and pulled to the bank. They soon went dry and black, and, after a brief discussion as to whether they should be kept in a showcase, they were thrown in the bin.

This system of pruning the leaders bore excellent fruit. In exchange for relatively small physical impairment, a great improvement in morale was achieved. The leaders' authority grew with periodic mutilation. When a hand with missing fingers was raised above the barricades, the demonstrators rallied round and the lancers on their horses were submerged in a crowd they couldn't break up. The singing, the thuds, the neighing, the shouts – 'Volja i Raviopravie!', 'Death to the Tsar!' 'Victorious and honoured the day after shall fall!' – ranged in the icy air, wafted over the banks of the Nevà, reached the Peter and Paul fortress, penetrated the deepest cells where imprisoned comrades beat their chains to the rhythm and stretched out their stumps through the bars.

4

Every time they reached out a hand to sign a document or make the kind of terse gesture that would stress something in a speech, the young leaders found themselves looking at their amputated fingers, and this had an immediate mnemonic effect, establishing an association of ideas between the organ of command and time getting shorter. More than anything else it was a practical system: the amputations could be carried out by simple students and nurses, in improvised operating rooms, with whatever instruments came to hand; if found and arrested by the ever menacing police, the punishment for a simple mutilation was not serious, or at least nowhere near as severe as those they would bring on themselves if the theory's prescriptions were followed to the letter. It was a time when the straightforward killing of the leaders would not have been understood, either by the authorities or public opinion; the executioners would have been condemned as murderers, the imagined motive, rivalry or revenge.

In every local organization and at every level of the movement, a group of activists, distinct from the leaders and whose members were constantly being changed, took charge of the amputations; they established the frequency and the parts of the body, they arranged for the purchase of disinfectants, and, availing themselves of the advice of an expert or two, they themselves handled the instruments. It was a sort of committee of wise men, but with no influence over political decisions which remained strictly in the hands of the Executive Committee.

When the leaders began to run short of fingers, they looked into the possibility of one or two anatomical variations. The first thing to attract their attention was the tongue: not only did it lend itself to further resections of slivers or fibrils, but in symbolic and mnemonic terms it was exactly what they were after: every little cut directly affected vocal and oratorical ability. But the technical difficulties inherent in the delicacy of the organ were greater than was at first thought. After an early series of operations, tongues were discarded, and the committee fell back on more obvious but less taxing mutilations: ears, noses, a tooth or two. (As far as amputation of the testicles was concerned, though not absolutely ruled out, it was almost always avoided, since it could lend itself to sexual innuendo.)

There's a long way to go. The hour of revolution has yet to strike. The leaders of the movement continue to subject themselves to the scalpel. When will they take power? However late it is, they will be the first leaders not to disappoint the hopes others have placed in them. Already we see them parading through flag-draped streets the day of their investiture: lurching on wooden legs if they still have one of their own intact; pushing walking frames with one arm if they still have an arm to push with, faces hidden in feathered masks to hide the more repugnant mutilations, some holding aloft their own scalps as trophies. At that point it will be clear that it's only in what little flesh is left them that power can be incarnated, if any power there is still to be.

The Burning of the Abominable House

In a few hours' time Skiller, the insurance agent, will be coming to ask me for the computer results, and I still haven't keyed in the orders to the electronic circuits which will have to grind to a fine dust of bits both Widow Roessler's secrets and her hardly to be recommended boarding house. Where the house once stood, between railway lines and iron stockyards, on one of those humps of wasteland our city's suburbs leave behind like heaps of dirt that have escaped the broom, nothing is left but charred rubble now. It could have been a smart villa originally, or it may have looked no better than a ghostly hovel: insurance company reports have nothing to say on the matter; and now it has burnt down, from eaves to cellar, and the incinerated corpses of its four inhabitants have left no clue that might serve to reconstruct the events that led up to this secluded slaughter.

Rather than the bodies, what does offer a clue is a copybook found in the ruins, entirely burnt except for its cover which was protected by a plastic folder. On the front it says: *An Account of the Abominable Deeds Committed in this House* and on the back there is an index with twelve entries in alphabetical order: Blackmail, Drugging, Incitement to Suicide, Knifing, Prostitution, Threatening with a Gun, Tying and Gagging, Rape, Seduction, Slander, Snooping, Strangling.

It isn't known which of the house's inhabitants penned this sinister summary, nor to what end: to report the matter to the police, to confess, to defend themselves, to gratify their fascinated contemplation of evil. All we have is this index which doesn't tell us the names of the perpetrators or the victims of the twelve deeds – criminal or merely immoral as they may be – nor does it explain the order in which they were committed, something that would offer a good start for reconstructing a story: the entries in alphabetical order refer us to page numbers obliterated by a black streak. To complete the list would require one additional word, Arson, doubtless the final deed in this grim chain of events. But who did it? In order to hide, or to destroy?

Even if we accept that each of the twelve deeds was committed by just one person and inflicted upon just one other person, reconstruction would still be a tall order: given that there are four characters to be considered, then taken two by two we have twelve possible relationships for each of the twelve kinds of relationship listed. The number of possible combinations is thus twelve to the twelfth, meaning that we shall have to choose from a total of eight thousand eight hundred and seventy-four billion, two hundred and ninety-six million, six hundred and seventy-two thousand, two hundred and fifty-six potential solutions. It is hardly surprising that our already overworked police force has chosen not to pursue its enquiries, on the good grounds that, however many crimes may have been committed, the perpetrators doubtless died together with their victims.

Only the insurance company is eager to know the truth: mainly on account of a fire insurance policy taken out by the owner of the house. The fact that the young Inigo, the policy holder, likewise perished in the flames only serves to make the matter more problematic: his powerful family, despite having ejected and disinherited this degenerate son, is notoriously disinclined to give up anything owed to them. Then one can level the worst possible charges (whether or not included in the abominable index) against a young man who, as a hereditary member of the British House of Lords, dragged an illustrious title down to the steps of those public squares that serve as beds to a nomadic, introspective generation, a man who was wont to soap his long hair under the water of municipal fountains. The small house he rented to the old landlady was the last property left to him, and he had taken a room there subletting from his own tenant in return for a reduction in the already low rent he charged. If he, Inigo, was the arsonist, perpetrator and victim of a criminal plan executed with the carelessness and imprecision that appear to have been typical of his way of behaving, and if the insurance company could demonstrate as much, then they wouldn't have to pay the damages.

But this is not the only claim the company is obliged to honour as a result of the calamity: every year Widow Roessler would renew a policy insuring her own life in favour of her adopted daughter, a fashion model familiar to anyone in the habit of leafing through the pages of the more stylish magazines. Of course Ogiva herself is likewise dead, incinerated together with the collection of wigs that would transform her features with their terrifying charm (how else describe a beautiful and delicate young woman with a completely bald skull) into those of hundreds of different and exquisitely asymmetrical faces. But it turns out that the model had a three-year-old child, entrusted to relatives in South Africa, who will waste no time in claiming the rewards of the policy, unless it can be demonstrated that it was she, Ogiva, who killed (*Knifing? Strangling?*) Widow Roessler. Or again, given that Ogiva had taken the trouble to insure her wig collection, the child's guardians could claim on this policy too, unless it can be demonstrated that she was responsible for their destruction.

Of the fourth person who died in the fire, the gigantic Uzbek wrestler, Belindo Kid, we know that in Widow Roessler he had found not only a zealous landlady (he was the only paying occupant of the boarding house) but also an agent with a keen eye for business. Indeed the old lady had recently agreed to finance the ex-middleweight champion's seasonal tour, covering herself by insuring against the eventuality that illness, incapacity or injury might prevent him from honouring his contracts. A consortium of wrestling match organizers are now claiming damages against this policy; but had the old woman *induced* Belindo *to suicide*, perhaps by *slandering* him or *blackmailing* him or *drugging* him (the giant was renowned on the international scene for his impressionable character), then the company could easily have them desist.

I can't prevent the slow tentacles of my mind from advancing one hypothesis at a time, exploring labyrinths of consequence that magnetic memories would run through in a nanosecond. It is from my computer that Skiller is expecting a solution, not from me.

Of course each of the four catastrophic characters appears better suited to be perpetrator of some of the abominable deeds and victim of others. But who can rule out the notion that the most improbable alternative might be the only one possible? Take what you would suppose to be the most innocent of the twelve relationships, that implied by *seduction*. Who seduced whom? I have to work hard to concentrate on my permutations here: a flow of images swirls unceasingly in my mind, breaking up and re-forming as though in a kaleidoscope. I see the long fingers of the fashion model with their green and purple varnished nails skimming the listless chin, the grassy stubble of the slummy young aristocrat, or tickling the solid predatory nape of the Uzbek champion who, aware of a remote and pleasant sensation, arches his deltoids like a purring cat. But immediately afterwards I also see the volatile Ogiva allowing herself to be seduced, captivated by the taurine flattery of the middleweight or the consuming introversion of the feckless youth. And I can also see the old widow, haunted by appetites that age may discourage but not extinguish, painting her face and dolling herself up to lure one or the other of her male prey (or both), and overcoming opposition very different in terms of weight but equally feeble in terms of character. Or I see her herself as the object of a seduction whose perversity might be due to youthful lust's readiness to confuse life's seasons, or alternatively to sinister calculation.

159

Until finally, to complete the picture, the shadow of Sodom and Gomorrah unleashes the whirligig of loves between the same sex.

Does the range of possibilities shrink a little for the more criminal deeds? Not necessarily: anybody can *knife* anybody else. Already I can imagine Belindo Kid being treacherously skewered in the back of the neck by a switchblade that slices through his spinal cord the way the toreador's sword dispatches the bull. Behind the perfectly aimed blow we might find the slender, bracelet-tinkling wrist of an Ogiva seized by cold and bloody frenzy, or Inigo's playful fingers, rocking the dagger to and fro by the blade, then flinging it through the air with inspired abandon along a trajectory that strikes its target almost by chance; or we might find LandLady Macbeth's claw, shifting the curtains of the bedrooms at night as she imposes her presence on the sleepers' breathing. Nor are these the only images that throng my mind: Ogiva or Widow Roessler slaughter Inigo like a lamb, knifing through his windpipe; Inigo or Ogiva grab the big knife the widow is using to slice the bacon and hack her to bits in the kitchen; the widow or Inigo dissect Ogiva's nude body like surgeons while she struggles (*tied up and gagged?*) to escape. Then if Belindo had found the knife in his hand, at a moment of exasperation perhaps, or perhaps when someone had stirred him up against someone else, he could have had all the others in pieces in no time. But why should he, Belindo Kid, go for a *knifing*, when both the copybook index and his own motor sensory circuits offer the possibility of *strangling*, something far more congenial to his physical tendencies and technical training? And furthermore, this would be an action of which he could only be the subject and not the object: I'd like to see the other three trying to strangle the middleweight wrestler; their puny fingers wouldn't even go round his tree-trunk neck!

So this is a piece of data the programme will have to take into account: Belindo doesn't *knife* but prefers to *strangle*; and he can't be *strangled*, only if *threatened with a gun* can he be *tied up and gagged*; once *tied up and gagged* anything can happen to him, he can even be *raped*, by the ruttish widow, or the impassive model, or the eccentric youth.

Let's start laying down exclusions and orders of precedence. Someone may first *threaten someone with a gun*, then *tie them up and gag them*; it would be to say the least superfluous to *tie up* someone first then *threaten* them afterwards. On the other hand someone *knifing* or *strangling* who at the same time *threatened with a gun*, would be engaging in a gesture at once awkward and unnecessary, unforgivable. Someone who wins over the object of his or her desires by *seduction* has no need to *rape* that person; and vice versa. Someone inciting someone else to *prostitution* may have previously *seduced* or *raped* them; doing so afterwards would be a pointless waste of time and energy. One may *snoop* on someone in order to *blackmail* them, but if you have already *slandered* them then further scandalous revelations can frighten them no more; hence the person *slandering* is not interested in *snooping*, nor has any further reasons for *blackmail*. Someone *knifing* one victim may well *strangle* another, or *incite them to suicide*, but it is unlikely that the three deadly deeds could be committed at the expense of the same person.

Following this method allows me to rewrite my flow-chart: to establish a system of exclusions that will enable the computer to discard billions of incongruous combinations, to reduce the number of plausible concatenations, to approach a selection of that solution which will present itself as true.

But will we ever get to that? Half I'm concentrating on constructing algebraic models where factors and functions are anonymous and interchangeable, thus dismissing the faces and gestures of those four phantoms from my thoughts; and half I am identifying with the characters, evoking the scenes in a mental film packed with fades and metamorphoses. Maybe it's around the word *drugging* that the cog that drives all the others turns: at once my mind associates the word with the pasty face of the last Inigo of an illustrious stock; if *drugging* meant the reflexive *drugging oneself*, there would be no problem here: it's highly likely that the

161

boy took drugs, something that does not concern me; but the transitive sense of *drugging* implies a drugger and a person drugged, the latter consenting, unknowing or compelled.

It is equally likely that Inigo gets himself so high on drugs that he tries to preach stupefaction to others; I imagine spindly cigarettes being passed from his hand to Ogiva's or old Widow Roessler's. Is it the young nobleman who transforms the lonely boarding house into a smoke-filled den of kaleidoscopic hallucinations? Or is it the landlady who lures him there in order to exploit his inclination toward states of ecstasy? Perhaps it is Ogiva who procures the drug for the old opium addict, Roessler, and Inigo who, while *snooping* on her, discovers where she hides it and bursts in on her *threatening her with a gun* or *blackmailing* her; Widow Roessler shouts to Belindo for help, then *slanders* Inigo accusing him of having *seduced* and *prostituted* Ogiva, the Uzbek's chaste passion, at which the wrestler takes his revenge by *strangling* the boy; to get out of trouble the landlady now has no alternative but to incite the wrestler *to suicide*, not a problem since the insurance company will pay the damages, but Belindo, in for a penny in for a pound, *rapes* Ogiva, *ties and gags* her and sets fire to the obliterating pyre.

Slowly does it: no point in imagining I can beat the electronic brain to it. The drug might just as well have to do with Belindo: old and over the hill he can't climb into the ring these days without stuffing himself full of stimulants. It's Widow Roessler who doles them out, slipping them in his mouth with a soup spoon. *Snooping* through the keyhole, Inigo, a glutton for psychodrugs, interrupts and demands a dose for himself. When they refuse, he *blackmails* the wrestler threatening to have him banned from the championship; Belindo *ties and gags* him, then *prostitutes* him for a few guineas to Ogiva who has for some time been infatuated with the elusive aristocrat; impervious to eros, Inigo can only achieve an amorous state if on the point of being *strangled*; Ogiva presses on his carotid artery with her slim fingertips; perhaps Belindo lends a hand; just two of his fingers and the little lord rolls his eyes and gives up the ghost; what to do with the corpse? To simulate a suicide they *knife* him ... Stop! Have to rewrite the whole programme: have to cancel the instruction now stored in the central memory that someone *strangled* cannot be *knifed*. The ferrite rings are demagnetized and remagnetized; I'm sweating.

Let's start again from scratch. What is the job my client expects of me? To arrange a certain amount of data in a logical order. It is information I am dealing with, not human lives, with their good and evil sides. For reasons that need not concern me the data available to me only has to do with the evil side, and the computer must put it in order. Not the evil, which cannot perhaps be put in order, but the information relative to the evil. On the basis of this data, contained in the alphabetical index of the *Abominable Deeds*, I must reconstruct the lost *Account*, true or false as that may be.

The *Account* presupposes the existence of a writer. Only by reconstructing it will we know who that was: certain data, however, can already be placed on his or her file. The author of the *Account* couldn't have been killed by *knifing* or *strangling*, because he wouldn't have been able to include his or her own death in the report; as far as suicide is concerned, the writer could have decided on it before writing out the copybook-testament, and carried it out later; but someone who believes they have been *incited to suicide* by the force of someone else's will does not commit suicide; every exclusion of the author of the copybook from the role of victim automatically increases the likelihood of our being able to attribute to him or her the role of perpetrator: hence this person could be both the originator of the evil and of the information regarding that evil. This presents no problems for my work: evil and information regarding evil are coincident, both in the burnt book and in the electronic files.

The memory has also been fed another series of data to be compared with the first: the four insurance policies taken out with Skiller, one by Inigo, one by Ogiva and two by the Widow

163

(one for herself and one for Belindo). An obscure thread may link the policies to the *Abominable Deeds* and the photoelectric cells must follow that thread in a bewildering blind man's bluff, seeking it out amongst the tiny holes of the punch cards. Even the policy data, now translated into binary code, is capable of evoking images in my mind: it's evening, there's fog; Skiller rings at the door of the house on the hump of wasteland; the landlady imagines he's a new tenant and greets him accordingly; he gets his insurance brochures out of his bag; he's sitting in the lounge; he accepts a cup of tea; clearly he can't get the four contracts signed in just one visit; he makes sure he is thoroughly familiar with the house and its four inhabitants. I imagine Skiller helping Ogiva to brush out the wigs in her collection (and in so doing his lips brush the model's bald scalp); I imagine him as, with a touch as sure as a doctor's and as thoughtful as a son's, he measures the widow's blood pressure, enclosing her soft white arm in the sphygmomanometer; or again I see him trying to get Inigo interested in home maintenance, pointing out problems with the plumbing, subsidence in the loadbearing beams, while in a fatherly voice telling him not to bite his nails; I see him reading the sports papers with Belindo, complimenting him with a slap on the back when he has guessed a winner.

I must admit, I don't really like this Skiller. A web of complicity stretches out wherever he ties his threads; if he really did have so much power over Widow Roessler's boarding house, if he was the factotum, the *deus ex machina*, if nothing happened between those walls but that he knew about it, then why did he come to me for a solution to the mystery? Why did he bring me the charred copybook? Was it he who found the copybook in the ruins? Or did he put it there? Was it he who brought this mass of negative information, of irreversible entropy, he who introduced it into the house, as now into the circuits of the computer?

The Roessler boarding-house massacre doesn't have four characters: it has five. I translate the data of insurance agent Skiller into holes on punchcards and add it to the other information. The abominable deeds could be his doing as much as any of the others: he could have *Blackmailed, Drugged, Induced to Suicide,* etc., or better still he could have made somebody *prostitute* themselves or *strangle* someone and all the rest. The billions of combinations multiply, but perhaps a shape is beginning to emerge. Merely for the purposes of a hypothesis I could construct a model in which all the evil stems from Skiller, before whose entrance on the scene the boarding house basked in Arcadian innocence: old Widow Roessler plays a *Lied* on her Bechstein which the gentle giant Belindo humps from room to room for the sake of the tenants' enjoyment, Ogiva waters the petunias, Inigo paints petunias on Ogiva's head. The bell rings: it's Skiller. Is he looking for a bed and breakfast? No, but he has some useful insurance policies to offer: life, accident, fire, house and contents. The conditions are good; Skiller invites them to think it over; they think it over; they think of things they never thought of before; they are tempted; temptation starts its trail of electronic impulses through the channels of the brain . . . I'm aware that I am undermining the objectivity of the operation with these subjective dislikes. In the end, what do I know about this Skiller? Perhaps his soul is without stain, perhaps he is the only innocent person in the story, while all the data depict Widow Roessler as a sordid miser, Ogiva as a ruthless narcissist, Inigo as lost in his dreamy introversion, Belindo as condemned to muscular brutality for lack of alternative role models . . . It is they who called Skiller, each with a sinister plan against the other three and the insurance company. Skiller is the dove in a nest of serpents.

The computer stops. There's an error, and the central memory has picked it up; it cancels everything. There are no innocents to be saved, in this story. Start again.

No, it wasn't Skiller who rang at the door. Outside it's drizzling, there's fog, no one can make out the visitor's face. He comes into the passage, takes off his wet hat, unwraps his woollen scarf. It's me. I introduce myself. Waldemar, computer programmer and systems analyst. You're looking well, you know,

Signora Roessler? No, we've never met, but I remember the data on the analogical-digital convertor and I recognize all four of you perfectly. Don't hide, Signor Inigo! You're looking good, Belindo Kid! Is that purple hair I see peeping over the stairs Signorina Ogiva? Here you are all together; good: let me explain why I've come. I need you, yes, you, just as you are, for a project that's kept me nailed to my programming console for years. During office hours I work freelance for clients, but at night, shut up in my laboratory, I spend my time researching a system that will transform individual passions – aggression, private interest, selfishness, various vices – into elements necessary for the universal good. The accidental, the negative, the abnormal, in a word the human, will be able to develop without provoking general destruction, by being integrated into a harmonious plan . . . This house is the ideal terrain for determining if I am on the right track. Hence I am asking you to accept me here as a tenant, a friend . . .

The house is burnt down, everybody is dead, but in the computer I can arrange the facts according to a different logic, get into the computer myself, insert a Waldemar programme, bring the number of characters to six, introduce new galaxies of combinations and permutations. The house rises from the ashes, all its inhabitants are alive again, I turn up at the door with my collapsible suitcase and golf clubs, and ask for a room to rent . . .

Signora Roessler and the others listen in silence. They don't trust me. They suspect I'm working for the insurance company, that I've been sent by Skiller . . .

One can hardly deny that their suspicions are well founded. It's Skiller I'm working for of course. It would have been he who asked me to gain their confidence, to study their behaviour, to forecast the consequences of their evil intentions, to classify stimuli, tendencies, gratifications, quantify them, store them in the computer . . .

But if this Waldemar programme is nothing but a duplicate of the Skiller programme, then it is pointless keying it in. Skiller and Waldemar must be enemies, the mystery will be sorted out in the struggle between us.

In the drizzly evening two shadows brush against each other on the rusty overpass that leads to what must once have been a residential suburb, though there's nothing left now but a crooked house on a hump of ground surrounded by derelict car dumps; the lighted windows of the Roessler boarding house emerge from the fog as though on a short-sighted retina. Skiller and Waldemar don't know each other as yet. Each unaware of the other, they stalk around the house. Who will make the first move? Indisputably the insurance agent takes precedence.

Skiller rings the doorbell. 'Please excuse me, on behalf of my company I am carrying out some research into the role played by household factors in disasters. This house has been chosen for our representative sample. With your permission, I would like to keep your behaviour under observation. I hope this won't put you to too much trouble: it's just a question of filling in some forms from time to time. In return the company is offering the chance to enjoy special discounts on insurance policies of various kinds: life, property . . .'

The four listen in silence; already each of them is thinking how they can get something from the situation, each is concocting a plan . . .

But Skiller is lying. His programme has already forecast what each member of the household will do. Skiller has a copybook listing a series of violent or dishonest acts whose probability he merely has to establish. He already knows there will be a series of maliciously provoked injuries, but that the company won't have to pay any damages, because all the beneficiaries will have killed each other. All these forecasts were given him by a computer: not my own, so I am bound to imagine the existence of another programmer, Skiller's accomplice in a criminal plot. The plot goes like this: a databank brings together the names of those fellow citizens of ours driven by fraudulent and destructive impulses; there are several hundred thousand of them; a system of persuasion and follow-ups leads them to become clients of the company, to insure everything insurable, to produce fraudulent

167

accidents and to kill each other off. The company will have taken care to record evidence to its own advantage, and since those committing crimes always tend to overdo it, the amount of information will include a considerable percentage of useless data that will function as a smokescreen to cover up the company's involvement. Indeed this coefficient of entropy has already been programmed: not all the *Abominable Deeds* of the index have a role in the story; some just create a 'noise' effect. The Roessler boarding-house operation is the first practical experiment the diabolical insurance agent has attempted. Once the disaster has taken place, Skiller will go to another computer, whose programmer is ignorant of all the facts, to check if it is possible to trace consequence back to cause. Skiller will give this second programmer all the necessary data together with a certain amount of 'noise' such as to produce circuit overload and debase the information: the evil intent of those insured will be sufficiently demonstrated, but not that of the insurer.

I am the second programmer. Skiller has set it up well. Everything fits. The programme was set up beforehand, and the house, the copybook, my own flowchart and my computer were to do nothing more than carry it out. I'm stuck here inputting and outputting the data of a story I can't change. There's no point in my putting myself in the computer: Waldemar will not go up to the house on the hump of wasteland, nor will he meet the four mysterious inhabitants, nor will he be (as he had hoped) the perpetrator of a *seduction* (victim: Ogiva). Perhaps even Skiller only has an input-output function: the real computer is elsewhere.

But a game between two computers is not won by the one that plays better than the other, but by the one that understands how its opponent is managing to play better than itself. My computer has now been fed its opponent's winning game: so has it won?

Someone rings at the door. Before going to open it, I must quickly work out how Skiller will react when he finds out his plan

168

has been discovered. I too was persuaded by Skiller to sign a fire insurance policy. Skiller has already provided for killing me and setting fire to the laboratory: he will destroy the punchcards that accuse him and demonstrate that I lost my life attempting arson. I hear the fire brigade's siren approaching: I called them in time. I click off the safety catch on my gun. Now I can open the door.

The Petrol Pump

I should have thought of it before, it's too late now. It's after twelve thirty and I didn't remember to fill up; the service stations will be closed until three. Every year two million tons of crude are brought up from the earth's crust where they have been stored for millions of centuries in the folds of rocks buried between layers of sand and clay. If I set off now there's a danger I'll run out on the way; the gauge has been warning me for quite a while that the tank is in reserve. They have been warning us for quite a while that underground global reserves can't last more than twenty years or so. I had plenty of time to think about it, as usual I've been irresponsible; when the red light begins to wink on the dashboard I don't pay attention, or I put things off, I tell myself there's still the whole reserve to use up, and then I forget about it. No, maybe that's what happened in the past, being careless like that and forgetting about it: in the days when petrol still seemed as plentiful as the air itself. Now when the light comes on it transmits a sense of alarm, of menace, at once vague and impending; that is the message I pick up and record along with the many angst-ridden signs sedimenting down among the folds of my consciousness, dissolving in a state of mind that I can't shake off, but that doesn't prompt me to any precise practical action as a consequence, such as, for example, stopping at the first pump I find and filling up. Or is it an instinct for making savings that has gripped me, a reflex miserliness: as I become aware that my tank is about to run out, so I sense re-

170

finery stocks dwindling, and likewise oil pipeline flows, and the loads in tankers ploughing the seas; drill-bits probe the depths of the earth and bring up nothing but dirty water; my foot on the accelerator grows conscious of the fact that its slightest pressure can burn up the last squirts of energy our planet has stored; my attention focuses on sucking up the last dribbles of fuel; I press the pedal as if the tank were a lemon that must be squeezed without wasting a drop; I slow down; no: I accelerate, my instinctive reaction being that the faster I go, the further I'll get with this squeeze, which could be the last.

I don't want to risk leaving town without having filled up. Surely I'll find one station open. I start patrolling the avenues, searching the pavements and flowerbeds where the coloured signs of different petroleum companies bristle, though less aggressively than they used to, in the days when tigers and other mythical animals blew flames into our engines. Again and again I'm fooled by the 'Open' signs which only mean that the station is open today during regular hours, and hence closed during the lunch break. Sometimes there's a pump attendant sitting on a folding chair eating a sandwich or half asleep: he spreads his arms in apology, the rules are the same for everybody and my questioning gestures are pointless as I knew they would be. The time when everything seemed easy is over, the time when you could believe that human energy like natural energy was unconditionally and endlessly at your service: when filling stations blossomed enticingly in your path all in a line with the attendant in green or blue or striped dungarees, dripping sponge at the ready to cleanse a windscreen contaminated by the massacre of swarms of gnats.

Or rather: between the end of the times when people with certain jobs worked round the clock and the end of the times when you imagined that certain commodities would never be used up, lies a whole era of history whose length varies from country to country, person to person. So let me say that right now I am experiencing simultaneously the rise, apex and decline of the so-called opulent societies, the same way a rotating drill pushes in an instant from one millennium to the next as it cuts through the sedimentary rocks of the Pliocene, the Cretaceous, the Triassic.

I take stock of my situation in space and time, confirming the data supplied by the kilometre clock, just returned to zero, the fuel gauge now steady on zero, and the time clock, whose short hand is still high in the meridian quadrant. In the meridian hours, when the Water Truce brings thirsty tiger and stag to the same muddy pool, my car searches in vain for refreshment as the Oil Truce sends it scurrying from pump to pump. In the meridian hours of the Cretaceous living creatures surged on the surface of the sea, swarms of minute algae and thin shells of plankton, soft sponges and sharp corals, simmering in the heat of a sun that will go on living through them in the long circumnavigation life begins after death, when reduced to a light rain of animal and vegetal detritus they sediment down in shallow waters, sink in the mud, and with the passing cataclysms are chewed up in the jaws of calcareous rocks, digested in the folds of syncline and anticline, liquefied in dense oils that push upward through dark subterranean porosities until they spurt out in the midst of the desert and burst into flames that once again warm the earth's surface in a blaze of primordial noon.

And here in the middle of the noonday urban desert I've spotted an open service station: a swarm of cars surges around it. There are no attendants; it's one of those self-service pumps that take notes in a machine. The drivers are busy pulling chrome pump nozzles out of their sheaths, they stop in mid-gesture to read instructions, uncertain hands push buttons, snakes of rubber arch their retractable coils. My hands fiddle with a pump, hands that grew up in a period of transition, that are used to waiting for other hands to perform those actions indispensable for my survival. That this state of affairs wasn't permanent I was always aware, in theory; in theory my hands would like nothing better than to regain their role of performing all the manual operations of the race, just as in the past when inclement nature beset a man armed with no more than his two bare hands, so today we are beset by a mechanical world that is doubtless more easily manipulated than brute nature, the world in which our hands will henceforth have to go back to managing on their own, no longer able to pass on to other hands the mechanical labour our daily life depends on.

As it turns out my hands are a little disappointed: the pump is so easy to work you wonder why on earth self-service didn't become commonplace ages ago. But the satisfaction of doing it yourself isn't much greater than that of using an automatic chocolate bar dispenser, or any other money munching device. The only operations that require some attention are those involved in paying. You have to place a thousand-lire note in the right position in a little drawer, so that a photoelectric eye can recognize the effigy of Giuseppe Verdi, or perhaps just the thin metal strip that crosses every banknote. It seems the value of the thousand lire is entirely concentrated in that strip; when the note is swallowed up a light goes on, and I have to hurry to push the nozzle of the pump into the mouth of the tank and send the jet gushing in, compact and trembling in its iridescent transparency, have to hurry to enjoy this gift that is incapable of gratifying my senses but nevertheless avidly craved by that part of me which is my means of locomotion. I have just enough time to think all this when with a sharp click the flow stops, the lights go off. The complicated mechanism set in motion a few seconds ago is already stilled and inert, the stirring of those telluric powers my rituals called to life lasted no more than an instant. In return for a thousand lire reduced to a meagre metal strip the pump will concede only a meagre quantity of petrol. Crude costs eleven dollars a barrel.

I have to start all over again, feed in another note, then others again, a thousand lire a go. Money and the subterranean world are family and they go back a long way; their relationship unfolds in one cataclysm after another, sometimes desperately slow, sometimes quite sudden; as I fill my tank at the self-service station a bubble of gas swells up in a black lake buried beneath the Persian Gulf, an emir silently raises hands hidden in wide white sleeves and folds them on his chest, in a skyscraper an Exxon computer is crunching numbers, far out to sea a cargo fleet gets the order to change course, I rummage in my pockets, the puny power of paper money evaporates.

I look around: I'm the only one left by the deserted pumps. The to-ing and fro-ing of cars round the only filling station open at this hour has unexpectedly stopped, as if at this very moment the convergence of creeping cataclysms had suddenly produced the ultimate cataclysm, the simultaneous drying up perhaps of oilwells pipelines tanks pumps carburettors oil sumps. Progress does have its risks, what matters is being able to say you foresaw them. For a while now I've been getting used to imagining the future without flinching, I can already see rows of abandoned cobweb-draped cars, the city reduced to a plastic scrap heap, people running with sacks on their backs chased by rats.

All of a sudden I'm seized by a craving to get out of here; but to go where? I don't know, it doesn't matter; perhaps I just want to burn up what little energy is left us and finish off the cycle. I've dug out a last thousand lire to siphon off one more shot of fuel.

A sports car stops at the filling station. The driver, a girl wrapped in the spirals of her flowing hair, scarf and woollen turtle-neck, lifts a small nose from this tangled mass and says: 'Fill her up.'

I'm standing there with the nozzle in the air; I may as well dedicate the last octanes to her, so they at least leave a memory of pleasant colours when they burn, in a world where everything is so unattractive: the operations I perform, the materials I use, the salvation I can hope for. I unscrew the fuel cap on the sports car, slip in the pump's slanted beak, press the button, and as I feel the jet penetrate, I at last experience something like the memory of a distant pleasure, the sort of vital strength that establishes a relationship, a liquid flow is passing between myself and the stranger at the wheel.

174

She has turned to look at me, she lifts the big frames of her glasses, she has green eyes of iridescent transparency. 'But you're not a pump attendant . . . What are you doing . . . Why . . .' I want her to understand that this is an extreme act of love on my part, I want to involve her in the last blast of heat the human race can make its own, an act of love that is an act of violence too, a rape, a mortal embrace of subterranean powers.

I make a sign for her to shush and point down with my hand in the air as though to warn her that the spell could break any second, then I make a circular gesture as if to say it's all the same, and what I mean is that through me a black Pluto is reaching up from the underworld to carry off, through her, a blazing Persephone, because that's how that ruthless devourer of living substances, the Earth, starts her cycle over again.

She laughs, revealing two pointed young incisors. She's uncertain. The search for oil deposits in California has brought to light skeletons of animal species extinct these fifty thousand years, including a sabre-toothed tiger, doubtless attracted by a stretch of water lying on the surface of a black lake of pitch which sucked the animal in and swallowed it up.

But the short time granted me is over: the flow stops, the pump is still, the embrace is broken off. There's a deep silence, as if all engines everywhere had ceased their firing and the wheeling life of the human race had stopped. The day the earth's crust reabsorbs the cities, this plankton sediment that was humankind will be covered by geological layers of asphalt and cement until in millions of years' time it thickens into oily deposits, on whose behalf we do not know.

I look into her eyes: she doesn't understand, perhaps she's only just beginning to get scared. Well, I'll count to a hundred: if the silence goes on, I'll take her hand and we'll start to run.

Neanderthal Man

INTERVIEWER: I'm speaking from the picturesque Neander valley, near Düsseldorf. Around me lies a contorted landscape of
calcareous rocks. My voice resounds against the walls both of
natural caves and man-made quarries. It was during work on
these stone quarries that in 1856 one of the oldest inhabitants
of this valley was found, someone who settled here about
thirty-five thousand years ago. Neanderthal Man: that was how
they agreed to call him, after the valley. I have come to Neanderthal to interview him. Mr Neander – I will address him with
this simplified appellation throughout our interview – Mr
Neander, as you may know, is somewhat diffident by nature,
bad-tempered even, partly it's his old age, and he doesn't seem
particularly impressed by the international fame he enjoys.
Nevertheless he has politely agreed to answer a few questions
for our programme. Here he comes now, with his charac-
teristic rather lolloping gait, looking me over from beneath the
prominent arch of his eyebrows. This immediately prompts me
to ask him a somewhat indiscreet question out of a curiosity
doubtless shared by many of our listeners. Mr Neander, did
you expect to become so famous? I mean: as far as we know,
you never did anything remarkable in your life: then all of a
sudden you found you were a very important person. How do
you explain this?

NEANDER: That's what you say. Were you there? Me yes, I was
there. You no.

INTERVIEWER: Agreed, you were there. Well, do you feel that is sufficient?

NEANDER: I was already there.

INTERVIEWER: That's a useful point I think. Mr Neander's great merit isn't so much the simple fact of being there, but of having *already* been there, having been there then, before so many others. Precedence is a quality no one would wish to deny Mr Neander. However much ... even before that, as further research has demonstrated – and as you yourself can confirm, isn't that right, Mr Neander? – we find traces, many traces and on a number of continents, of human beings, yes, already human humans ...

NEANDER: My dad ...

INTERVIEWER: Right back as far as a million years before ...

NEANDER: My gran ...

INTERVIEWER: Hence your precedence, Mr Neander, no one can deny you, though it would seem to be a relative precedence: let's say that you are the first ...

NEANDER: Before you anyway ...

INTERVIEWER: Agreed, but that's not the point. What I mean is that you were the first to be believed to be the first by those who came after.

NEANDER: That's what you think. Before that there's my dad ...

INTERVIEWER: Not only him, but ...

NEANDER: My gran ...

INTERVIEWER: And before that? Concentrate now, Mr Neander: your gran's gran!

NEANDER: No.

INTERVIEWER: What do you mean, no?

NEANDER: The bear!

INTERVIEWER: The bear! A totemic ancestor! As you have heard, Mr Neander considers the forefather of his family tree to have been a bear, no doubt the animal-totem taken as the symbol of his clan, his family!

177

NEANDER: Your family you mean! First there's the bear, then the bear goes and eats up gran ... Then there's me, then I go and I kill the bear ... Then I eat up the bear.

INTERVIEWER: Allow me to explain to our listeners for a moment, Mr Neander, the valuable information you are giving us. First there's the bear! how well you express it, asserting with great clarity the precedence of raw nature, of the biological world, which forms the backdrop, isn't that right, Mr Neander?, the lush backdrop to the advent of man, and it is when man steps so to speak into the limelight of history that the great adventure of our struggle with nature begins, a nature that is first our enemy, then is gradually subdued to our will, a process lasting thousands of years that Mr Neander has evoked so powerfully in the dramatic scene of the bearhunt, a myth almost of the founding of our history ...

NEANDER: It was me was there. Not you. There was the bear. Where I go the bear comes. The bear is all around where I am, if not, not.

INTERVIEWER: Right. It seems that our Mr Neander's mental horizon goes no further than that part of the world that lies in his immediate field of perception, excluding any representation of events occurring beyond that in time or space. The bear is where I see the bear, he says, if I don't see it, it's not there. This is certainly a limitation one would wish to bear in mind during the rest of the interview, taking care not to ask him questions that exceed, isn't that right?, the intellectual capacities of a still rudimentary stage in the cycle of evolution ...

NEANDER: That's you. What are you talking about? What do you know? Food, right? It's the same food I'm after and the bear's after. The best at catching the quick animals is me; the best at catching the big animals is the bear. Right? And then either it's the bear takes them off me or me takes them off the bear. Right?

INTERVIEWER: Perfectly clear, I agree, Mr Neander, no need to get worked up. It's a case, how can we say, of symbiosis be-

178

tween two species, one species of the genus *homo* and the other of the genus *ursus*; or rather, what we have is a biological equilibrium, if you like: in the midst of the ruthless ferocity of the fight for survival, a tacit understanding is established ...

NEANDER: And then, either it's the bear kills me, or me that kills him, the bear ...

INTERVIEWER: There we are, the fight for survival flares up again, the best adapted wins, not just the strongest that is – and Mr Neander, despite his rather short legs, is very muscular – but above all the most intelligent, and Mr Neander, despite the concave curve to his almost horizontal forehead, displays surprising mental faculties ... Here is the question I've been wanting to ask you, Mr Neander: was there a moment when you feared the human race might go under? You understand me, Mr Neander, might disappear from the face of the earth?

NEANDER: My gran ... My gran on the ground ...

INTERVIEWER: Mr Neander goes back to this episode that must have been a, let's say, traumatizing experience in his past ... Or rather: in *our* past.

NEANDER: The bear on the ground ... I ate the bear ... Me: not you.

INTERVIEWER: Precisely, that's another thing I wanted to ask: was there a moment when you had the clear impression of the human race's having won, the certainty that it would be the bear that would die out, not us, because nothing could stop our onward march, and that you Mr Neander would one day deserve our gratitude, I mean the gratitude of a humanity that has reached the highest point of its evolution, a gratitude I now extend to you today from this microphone ...

NEANDER: Mmm ... Me if I have to go on I go on ... if I have to stop I stop ... if I have to eat the bear I stop and eat the bear ... Afterwards I go on, the bear stops still, a bone here, on the ground, a bone there, on the ground ... Behind me come the others, they come on, up to where the bear is, stopped still, the others stop, they eat the bear ... My son gnaws at a bone, another son of mine gnaws at another bone, another son of mine gnaws at another bone . . .

INTERVIEWER: Mr Neander is now bringing to life for us one of the culminating moments in the life of a clan of hunters: the ritual banquet after a successful hunt . . .

NEANDER: My brother-in-law gnaws another bone, my wife gnaws another bone . . .

INTERVIEWER: As you will have heard in Mr Neander's own words, women were the last to help themselves at the ritual banquet, which constitutes an admission of the inferior social status to which women were condemned . . .

NEANDER: Your woman you mean! First I bring the bear to my wife, my wife lights the fire beneath the bear, then I go off to pick some basil, then I get back with the basil and I say: well now, where is the bear's thigh? and my wife says: I ate it, right? to check if it was still raw, right?

INTERVIEWER: As early as the communities of hunters and ga-therers – for this is what emerges from Mr Neander's account – there was already a strict division of labour between men and women . . .

NEANDER: Then I go off to pick some marjoram, then I get back with the marjoram and I say: well now, where's the bear's other thigh? and my wife says: I ate it, right? to check if it was already burnt, right? And I say: well now, you know who's going to go and pick the oregano, don't you? You're going, I'm telling you, you're going for the oregano, yes you are.

INTERVIEWER: From this delightful little family vignette we can glean many hard facts about the life of Neanderthal man: first, his knowledge of fire and its use in cooking; second, the gathering of aromatic herbs and their gastronomic application; third, the consumption of meat in large detached portions, which would require the use of proper cutting implements and hence implies a highly developed ability to work flint. But let's hear if our guest has anything to tell us about this himself. I will formulate the question in such a way as not to influence

180

his response: Mr Neander, you with your stones, yes, those nice round stones you see so many of hereabouts, didn't you ever try, I don't know, to play with them, to bang them against each other a bit, to see if they were really that hard?

NEANDER: What's that you're saying about stones? Don't you know what you do with a stone! Clank! Clank! That's me with a stone: clank! You get the stone, right? you put it on a big stone, you get that other stone, you lay into it, sharp, clank! you know where to hit it sharp? there! that's where you hit it!: clank! a sharp hit! go on! ow! that way you squash your finger! Then you suck your finger, then you jump up and down, then you get hold of that other stone again, you put the stone back on the big stone, clank! You see it's split in two, a thick splinter and a thinner splinter, one curved this way, the other curved that way, you pick up this one that's easy to hold, this way, like this, you pick up the other with the other hand, that way, like that, and off you go: clunk! understand that you go clunk there, right there, go on! ow! you've stuck the point in your hand! then you suck your hand, turn round on one foot, then you get hold of the splinter again, the other splinter in the other hand, clunk!, a little splinter's split off, ow! in your eye! you rub your eye with your hand, kick the big stone, get hold of the thick splinter again and the thin splinter, clunk! you split off another splinter right nearby, clunk! another, clunk! yet another, and you see that where they've split off they've left a nick that goes in nice and round, and then another nick, and then another nick, like that up and down all around, and then on the other side too, clunk! clunk! see how it's coming off all around, finer and finer, sharper and sharper...

INTERVIEWER: Our thanks to...

NEANDER: ...then you give it little taps like this, clink! clink! and you split off tiny tiny splinters, clink! clink! and you see how that leaves lots of tiny tiny teeth, clink! clink!

INTERVIEWER: Yes, we've understood that perfectly. On behalf of our listeners let me thank...

181

NEANDER: Understood what? Now you can hit it here once: clonk! and then afterwards you can hit it again the other side, clunk!

INTERVIEWER: Clunk, exactly, let's move on to another...

NEANDER: ...that way you can hold it properly in your hand, this stone, now it's worked both sides, then the real work starts, because you get another stone and you put it on the big stone, clank!

INTERVIEWER: And so on, very clear, what matters is how you begin. Let's move...

NEANDER: Oh no, once I've begun, I don't want to stop, there's always a stone on the ground that looks better than the first one, so I throw away the first and get this other and clank! clank! and lots of the splinters flying off you chuck and lots are even better to work, so I get going on those, clink! clink! and it turns out I can have all these stones come out just how I want and the more nicks I make the more other nicks I can make, where I've made one I make two, and then in each of these two I make another two, and in the end the whole lot breaks to bits and I chuck it in the heap of the broken splinters which is growing and growing on this side, but on the other side I've got a whole mountain of rocks still to be turned into splinters.

INTERVIEWER: Now that Mr Neander has described for us this frustrating, monotonous work...

NEANDER: Monotonous! You're the one that's monotonous! Do you know how to make nicks in stones, you, nicks all the same, do you know how to make the nicks monotonous? No, so what are you talking about? I know how to do it all right! And ever since I started, ever since I saw I've got the thumb for it, you see this thumb? this thumb that I put here and the other fingers I put there and in the middle there's a stone, in my hand, gripped tight so it can't slip out, ever since I saw that I was holding the stone in my hand and hitting it, like this, or like that, well since then what I can do with the stones I can do with everything, with the sounds that come out of my

182

mouth, I can make sounds like this, a a a, p p p, ny ny ny, and so I never stop making sounds, I start speaking, I never stop speaking, I start speaking about speaking, I start working stones I can use for working stones, and meantime it occurs to me to think, I think of all the things I could think when I think, and it occurs to me I'd like to do something to have others understand things, paint some red stripes on my face for example, no reason in particular, just to let the others know I've put some red stripes on my face, and I think I'd like to make my wife a necklace of boar's teeth, no reason in particular, just to have people know that my wife has a necklace of boar's teeth, and yours doesn't, I don't know what you think you have that I didn't have, I had everything I wanted, everything that was done afterwards, I'd already done, everything that was said and thought and meant was already there in what I said and thought and meant, all the complication of complication was already there, I only have to pick up this stone with my thumb and the hollow of my hand and the other four fingers that fold over it, and everything's already there, I had everything that others had later, everything others knew and could do later I already had not because it was mine but because it *was*, because it was already, because it was there, whereas later others had it and knew it and could do it less and less, always a bit less than what might have been, than what there was before, what I had before, what I was before, I really was there then in everything and for everything, not like you, and everything was in everything and for everything, everything you need to be in everything and for everything, even everything wrong that came later was already there in that clank! clank! clink! clink! so what are you trying to say, what do you think you are, what do you mean thinking you're here when you are not, or if you are it's only because I really was and the bear was and the stones and the necklaces and the hammerings on the fingers and everything you need to be and that when it's there is there.

Montezuma

MYSELF: Your Majesty ... Your Holiness! ... Emperor! ... General!
... I don't know how to address you, am obliged to resort to
terms that only partially convey the prerogatives of your position,
forms of address that in my modern language have lost much of
their authority, sound like echoes of lost powers ... As your
throne high on the Mexican plateau is lost, the throne from which
you reigned over the Aztecs, most august of their sovereigns, and
the last too, Montezuma ... Even calling you by your name is a
problem for me: Motecuhzoma, it seems that's what your name
really sounded like, but in our European books it's distorted to
Moteczuma, Moctezuma ... A name that some writers say means
'sad man'. To tell the truth, it's a name you would have well
deserved, for you saw the prosperous, well-ordered empire the
Aztec world then was, invaded by incomprehensible beings,
armed with unheard-of instruments of death. It must have been
as if our cities here were suddenly to be invaded by extra-terrestrials. But we have already imagined that moment in every
possible way: or at least we think we have. And you? When did
you begin to realize that you were witnessing the end of a world?
MONTEZUMA: The end ... Day rolls towards sunset ... Summer
rots in muddy autumn. Thus every day – every summer ... You
can never be certain they will return. That's why man has to
ingratiate himself with the gods. So that the sun and stars may
continue to revolve over the fields of maize – one more day –
one more year ...

MYSELF: You mean to say that the end of the world is always there hanging over us, that amid all the extraordinary events you were witness to in your lifetime, the most extraordinary was that everything went on, not that everything was collapsing?

MONTEZUMA: It's not always the same gods who reign in the sky, not always the same empires collecting their taxes in city and country. Throughout my life I honoured two gods, one present and one absent: the Blue Hummingbird, Huitzilopochtli who led us Aztecs in war, and the banished god, the Plumed Serpent, Quetzacoatl, an exile beyond the ocean, in the unknown lands of the West. One day the absent god would return to Mexico to wreak his revenge on the other gods and those peoples faithful to them. I feared the threat that hung over my empire, the upheaval that would usher in the era of the Plumed Serpent, but at the same time I looked forward to it, inwardly I was impatient that this prophecy should come to pass, even though I knew it would mean the ruin of our temples, the slaughter of the Aztecs, my own death...

MYSELF: And you really believed that the god Quetzacoatl led the Spanish conquistadores off their ships, you recognized the Plumed Serpent in the iron helmet and black beard of Hernán Cortés?

MONTEZUMA (*a sorrowful wail*)

MYSELF: Forgive me, King Montezuma: that name reopens a wound in your heart...

MONTEZUMA: Oh enough... This story has been told too many times. That this god was traditionally depicted as having a pale bearded face, and that seeing (*he groans*) the pale and bearded Cortés we supposedly thought him our god... No, it's not that simple. Correspondences between signs are never conclusive. Everything must be interpreted: the scriptures handed down by our priests are not made of letters, like yours, but of images.

MYSELF: You mean that your pictographic scripture and reality

185

were each to be read in the same way: they both had to be deciphered...

MONTEZUMA: In the images of the holy books, the bas-reliefs in the temples, the feather mosaics, every line, every frieze, every coloured stripe can have a meaning... And in the things that come to pass, the events that unfold before our eyes, every tiny detail can have a meaning that points us to the intentions of the gods: the flutter of a robe, a shadow that forms in the dust... If it is thus for all things that have names, think how many things crossed my path that had no name, things I was constantly having to ask myself the meaning of! Wooden houses appear floating on the sea, their cloth wings bellied with wind... My army lookouts try to explain everything they see in words, but how to say something if you don't know what it is? Men land on the beaches dressed in a grey metal that glitters in the sun. They climb on beasts we have never seen before, a sort of sturdy stag but with no antlers and leaving half-moon prints on the earth. Instead of bows and spears they carry some kind of trumpet that unleashes thunder and lightning, smashing bones from afar. Which were the stranger, the images of our holy books, the small terrible gods all in profile under flashing heads of hair, or these bearded, sweaty, smelly beings? They pushed deeper into our daily space, they robbed the hens from our coops, roasted them, gnawed the flesh from the bones just as we did: yet they were so different from us, incongruous, inconceivable. What could we do, what could I do, I who had so long studied the art of interpreting ancient temple images and dream visions, but try to interpret these new apparitions? Not that the one resembled the other: but the questions I was prompted to ask in the face of the inexplicable events I was experiencing were the same as those I had asked myself when poring over gods grinding their teeth in parchment paintings or in sculpted blocks of copper plated with gold and studded with emeralds.

MYSELF: But what lay behind your hesitation, King Montezuma?

You saw that the Spanish didn't stop advancing, that sending ambassadors with lavish gifts only aroused their greed for precious metals, that Cortés was forging alliances with those tribes who suffered your oppression, stirring them up against you, that he massacred the tribes who at your instigation laid ambushes for him, and yet at the last you welcomed him and all his soldiers as guests in the capital, and very soon you were allowing this guest to become your master, accepting that he proclaim himself protector of your shaky throne, and, with this pretext, that he hold you prisoner... Don't tell me that you were so ingenuous as to believe in Cortés...

MONTEZUMA: That the whites were not immortal I knew; certainly they were not the gods we had been waiting for. But they possessed powers that seemed beyond the human: arrows broke against their armour; their fiery blowpipes — or whatever devilry it was — projected darts that were always lethal. And yet, and yet, one could hardly deny that we had our superior side too, and sufficient perhaps to even the scales. When I took the Spanish to see the marvels of our capital they were so amazed! It was we who really triumphed that day, over those rude conquerors from beyond the sea. One of them said that not even reading their books of adventures had they ever imagined such splendour. Then Cortés took me hostage in the palace where I had made him my guest; not content with all the presents I gave him, he had his men dig an underground tunnel to the treasure chamber and sacked it; my destiny was twisted and thorny as a cactus. But the boorish soldiers guarding me spent their days playing dice and cheating, making vulgar noises, fighting over the gold ornaments I tossed them as tips. And I was still king. I demonstrated as much every day: I was superior to them, I, not they, was the victor.

MYSELF: Were you still hoping to turn the tables?

MONTEZUMA: Perhaps there was a battle going on amongst the gods in the sky. A sort of equilibrium had established itself between us, as if our destinies were held in the balance. Surrounded by gardens, our lakes flashed with the sails of the brigs they had built; their arquebuses fired volleys from the shore. There were days when I was seized by an unexpected happiness, and laughed till I cried. And days when I only cried, amidst the laughter of my prison guards. Peace shone from time to time between clouds heavy with war. Don't forget that the foreigners were led by a woman, a Mexican woman, from a tribe hostile to our own, but of the same race. You say: Cortés, Cortés, and you think that Malitzin – Doña Marina, as you call her – was only his interpreter. No, she was Cortés's mind, or at least half of it: there were two heads directing the Spanish expedition; the plan for the Conquest arose from the union of a noble princess from our own land and a little man who was pale and hairy. Perhaps it would have been possible – I felt it would – to establish a new era in which the invaders' qualities – which I believed divine – would be fused with our own more ordered and refined civilization. Perhaps it would be we who absorbed them, with all their armour and horses and mortars, to appropriate their extraordinary powers for ourselves, to have their gods sit down to eat at our gods' banquet...

MYSELF: Wishful thinking, Montezuma, so as not to see your prison bars! Yet you knew there was another way: you could have resisted them, beaten them, overcome the Spanish. That was the way your grandson chose when he organized a conspiracy to free you...and you betrayed him, you lent the Spanish what was left of your authority to quell your people's rebellion...Yet Cortés only had four hundred men with him at the time, he was isolated in an unknown continent; and what's more he had fallen out with the authorities of his own government across the sea. Of course, whether for Cortés or against, the fleet and army of Emperor Charles V's Spain was a threat to the New Continent...Was it their intervention you were afraid of? Had you already realized that the balance of forces was crushingly against you, that defiance of Europe was hopeless?

MONTEZUMA: I knew we weren't equals, but not in the way you speak of, white man. The difference that held me back was not something to be weighed or measured... It was not the same as when two highland tribes – or two nations on your continent – seek to dominate each other, and courage and strength in battle decide the outcome. To fight an enemy you must move in the same space as he does, exist in the same time. Whereas we watched each other from different dimensions, without quite touching. The first time I received him, Cortés violated all the sacred rules and embraced me. The priest and dignitaries of my court covered their faces before this scandal. But to me it was as though our bodies hadn't touched. Not because my position placed me beyond any alien contact, but because we belonged to two worlds that had never met, nor could meet.

MYSELF: King Montezuma, that was Europe's first real encounter with the 'other'. Less than thirty years had passed since Columbus had discovered the New World, and so far it had been nothing but tropical islands and mud-hut villages... Now the first colonial expedition of a white army was meeting not the famous 'savages', survivors of a prehistoric golden age, but a complex and wealthy civilization. And it was precisely at that first meeting between our world and yours – I say your world as an example of every other possible world – that something irreparable happened. This is what I ask myself, what I ask you, King Montezuma. Faced with the unexpected, you were prudent, but hesitant and submissive too. And your approach certainly didn't spare your people or your country the massacres and ruin that have been going on for centuries. Had you met those first conquistadores with determined resistance perhaps that would have been enough to get the relationship between the two worlds going along different lines, to give it a different future. Warned by your resistance, the Europeans would perhaps have been more prudent and respectful. Perhaps there was still time for you to root out the

189

dangerous weeds just sprouting in European minds: the conviction that they had the right to destroy everything that was alien to them, to plunder the world's riches, to spread the uniform stain of misery and wretchedness across every continent. Then the history of the world would have taken a different path, you understand, King Montezuma, you do see, Montezuma, what a modern European is telling you, a man coming to terms with the end of a supremacy in which so many remarkable talents were turned to evil ends, in which everything we thought and did in the conviction that it was a universal good, bore the hallmark of a limitation ... Answer a man who feels he is, like yourself, a victim, and like yourself responsible ...

MONTEZUMA: You too speak as though reading from a book long written. For us, at that time, the only thing written was the book of our gods, the prophecies that could be read in a hundred ways. Everything had to be deciphered, the first thing we had to do with every new fact was to find a place for it in the order that upholds the world and outside of which there is nothing. Everything we did was a question waiting for an answer. And for every answer to have a further reliable confirmation I had to formulate my questions in two ways: one in one sense and the other in the opposite sense. I asked a question by making war and I asked a question by making peace. That's why I led the people in their resistance and at the same time stood beside Cortés as he cruelly subdued them. You say we didn't fight? Mexico City rebelled against the Spanish; rocks and arrows rained down from every roof. It was then my subjects stoned me to death, when Cortés sent me to appease them. Then the Spanish got reinforcements; the rebels were massacred; our peerless city was destroyed. The answer from that book I had been trying to decipher was: no. That is why you see my shadow creeping stooped about these ruins, as it has ever since that day.

MYSELF: But you were as alien to the Spanish as they were to

190

you. You were the other, the incomprehensible, the unimaginable for them. The Spanish had to decipher you as much as you them.

MONTEZUMA: You appropriate things for yourselves; the order that upholds your world is one of appropriation; all you had to understand was that we had something which, as you saw it, was more worthy of appropriation than anything else, while for us it was just an attractive material for jewellery and ornaments: gold. Your eyes sought gold, gold, gold; your thoughts circled like vultures around that one object of desire. For us on the other hand the order behind the world consisted in giving. Giving so that the gods' gifts might go on being heaped upon us, so that the sun might go on rising every morning slaking its thirst on the blood that issues forth . . .

MYSELF: The blood, Montezuma! I was afraid of mentioning it, and now you bring it up yourself, the blood of human sacrifice . . .

MONTEZUMA: That again. That. And what about yourselves? Let's add it up, let's add up the victims of your civilization and ours . . .

MYSELF: No, no, Montezuma, that argument won't wash, you know I'm not here to justify Cortés and his men, you certainly won't catch me playing down the crimes that our civilization has committed and still commits, but now it's *your* civilization we're talking about! Those young people lain on the altar, the stone knives dashing out the heart, the blood showering all around . . .

MONTEZUMA: And so? So what? Men of every time and clime toil to but one end: to keep the world together, to prevent it from falling apart. It's just the way they do it that differs. In our cities, all lakes and gardens, that sacrifice of blood was as necessary as turning the soil, as channelling the water of the rivers. In your cities, all wheels and cages, the sight of blood is terrifying, I know. But how many more lives are ground to pulp in your cogs!

191

MYSELF: Okay, every culture has to be understood from within, that much I've understood, Montezuma, the times of the Conquest that destroyed your temples and gardens are behind us now. I know that in many respects yours was a model culture, but by the same token I'd like you to admit its monstrous side: that prisoners of war had to meet that fate...

MONTEZUMA: Why would we have gone to war otherwise? Our wars were courteous and playful in comparison with yours, a game. But a game with a necessary end: to decide whose destiny it was to lie on their backs on the altar in the sacrificial festivals and bare their breasts to the obsidian blade brandished by the Great Sacrificer. That fate could befall any of us, for the good of all. What good do your wars do? Every time they happen the reasons you come up with are banal pretexts: conquests, gold.

MYSELF: Or not allowing ourselves to be dominated by others, not ending up like yourselves under the Spanish! If you had killed Cortés's men, no, I'll go further, listen carefully to what I'm going to say, Montezuma, if you had cut their throats one by one on the altar as sacrifices, well then I would have understood, because your survival as a people was at stake, your perpetuation through history...

MONTEZUMA: See how you contradict yourself, white man? Kill them... I wanted to do something far more important: conceive them. If I could have conceived the Spanish, brought them into my manner of thinking, been sure of their true nature, whether gods or evil demons it didn't matter which, or beings like ourselves subject to divine or demonic will, in short if I could have made of them – inconceivable as they were – something my mind could dwell on and grasp, then, and only then, would I have been able to have them as my allies or enemies, to recognize them as persecutors or victims.

MYSELF: For Cortés, on the other hand, everything was clear. He didn't worry about this kind of thing. He knew what he wanted, the Spaniard did.

192

MONTEZUMA: It was the same for him as for me. The real victory he sought to gain over me was the same: that of conceiving me.

MYSELF: And did he succeed?

MONTEZUMA: No. It may seem that he had his way with me: he tricked me many times, he sacked my treasures, he used my authority as a shield, he sent me to die stoned by my own subjects: but he didn't succeed in possessing me. What I was remained forever beyond his imagining, unattainable. His reasoning never managed to trap my reasoning in its net. That is why you come back to meet me amidst the ruins of my empire – of your empires. That is why you come asking me questions. Four and more centuries after my defeat you are no longer sure you conquered me. Real wars and real peace don't take place on earth, but between the gods.

MYSELF: Montezuma, now you've explained why it was impossible for you to win. The war between the gods means that behind Cortés's marauders lay the idea of the West, lay history that never stands still, that presses on, swallowing up those civilizations for whom time has stopped still.

MONTEZUMA: You too superimpose your gods on the facts. What is this thing you call history? Perhaps all you mean is the absence of equilibrium. Whereas when men live together in such a way as to establish a lasting equilibrium you say history has stopped. If you had managed to be less enslaved to this history of yours, you wouldn't be coming to reproach me for not having stopped you in time. What do you want from me? You've realized that you don't know what it is, this history of yours, and you are wondering if it mightn't have had a different course. And to your mind, I should have been the one giving history this different course. But how? By thinking the way you think? You too feel the need to classify everything new with the names of your gods, everything that turns your world upside down, and you are never sure whether those gods are real gods or evil spirits, and you are quick to become

193

their prisoners. The laws of the material world seem clear to you, yet that doesn't mean you stop expecting that from behind those laws the design that shapes the world's destiny will reveal itself. Yes, it's true, at the beginning of your sixteenth century the fate of the world was not yet settled perhaps. Your civilization of perpetual motion still didn't know where it was going – as today it no longer knows where it can go – and we, the civilization of permanence and equilibrium, might still have swallowed it up in our harmony.

MYSELF: It was too late! You Aztecs would have had to land near Seville and invade the Extremadura, not vice versa! History does have a sense, a direction that can't be changed!

MONTEZUMA: A direction that you want to impose on it, white man! Otherwise the world would crumble under your feet. I too had a world that sustained me, a world that was not your world. I too hoped that the sense of everything would not be lost.

MYSELF: I know why it mattered to you. Because if the sense of your world had been lost, then the mountains of skulls piled in the ossuaries of your temples would have had no sense either, and your altar stones would have become no more than butchers' slabs stained with the blood of innocent human beings!

MONTEZUMA: Now look with the same eyes on your own carnage, white man.

Before You Say 'Hello'

I hope you're still by the phone, that if someone else calls you'll ask him to hang up at once so as to keep the line free: you know my call could get through any moment. I've already dialled your number three times, but my signal got lost in bottlenecks of circuitry, whether here, in the city I'm calling from, or there in your city's network, I don't know. The lines are busy everywhere. All Europe is calling all Europe.

Only a few hours have passed since I said goodbye to you, in a mad rush; the trip is always the same, I do it mechanically every time, as though in trance: a taxi waiting for me in the street, a plane waiting for me at the airport, a company car waiting for me at another airport, then here I am, hundreds and hundreds of miles away from you. This is the moment that matters most for me: I have just put down my luggage, I still haven't taken off my coat, and already I'm lifting the receiver, dialling your city's area code, then your number.

My finger pushes each number slowly towards the end of the dial, I concentrate on the pressure of my fingertip as if it were that that determined the exactness of the journey each number must accomplish following a series of required steps far far away from each other and from us, until they set the bell ringing by your bed. It's rare for the operation to succeed first go: I don't know how long the labours of index finger thrust in dial will last, nor the uncertainties of ear glued to dark shell. To contain my impatience I remember a time not long ago when it was the invisible vestal virgins of the exchange who had the job of guaranteeing the continuity of this fragile flow of sparks, of fighting invisible battles against invisible fortresses: every internal impulse urging me to communicate was mediated procrastinated filtered through an anonymous and daunting procedure. Now that a network of automatic connections extends across entire continents and every subscriber can call every other subscriber at will without asking anybody's help, I must resign myself to paying for this extraordinary freedom with an expense of nervous energy, repetition of movements, time-wasting, growing frustration. (And to paying for it again in the form of extremely expensive bills, but the relationship between the act of telephoning and the experience of the cruel prices is not a direct one: the bills arrive every three months, a single direct-dial long distance call is drowned in an overall figure that generates the same stupor as those natural disasters in the face of which our resolve immediately finds the alibi of inevitability.) So great is the temptation the facility to telephone constitutes, that telephoning is becoming ever more difficult, even impossible. Everybody telephones everybody at every possible moment, and nobody can speak to anybody, signals go wandering up and down automatic search circuits, beating their wings like crazed butterflies, without managing to slip into a free line, each subscriber goes on firing off numbers into the exchanges convinced that it's no more than a temporary local hitch. The truth is that the vast majority of calls are made without people having anything to say to each other, hence it hardly matters whether they get through or not, all they do is harm those few who really would have something to say.

Certainly I can't claim as much. If I am in such a hurry to phone you after a few hours apart, it's not because there's something vital I forgot to tell you, nor am I impatient to re-establish that intimacy broken off at the moment of my leaving. If I tried to tell you something of the kind, I would immediately sense your sarcastic smile, or hear your voice icily calling me a liar. You'd be right: the last hours before I leave are full of silences and uneasiness between us; so long as I'm at your side the distance is insuperable. But that's precisely why I can't wait to call you: because it's only in a long-distance call, or better still an international call, that we can hope to achieve that state usually defined as 'togetherness'. That is the real reason for my journey, for my constant hopping about the map, the secret justification I should say, the one I give myself, without which I could only think of my professional activities as inspector of the European operations of a multinational company as a meaningless routine: I leave so as to be able to phone every day, because for you I have always been, as for me you have always been, at the other end of a wire, or rather a coaxial copper conductor cable, at the other pole of a tenuous modulated-frequency current that flows through the subsoil of the continents and across the ocean bed. And when we don't have this wire between us to make contact, when it is our lustreless physical presence that occupies the sensory field, immediately everything between us becomes commonplace superfluous automatic, gestures words facial expressions reciprocal reactions of pleasure or intolerance, all that direct contact can transmit between two people and which as such can also be said to be transmitted and received to perfection, always bearing in mind the rudimentary equipment human beings have at their disposal for communicating with each other; in short physical presence may be a wonderful thing for both of us, but hardly to be compared with the vibrational frequencies you get through the electronic switching system of a great telephone network, nor with the emotional intensity such frequencies can arouse in us.

The more the exchange is precarious, risky, insecure, the stronger the emotions are. If we are not satisfied with our exchanges when we are together, it is not because they are going badly, but because they are going how they have to go. Whereas now I find myself holding my breath as yet again I grind out the series of numbers on the rotating dial, draw in through my ear the ghostly sounds that surface in the receiver: a drumming engaged signal in the background, so vague as to have me hoping it's a chance interference that has nothing to do with us; or a muffled sputtering of charges that could be heralding the success of a complicated operation or at least an intermediate phase of that operation, or once again the ruthless silence of darkness and the void. In some unidentifiable point of the circuitry my call has lost its way.

I pick up the receiver and get the dial tone again, then with redoubled slowness repeat the first numbers of the code, numbers that do no more than find a way out of the city network, then the national network. In some countries there's a special tone at this point to let you know that the first part of the operation has succeeded; if you don't hear the trill of a little musical jingle there's no point in going on with the other numbers: you have to wait for a line to come free. At home they sometimes give you a very short whistle that comes at the end of the code, or halfway through: but not for all codes and not on every occasion. In short, whether you've heard that little whistle or not you can't be sure of anything: when they give the all-clear signal the line may be deaf or dead, or it may turn out to be unexpectedly live without having given any signs of life earlier on. So it's best not to be put off whatever happens, to dial the number down to the last digit and wait. Assuming that the engaged signal doesn't explode halfway through, to tell you you're wasting your time. But all the better if it does: I can hang up immediately, saving myself another pointless wait, and try again. Generally, though, having embarked on the exasperating business of tracing a dozen figures in the dial's rotations, I'm left with no indication as to the results of my efforts. What straits is my signal negotiating right now? Is it still stuck in the recorder of the exchange here in town, waiting its turn in a line of calls? Has it already been translated into commands for the selector switches, divided in groups of digits that are heading off to look for the way to successive intermediate exchanges? Or did it fly straight to the network of your city, your local area, without encountering so much as an obstacle, only to be caught there like a fly in a spider's web, reaching out towards your unreachable telephone?

The earpiece tells me nothing, and I don't know whether I'll have to accept defeat and hang up, or whether all of a sudden a light rustling crackle will tell me my call has found a free line, has set off like an arrow and in a few seconds will be waking your bell like an echo.

It's in this silence of circuitry that I speak to you. I'm well aware that when our voices finally get to meet along the wire we will have only banal and awkward comments to make; I'm not calling to say anything to you, nor because I imagine you have anything to say to me. We phone each other because it's only in these long-distance calls, this groping for each other along cables of buried copper, cluttered relays, the whirling contact points of clogged selector switches, only in this probing the silence and waiting for an echo that one prolongs that first call from afar, that cry that went up when the first great crack of the continental drift yawned beneath the feet of a human couple, when the depths of the ocean opened up to separate them, while, torn precipitously apart, one on one bank and one on the other, the couple strove with their cries to stretch out a bridge of sound that might keep them together yet, cries that grew ever fainter until the roar of the waves overwhelmed all hope.

Ever since then distance has been the warp that supports the weft of every love story, of every relationship between living beings, the distance the birds seek to bridge when they launch their subtly trilled archways into the morning air, as we launch bursts of electrical impulses into the earth's nerve systems, each translatable into commands for relays: the only way human beings still have of knowing that they are calling each other for no other reason than the need to call each other. Doubtless the birds have little more to say than I have to say to you, as I flounder on, finger turning in this number-crunching dial, hoping that one click will prove luckier than the rest and set your bell a-ringing.

199

Like a wood deafened by the twittering of birds, our telephonic planet rings with conversations achieved or attempted, with the trilling of sound equipment, with the whining of a line cut off, the whirr of a signal, tones, ticking; and the upshot of all this is a universal chirping, arising from each individual's need to demonstrate his existence to someone else, and from the fear of our finally understanding that only the telephone network exists, while we who call and answer perhaps don't exist at all.

I've got the code wrong yet again, from the depths of the network I pick up a sort of birdsong, then snatches of other people's conversations, a recorded message in a foreign language repeating: 'The number you have dialled is not presently assigned to a subscriber.' Then the insistent engaged sign swells up to black out every glimmer. I wonder whether you are trying to call me at the same time and running into the same obstacles, floundering in the dark, getting lost in the same thorny labyrinth. I am speaking as I never would if you were listening; every time I push down the cradle wiping out the fragile succession of numbers I'm also wiping out everything I've said or thought as though in a delirium: this anxious insecure frenetic search for each other holds the beginning and the end of everything; we will never know more about each other than this rustling that fades and is lost along the wire. A vain tension in the ear concentrates the electricity of the passions, the rages of love and hate, which I – with my executive career in a big financial company, my days regulated by the careful employment of time – have never had the chance to experience except in a superficial, inattentive fashion.

Obviously it's impossible to get through at this time of day. I'd better give up, but if I stop trying to speak to you I'll immediately have to go back and deal with the phone as a completely different instrument, another part of myself with other functions: I've got a series of business meetings in town here that need urgent confirmation, I'll have to unplug the mental circuit that connects me to you and plug in the one that corresponds to my periodic inspections of companies controlled by my group or with joint shareholdings; I'll have to perform a switching operation not in the phone but in myself, in my approach to the phone.

First I want to have one last try, once more I'll dial that sequence of numbers that has taken the place of your name, your face, you. If I get through, good, if not, I'll stop. Meanwhile I can go on thinking things I'll never say to you, thoughts addressed more to the phone than to you, that have to do with the relationship I have with you through the phone, or rather the relationship I have with the phone with you as pretext.

Distant mechanisms revolve, my thoughts revolving with them, and I start to see the faces of other recipients of long-distance calls, variously pitched voices vibrate, the disc assembles and dismantles accents, attitudes and moods, but I can't settle on the image of an ideal woman to satisfy my yearning for a long-distance connection. Everything starts getting mixed up in my mind: faces, names, voices, numbers in Antwerp or Zurich or Hamburg. Not that I expect anything more from one number than from another: either with regard to the likelihood of getting through, or to what, once through, I might say or hear. But that doesn't stop me going on to try to make contact with Antwerp or Zurich or Hamburg or whatever other city yours may be — already forgotten in the whirligig of numbers I've been calling one after another for an hour now without ever getting through.

There are things that, even if my voice doesn't reach you, I feel the need to tell you: and it doesn't matter if I'm talking to you in Antwerp, or you in Zurich, or you in Hamburg. I want you to know that the moment I am really together with you isn't when I see you at night, in Antwerp, or Zurich, or Hamburg, after my business meetings; that is only the banal and inevitable aspect of our relationship: the tiffs, the making up, the rancour, the flarings of old passion; in every city and with every woman I phone the ritual I've established with you is repeated. Just as, as soon as I'm back in your town, even before you know I'm there,

I'll be spasmodically calling (trying to call) a number in Göteborg, or Bilbao, or Marseilles: a number I could easily get through to now with a local call here in the network of Göteborg, or Bilbao, or Marseilles (I can't remember where I am). But I don't want to talk to that number now; I want to talk to you.

That's what – given that you can't hear me – I want to tell you. For an hour I've been trying a series of numbers turn and turn about, all as impossible to get through to as yours, in Casablanca, Salonica, Vaduz: I'm sorry you're all stuck by the phone waiting for me; the service is getting worse and worse. As soon as I hear a voice say, 'Hello!' I shall have to be careful not to make a mistake, to remember which of you the last number I called corresponds to. Will I still recognize your voices? I've been waiting so long listening to silence.

I might as well tell you at this point, tell you, tell all of you, given that none of your phones is answering: my great ambition is to transform the entire global network into an extension of myself, propagating and attracting amorous vibrations, to use this instrument as an organ of my own body through which to consummate an embrace with the whole planet. I've almost made it. Hang on by your phones. And that means you too, in Kyoto, in São Paolo, in Riyadh!

Unfortunately my phone keeps giving me the engaged signal, even when I put it down and pick it up again, even when I bang down on the cradle. There, now I can't hear anything at all, you'd think I was cut off from every possible line. Keep calm all of you. It must be a temporary hitch. Hang on.

Glaciation

With ice? Yes? I go to the kitchen a moment to get the ice. And immediately the word 'ice' expands between her and me, separates us, or perhaps unites us, but the way a fragile sheet of ice unites the shores of a frozen lake.

If there is one thing I hate it's preparing the ice. It obliges me to break off a conversation just started, at the crucial moment when I ask her: A drop of whisky? and she: Thanks, but really just a drop, and me: With ice? And already I'm heading towards the kitchen as though into exile, already I can see myself fighting with ice cubes that won't come out of the tray.

No problem, I say, it won't take a second, I always have ice with whisky myself. It's true, the tinkling in the glass keeps me company, separates me from the din of the others, at parties where there are lots of people it stops me from losing myself in the ebb and flow of voices and sounds, that back and forth she detached herself from when she appeared for the first time in my field of vision, in the inverted telescope of my whisky glass, her colours advancing along that corridor between two smoke-filled rooms booming with music, and I stood there with my glass without going to one room or the other, and she too, she saw me in a distorted shadow through the transparency of the icy whisky glass, and I don't know if she heard what I was saying to her because there was all that din or perhaps again because I hadn't spoken, had only moved the glass and the ice rising and falling went clink clink, and she too said something into her little bell of glass and ice, certainly I hadn't imagined she would be coming to my place tonight.

I open the freezer, no, close the freezer, first I have to find the ice bucket. Hang on, I'll be with you in a sec. The freezer is a polar cave, dripping with icicles, the tray is welded to the base by a crust of frost, I pull hard and snap it off, fingertips turning white. In her igloo the Eskimo bride waits for the seal hunter lost out on the pack-ice. Now just a slight pressure to separate the cubes from the walls of their compartments: but no, it's a solid block, even when I turn the tray over they won't come out, I put it under the tap in the sink, turn on the hot water, the jet crackles on the frost-encrusted metal, my fingers turn from white to red. I've got my shirt cuff wet, that's very annoying, if there's one thing I hate it's feeling shapeless wet cloth clinging to my wrist.

Put a record on, I'll be back in a sec with the ice, can you hear me? She can't hear me with the tap on, there's always something stops us hearing and seeing each other. In the corridor too she was talking through hair falling half across her face, she was speaking over the edge of her glass and I heard her teeth laughing on the rim, on the ice, she was repeating: gla-ci-a-tion? as if of everything I'd said to her only that word had got through, and my hair was falling over my eyes too as I spoke into slowly melting ice.

I bang the edge of the tray against the edge of the sink, only one cube comes away, it falls outside the sink, it'll make a puddle on the floor, I'll have to pick it up, it's gone and got under the cupboard, I'll have to get down on my knees, reach a hand under, it slips through my fingers, there, I've got it and I throw it in the sink, go back to passing the tray upside down under the tap.

It was I who spoke to her about the great glaciation, now due to return and cover the earth, the whole of human history has taken place in a period between two ice ages, a period which is almost over now, the numbed rays of the sun can barely reach the earth's frost-sparkling crust, grains of malt accumulate the sun's dissipating strength, then set it flowing again, fermenting into alcohol, at the bottom of the glass the sun is still fighting its war with the ice, in the maelstrom's curving horizon the icebergs roll.

All at once three or four pieces of ice break off and fall into the sink, before I have time to turn the tray right way up they all tumble down drumming on the zinc. I grope around to grab them and put them in the ice bucket, now I can't find the cube that got dirty on the floor, to save them all I'd better wash them one by one, with warm water, no, with cold, they're already melting, a snowy lake is forming in the bottom of the bucket.

Adrift on the Arctic Sea the icebergs form a white embroidery along the Gulf Stream, pass beyond it, head down towards the tropics like a flock of giant swans, block harbour mouths, sail up river estuaries, tall as skyscrapers they drive their sharp spurs between skyscrapers, ice rasping on walls of glass. The silence of the northern night is broken by the roar of cracks that yawn to swallow up entire cities, then by the hiss of ice slides that deaden muffle soften.

I wonder what she's getting up to in there, so silent, no sign of life, she could have given me a hand, couldn't she, very nice, didn't even occur to her to ask: would you like me to help? Thank heaven I've finished now, I'll wipe my hands with this kitchen cloth, but I wouldn't want that kitchen cloth smell to linger, better wash them again, now where can I dry them? The problem is whether the solar energy accumulated in the earth's crust will be enough to maintain body heat throughout the next ice age, the solar heat of the Eskimo bride's igloo alcohol.

Off back to her then so we can drink our whisky in peace. See what she's been up to in here, without making a sound? She's taken her clothes off, she's naked on the leather couch. I'd like to go over to her but the room's been invaded by ice: dazzling white crystals piled on the carpet, on the furniture; translucent stalactites hang from the ceiling, weld themselves into diaphanous columns, a vertical sheet of solid ice has formed between her and me, our two bodies are prisoners in the thickness of the iceberg, we can barely see each other through a wall all sharp spikes glittering in the rays of a distant sun.

205

The Call of the Water

I move my arm towards the shower, place my hand on the knob, turn it slowly, rotating to the left.

I've just woken up, my eyes are still full of sleep, but I am perfectly aware that this gesture I'm performing to start my day is a decisive and solemn act, one that puts me in touch with both culture and nature together, with thousands of years of human civilization and with the birth pains of those geological eras that gave our planet its shape. What I expect most from the shower is that it confirm my mastery over water, my membership of that part of humanity which thanks to the efforts of previous generations has inherited the prerogative to summon water to itself with the simple turning of a tap, my privileged state of living in a century and a place where one may enjoy the most generous abundance of clean water whenever one likes. And I know that in order for this miracle to be renewed every day a series of complex conditions have to be met, so that turning on a tap can never be a distracted, automatic gesture, but requires concentration, mental participation.

There! In response to my summons the water climbs the piping, surges in the siphons, raises and lowers the ballcocks that control the flow into the cisterns, as soon as a pressure-change attracts it it rushes there, sends out its message along connecting pipes, spreads out across a network of collectors, drains and refill tanks, presses against reservoir dams, runs out from purifiers, advances along the entire front of the pipelines that bring it towards the city, having collected and stored it in one phase of its endless cycle, perhaps trickling from glacier mouths into rocky streams, perhaps pumped up from subterranean strata, draining down through veins in the rock, absorbed by cracks in the soil, fallen from the sky in a thick curtain of snow rain hail.

While my right hand adjusts the mixer, I stretch out my left and cup it to toss the first splashes on my eyes and wake myself up properly, and as I do so I sense far far away the thin, cold, transparent waves flowing towards me along miles and miles of aqueduct across plains valleys mountains, hear the water nymphs from the wellsprings coming towards me along their liquid ways, any moment they'll be folding me in their threadlike caresses under the shower here.

But before a drop appears at each hole in the shower head to lengthen in a still uncertain dribble then suddenly swell all together in concentric circles of vibrant jets, I have to wait a whole second, a second of uncertainty during which there's no way of knowing whether the world still contains any water, whether it hasn't become a dry, dust-covered planet like the other celestial bodies in our vicinity, or in any event whether it contains enough water for me to be able to take it in the hollow of my hands, far as I am from any reservoir or spring, in the heart of this fortress of asphalt and cement.

Last summer there was a big drought in Northern Europe, pictures on the TV showed wastes of fields reduced to a cracked and arid crust, once prosperous rivers shyly revealing their dry beds, cattle nuzzling in the mud to get some relief from the heat, queues of people with jugs and jars by a meagre fountain. It occurs to me that the abundance I have been wallowing in until today is precarious and illusory, water could once again become a scarce resource, hard to distribute, the water carrier with his little barrel slung over his shoulder raising his cry to the windows to call the thirsty down to buy a glass of his precious merchandise.

If I almost succumbed a moment ago to a sense of titanic

207

pride as I took hold of the command levers of the shower, it's taken less than a second to have me thinking how unjustified and fatuous my illusion of omnipotence was, and it's with trepidation and humility that I now watch for the arrival of the gush announced by a subdued quivering higher up the tube. But what if it were just an air bubble passing through the empty pipes? I think of the Sahara inexorably advancing a few inches every year, I see the lush mirage of an oasis trembling in the haze, I think of the arid plains of Persia drained by underground channels towards cities with blue majolica domes, crossed by nomad caravans that set out each year from the Caspian Sea to the Persian Gulf, camping under black tents where, crouched on the ground, a woman holds her gaudy veil with her teeth as she pours water for the tea from a leather bag.

I raise my face towards the shower waiting out that second before the spurts rain down on my half-closed lids to liberate sleepy eyes that are now exploring the chrome-plated showerhead peppered with little holes rimmed by calcium, and all at once I see it as a lunar landscape riddled with calcareous craters, no, it's the deserts of Iran I'm seeing from the air, dotted with small white craters all in rows at even intervals, showing the route the water follows along conduits three thousand years old: the *qanat* that run underground for fifty yards at a time, communicating with the surface via these wells where a man can climb down securing himself to a rope to carry out maintenance work. I too project myself into one of those dark craters, in an upsidedown world I drop into the showerhead holes as though into the *qanat* wells towards the water running there invisibly with a muffled hiss.

A fraction of a second is all it takes for me to rediscover the notion of up and down: it's from above that the water is about to reach me, after a jerky uphill journey. In thirsty civilizations artificial watercourses run below or along the ground, much as in nature itself, while the great luxury of civilizations lavish with the vital lymph has been that of having water overcome the force of gravity, having it rise up to then fall down again; hence the profusion of fountains with plays and sprays of water, the tall pillars of overhead aqueducts. The imposing masonry of Roman arches supports the lightness of a torrent suspended up above; it's an idea that expresses a sublime paradox: the most solidly, lastingly monumental at the service of the fluid and transitory, the elusive and diaphanous.

I listen hard to the network of waterflows suspended above and around me, to the vibration spreading through a forest of pipes. Above I sense the sky of the Roman Campagna crossed by conduits perched on gently descending arches, and higher up still by clouds that vie with the aqueducts to draw up immense quantities of running water.

The point of arrival for an aqueduct is always the city, the great sponge made for absorbing and spraying, Nineveh and its gardens, Rome and its baths. A transparent city never ceases to flow within the compact thickness of stones and cement, a fine filigree of water swathes the walls and streets. Superficial metaphors define the city as an agglomerate of stone, many-sided diamond or sooty coal, but every metropolis can also be seen as a grand liquid structure, a space defined by vertical and horizontal lines of water, a stratification of locations subject to tides and floods and undertow, where the human race realizes an ideal of amphibian life that satisfies its deepest vocation.

Or perhaps it is water's deepest vocation that is realized in the city: climbing, gushing, flowing upwards. It's in their height that cities find their identity: Manhattan raising up its watertanks on top of skyscrapers, Toledo which for centuries had to draw off barrel after barrel from the Tagus way below and plod them uphill on muleback, until for the delight of the melancholy Philip II *el artificio de Juanelo* lurched into creaking motion and, miracle of brief duration, brought the contents of its swinging buckets up the cliff to the Alcázar.

Here I am then ready to welcome the water not as something naturally due to me but as a lovers' tryst, an encounter whose freedom and felicity are proportional to the obstacles it has had to overcome. To live in complete intimacy with water the Romans placed the baths at the centre of their public life; today this intimacy is the heart of our private life, here under this shower whose streams I have so often seen running down your skin, naiad nereid undine, thus I see you once again appearing and disappearing as the jets fan out, now that the water comes gushing in swift obedience to my call.

The Mirror, the Target

When I was a boy, I spent hours and hours in front of the mirror pulling faces. Not that I thought my face so handsome as never to tire of looking at it; on the contrary, I couldn't bear it, that face of mine, and pulling faces gave me the chance to try out different ones, faces that appeared and were immediately replaced by other faces, so that I could believe I was a different person, many people of every kind, a host of individuals who one after the other became myself, that is I became them, that is each of them became another of them, while as for me, it was as if I didn't exist at all.

Sometimes after trying three or four different faces, or ten perhaps, or twelve, I would decide that just one of these was the one I preferred, and I would try to make it come back, to arrange my features so as once again to set them in that face that had looked so good. No chance. Once a face had gone, there was no way of getting it back, of having it merge with my face again. In the attempt I would assume constantly changing faces, unknown, alien, hostile faces, which seemed to take me further and further from that lost face. Frightened, I would stop pulling faces and my old everyday face would surface again, and I thought it duller than ever.

But these exercises of mine never lasted too long. There was always a voice to bring me back to reality.

Fulgenzio! Fulgenzio! Where's Fulgenzio sneaked off to? Typical! I know how that idiot spends his days well enough! Fulgenzio! Caught you in front of the mirror pulling faces! Again!

Frenetically I would improvise guilty, caught-red-handed faces, soldiers' standing-at-attention faces, obedient, good-boy faces, moron-from-birth faces, gangster faces, angel faces, monster faces, one after the other.

Fulgenzio, how many times do we have to tell you not to get so wrapped up in yourself! Look outside the windows! See how nature burgeons sprouts rustles whirrs blossoms! See how the busy town seethes pulsates throbs churns produces! Every member of my family would raise an arm to point me to something out there in the landscape, something that as they saw it would have the power to attract me excite me give me the energy that — as they saw it of course — I lacked. I would look and look, my eyes would follow their pointing fingers, I would try to get interested in what father mother aunts uncles grandmothers grandfathers older brothers older sisters younger brothers and sisters once twice third removed cousins teachers supervisors supply teachers schoolfriends and holiday friends were suggesting to me. But I couldn't find absolutely anything extraordinary in things as they were.

But perhaps there were other things hidden behind these things, and those, yes, those might interest me, indeed I was extremely curious about them. Sometimes I would see something, or someone, or some woman appear and disappear, I wasn't quick enough to identify what or whom, and at once I would race off after them. It was the hidden side of everything that intrigued me, the hidden side of houses, the hidden side of gardens, the hidden side of streets, the hidden side of towns, the hidden side of televisions, the hidden side of dishwashers, the hidden side of the sea, the hidden side of the moon. But when I managed to get to that hidden side, I realized that what I was looking for was the hidden side of the hidden side, or rather, the hidden side of the hidden side of the hidden side, no; the hidden side of the hidden side of the hidden side of the hidden side...

Fulgenzio, what are you doing? Fulgenzio, what are you looking for? Are you looking for somebody, Fulgenzio? I didn't know what to answer.

212

Sometimes, at the back of the mirror, behind my reflection, I thought I saw a presence I wasn't quick enough to identify and which immediately hid. I tried to study not myself in the mirror but the world behind me: nothing caught my attention. I was about to turn away when, there, I would see it peep out from the opposite side of the mirror. I would always catch it with the corner of my eye in the place where I least expected it, but as soon as I tried to get a good look it had gone. Despite the speed of its movements this creature was flowing and soft, as if swimming underwater.

I left the mirror and started to look for the spot where I'd seen the presence disappear. 'Ottilia! Ottilia!' I called it, because I liked that name and thought a girl I liked could have no other. 'Ottilia! Where are you hiding?' I always had the impression she was near, there in front, no: there behind, no; there round the corner, but I always arrived a second after she'd gone. 'Ottilia! Ottilia!' But if they had asked me: who is Ottilia? I wouldn't have known what to say.

Fulgenzio, a person has to know what he wants! Fulgenzio, you can't always be so vague about your plans! Fulgenzio, you must set yourself an end to achieve – an objective – an aim – a target – you must press on to your goal – you must learn your lesson, you must win the competition, you must earn a lot and save a lot!

I aimed at where I planned to get to, I concentrated my strength, I tensed my will, but my point of arrival was departing, my energies were centrifugal, my will tended only to distend. I gave it all I'd got, I worked hard to study Japanese, to get my astronaut's diploma, to win the weight-lifting championship, to collect a billion in hundred-lire pieces.

You keep right on on the path you've chosen, Fulgenzio! And I stumbled. Fulgenzio, don't wander from the line you've set yourself! And I muddled myself up in zigzags and ups and downs. Leap over the obstacles, my son! And the obstacles fell on me.

In the end I was so disheartened that not even the faces in the mirror were any help. The mirror wouldn't reflect my face any more and not even a shadow of Ottilia, just an expanse of scattered stones as though on the surface of the moon.

To strengthen my character I took up archery. My thoughts and actions must become like arrows that dart through the air along the invisible line that ends in an exact point, the centre of all centres. But my aim was no good. My arrows never hit the bull's eye.

The target seemed as far away as another world, a world that was all precise lines, sharp colours, regular, geometric, harmonious. The inhabitants of that world must make only precise and sudden movements, with nothing vague about them; for them there could be only straight lines, compass-drawn circles, set square corners . . .

The first time I saw Corinna, I realized that that perfect world was made for her, while I was still excluded.

Corinna would shoot her bow and wham! wham! wham! one after another the arrows thudded into the centre.

'Are you a champion?'

'Of the world.'

'You know how to bend your bow in so many different ways and every time the arrow's trajectory takes it right to the target. How do you do it?'

'You think that I'm here and the target there. No: I'm both here and there, I'm the archer and I'm the target that draws the archer's arrow to it, and I'm the arrow that flies and the bow that releases the arrow.'

'I don't understand.'

'If you become like me, you will understand.'

'Can I learn too?'

'I can teach you.'

In the first lesson Corinna said to me: 'To give your eye the steadiness you lack you must look at the target a long time, intensely. Just look at it, stare, until you lose yourself in it, until you convince yourself there's nothing else in the world than that target, and that you are in the centre of the centre.'

I gazed at the target. The sight of it had always communicated a feeling of certainty; but now, the more I looked, the more this certainty was overcome by doubts. There were moments when the red areas seemed to rise in relief against the green, others when the green areas seemed to be higher while the red sank back. Gaps opened up between the lines, precipices, chasms, the centre was in the bottom of a gorge or on the tip of a steeple, the circles opened up dizzying perspectives. I felt that a hand would come out from between the lines of the pattern, an arm, a person ... Ottilia! I immediately thought. But I was quick to banish the idea. It was Corinna I had to follow, not Ottilia, her image was enough to make the target dissolve like a soap bubble.

In the second lesson Corinna said: 'It's when it relaxes that the bow releases the arrow, but to do that it must first be properly tensed. If you want to become precise as a bow you have to learn two things: to concentrate yourself within yourself and to leave every tension outside.'

I tensed and relaxed myself like a bowstring. I went wham! but then I also went whim! and whum!, I vibrated like a harp, the vibrations spread through the air, they opened parentheses of emptiness whence the winds sprung. Between the whim! and the whum! a hammock was swinging. I climbed spirally screwing myself through space and it was Ottilia I saw rocking herself in the hammock amongst arpeggios. But the vibrations faded. I fell.

In the third lesson Corinna said to me: 'Imagine you are an arrow and run towards the target.'

I ran, I cut through the air, I persuaded myself I was like an arrow. But the arrows I was like were arrows that wandered off in every direction but the right one. I ran to gather the fallen arrows. I pressed on into desolate, stony wastes. Was it my own reflection in a mirror? Was it the moon?

Amid the stones I found my blunted arrows, stuck in the

215

sand, twisted, featherless. And there in the midst of them all was Ottilia. She was walking about calmly as though in a garden, gathering flowers and snatching at butterflies.

Me – Why are you here, Ottilia? Where are we? On the moon?

Ottilia – We are on the hidden side of the target.

Me – Is this where all the bad shots go?

Ottilia – Bad? No shot is ever bad.

Me – But the arrows don't have anything to hit here.

Ottilia – Here the arrows put down roots and become forests.

Me – All I can see is junk, fragments, rubble.

Ottilia – Lots of rubble piled up makes a skyscraper. Lots of skyscrapers piled up make rubble.

Corinna – Fulgenzio! Where have you got to? The target!

Me – I've got to go, Ottilia. I can't stay here with you. I've got to aim for the other side of the target.

Ottilia – Why?

Me – Everything's out of shape here, opaque, formless . . .

Ottilia – Look carefully. From very very very close. What can you see?

Me – A granulous, pitted, bumpy surface.

Ottilia – Go between bump and bump, grain and grain, crack and crack. You'll find the gate to a garden, with green flowerbeds and clear pools. I'm there at the bottom.

Me – Everything I touch is rough, arid, cold.

Ottilia – Pass your hand slowly over the surface. It's a cloud soft as whipped cream . . .

Me – Everything's uniform, muted, compact.

Ottilia – Open your eyes and ears. Hear the bustle of the city, see the glitter of windows and bright shop displays, and bugling and bell-ringing, and people white and yellow and black and red, dressed in green and blue and orange and saffron.

Corinna – Fulgenzio! Where are you!

But this time I couldn't tear myself away from Ottilia's

world, from the city that was cloud and garden too. Here, instead of going straight, the arrows turned and twirled along invisible lines that tangled and untangled and coiled themselves up and unwound, but in the end always hit the target, though perhaps a different target from the one you expected.

The strange thing about it was this: the more I realized the world was complicated interlocking inextricable the more it seemed to me that the things I really needed to understand were few and simple, and if I understood them, everything would be clear as the lines in a pattern. I would have liked to say this to Corinna, or to Ottilia, but it was a while now since I'd seen them, either of them, and, here's another strange thing, thinking about them I often confused the one with the other.

I hadn't looked at myself in the mirror for a long time now. One day when I happened to walk by a mirror I saw the target, with all its fine colours. I tried to put myself in profile, three quarter profile: I was still seeing the target. 'Corinna!' I cried. 'Here, Corinna! Look: I'm just the way you wanted me!' But then I thought that what I was seeing in the mirror wasn't just myself, but the world too, so I would have to look for Corinna there, amongst those coloured lines. And Ottilia? Perhaps Ottilia was there too appearing and disappearing. And when I gazed at the target-mirror long enough, was it Corinna or Ottilia I saw peeping out from between concentric circles?

Sometimes I get the impression I've run into her, one or the other of them, in the city streets, and that she wants to say something to me, but it happens when two subway trains pass in opposite directions, and Ottilia's image – or Corinna's? – comes towards me and flits away, followed by a series of extremely rapid faces framed in the windows, like the faces I once pulled in the mirror.

The Other Eurydice

You have won, men of without, you have recast the stories to suit yourselves, to condemn us of within to the role you like to give us, the role of powers of darkness and of death, and the name you have given us, Hades, is laden with tones of doom. Truly, if all should forget what really happened between us, between Eurydice and Orpheus and myself, Pluto, a story quite the reverse of the one you tell, if no one at all now remembers that Eurydice was one of us and that she never did live on the surface of the Earth until Orpheus snatched her away from me with his deceitful music, then our ancient dream of making the Earth a living sphere will be lost for ever.

Even now hardly anyone still remembers what we meant by making the Earth live: not what you imagine, content with your dustcloud life set down on the border between water, earth and air. I wanted life to expand outwards from the centre of the Earth, to spread upwards through its concentric spheres, to circulate around its metals, liquid and solid. Such was Pluto's dream. It was the only way the Earth might have become an enormous living organism, the only way we could have avoided that condition of precarious exile to which life has been forcibly reduced, the dull weight of an inanimate ball of stone beneath, and above, the void. You can no longer even imagine that life might have been something different from what now goes on without, or rather, almost without, since above you and the Earth's crust, there is always the other tenuous crust of the air. Still, there's no comparing this to the succession of spheres in whose interstices we creatures of the depths have always lived, and from which we still rise up to throng your dreams. The Earth is not solid inside, but disjointed, made up of superimposed layers of different densities one below the other, right down to the iron and nickel nucleus, which again is a system of nuclei one inside the other, each rotating separately from the others according to the greater or lesser liquidity of its element.

I don't know what right you have to call yourself terrestrial creatures. Your true name would be extra-terrestrials, people who live without: we who live within are the terrestrials, myself and Eurydice for example, until the day you tricked her and took her away from me, to your desolate without.

This is the realm of Pluto, since it is here that I have always lived, together with Eurydice at first, then alone, in one of these lands within. A sky of stone wheeled above our heads, clearer than your sky and crossed, like yours, by clouds, gathering suspensions of chrome and magnesium. Winged shadows take flight: these skies within have their birds, concretions of light rock tracing out spirals that wind upwards and out of sight. The weather is subject to brusque changes: when showers of leaden rain beat down, or zinc crystals hail, there's nothing for it but to worm your way into the shelter of some porous rock. Sometimes a fiery streak zigzags through the dark: it's not lightning, but an incandescent metal snaking down through a vein.

We thought of the Earth as the internal sphere where we happened to be, the sky as the sphere that surrounded that sphere: the same way you do really, except that here these distinctions were always temporary, arbitrary, since the consistency of the elements was constantly changing, and sometimes we would realize that our sky was hard and solid, a millstone crushing us, while the earth was a sticky glue of whirling eddies and bubbling gasses. I tried to take advantage of the downward melt of heavier elements to get closer to the true centre of the Earth, the nucleus of all nuclei, and I held Eurydice by the hand, leading her in the descent. But every downward infiltration that opened a way towards the centre, would displace other material and force it back towards the surface: sometimes, as we sank down we would be caught by the upward gushing tide and whirled along on the crest of its wave. So we went back up the terrestrial radius; passages would open in the mineral layers and suck us in and beneath us the rock would harden again. Until we found ourselves standing on another soil with another stony sky above our heads, hardly knowing if we were higher or lower than the point we had set out from.

No sooner did she see the metal of a new sky liquefy above us than Eurydice was seized by a yearning to fly. She flung herself upwards, swam across the dome of a first sky, then another, then a third, grabbing on to the stalactites that hung from the highest vaults. I followed, partly to join in her game and partly to remind her that we were supposed to be going in the opposite direction. Of course, Eurydice was as convinced as I was that the place we must get to was the centre of the Earth. Only by reaching the centre could we call the whole planet our own. We were the forefathers of terrestrial life and hence we had to begin to make the Earth live from its nucleus, gradually irradiating our condition throughout the globe. Terrestrial life was our goal, a life *of* the earth and *in* the earth; not what sprouts on the surface and which you think you can call terrestrial life, when it is no more than a mould that spreads its stains on the wrinkly peel of the apple.

We could already see the plutonic cities we meant to found rising under basalt skies, surrounded by walls of jasper, spherical, concentric cities sailing on oceans of mercury, washed by rivers of incandescent lava. What we wanted was a living-body-city-machine that would grow and grow until it filled the whole globe, a telluric machine that would use its boundless energy in ceaseless self-construction, combining and transforming all substances and shapes, performing, with the speed of a seismic shock the work that you without have had to pay for with centuries of

sweat. And this city-machine-living-body would be inhabited by
beings like ourselves, giants stretching out their powerful arms
across wheeling skies to embrace giantesses, who, with the rotating of concentric earths, would expose themselves in ever new
attitudes giving rise to ever new couplings.

These minglings, these vibrations were to give birth to a
realm of diversity and completeness, a realm of silence and of
music. Constant vibrations, propagating themselves at varying
slownesses, according to the depth and discontinuity of the materials, would ruffle the surface of our great silence, transforming
it into the ceaseless music of the world, harmonizing the deep
voices of the elements.

This to show you how mistaken your way is, your life where
work and pleasure are at odds, where music and noise are two
different things; this to show you how even then all this was
clear, and the song of Orpheus none other than a sign of your
partial and divided world. Why did Eurydice fall into the trap?
She belonged entirely to our world, Eurydice, but her enchanted
spirit was such that she delighted in every possible state of sus-
pension, and as soon as she got the chance to launch herself in
flight, in leaps, in ascents up volcanic vents, you would see her
bending her body into twists and turns and curvets and capers.

Boundary zones, the passages that led from one terrestrial
layer to another, gave her a keen sense of vertigo. I have said that
the Earth is made up of roofs laid one above another, like the
skins of an immense onion, and every roof leads to a higher roof,
and all together look forward to the final roof, there where the
Earth stops being Earth, where everything within is left on this
side and on the other there is only what is without. You identify
the Earth's boundary with the Earth itself; you believe that the
sphere is the surface that wraps around it, not the volume beneath; you have always lived in that flat dimension and you
never even imagine that an elsewhere and an otherwise could
exist; at the time we knew that this boundary was there, but we
didn't imagine one could see it, without leaving the Earth, an idea

221

that wasn't so much frightening as absurd. Everything the Earth expelled from its guts in eruptions and bituminous jets and fumaroles was sent flying out there: gases, liquid mixtures, volatile elements, worthless materials, refuse of every kind. The outside was the world's negative, something we couldn't even picture in our minds, the mere abstract idea of which was enough to provoke a shiver of disgust, no, of horror, or rather, a stupor, yes that's it, a sense of vertigo (certainly our reactions were more complicated than you would imagine, especially Eurydice's), into which would creep a certain fascination, an attraction to the void, the Janus-faced, the ultimate.

Following Eurydice on one of her wandering whims we entered the throat of a spent volcano. Above us, the other side of something like the narrow passage of an hourglass, the crusty grey cavity of the crater opened out into a landscape hardly different in shape and substance from those we lived in deep below; but what bewildered us was that the Earth ended here, it didn't begin to weigh down on itself again in another form, from here on was emptiness, or at least a substance incomparably more tenuous than those we had so far encountered, a transparent, vibrant substance, the blue air.

It was these vibrations that lost Eurydice, vibrations so different from those that spread slowly through basalt and granite, different from all the cracks, clangs and dull boomings that shudder sluggishly through masses of fused metal or great walls of crystals. Here, minute pointed sound-sparks darted towards her one after another from every possible direction and at a speed that was unbearable to us: it was a sort of tickling that filled you with unseemly cravings. We were seized – or at least I was seized, since from here on I shall have to distinguish between my own state of mind and Eurydice's – by the desire to retreat into that dark depth of silence over which the echo of earthquakes passes softly and is lost in the distance. But Eurydice, drawn as ever to the unusual and the rash, was eager to make this unique thing her own, regardless of whether it was good or bad.

It was then that the trap was sprung: beyond the edge of the crater the air vibrated continuously, or rather, it vibrated continuously but in a way that involved different discontinuous vibrations. It was a sound that rose to fullness, faded, swelled again, and this modulation was part of an invisible pattern it followed, extended across time like a chequer of solids and spaces. Further vibrations were superimposed on these, and they were shrill and sharply separate, yet drew together in a halo, first sweet then bitter, and as they contrasted or followed the movement of the deeper sound, they imposed a sort of circle or field or dominion of sound.

My immediate instinct was to get out of that circle, to get back to padded density: and I slipped inside the crater. But that same moment Eurydice had leapt up the rocks in the direction of the sound, and before I could stop her she was over the brim of the crater. Oh, it was an arm, something I thought might be an arm, that snatched her, snake-like, and dragged her out; I just heard a cry, her cry, join with the earlier sound, in harmony with it, in a single song that she and the unknown singer struck up together, to the rhythm of a stringed instrument, descending the outer slopes of the volcano.

I don't know whether this image corresponds to something seen or something imagined: I was already sinking down into my darkness, the inner skies were closing one by one above me: the siliceous vaults, aluminium roofs, atmospheres of viscous sulphur; and the dappled subterranean silence echoed around me with its restrained rumblings, its muttered thunder. My relief at finding myself once again far away from the sickening edge of the air and the torment of those soundwaves was matched only by my desperation at having lost Eurydice. I was alone now: I hadn't been able to save her from the torture of being torn from the Earth, exposed to the constant percussion of strings stretched in that air with which the world of the void defends itself from the void. My dream of making the Earth live by reaching the ultimate centre together with Eurydice had failed.

223

Eurydice was a prisoner, exiled in the roofless wastes of the world without.

What followed was a time of waiting. My eyes studied the closely packed landscapes which, one above the other, fill the volume of the globe: threadlike caverns, chains of mountains stacked in scales and sheets, oceans wrung out like sponges: the more I acknowledged and was moved by our crammed, concentrated, compact world, the more I suffered that Eurydice was no longer there to live in it.

Freeing her became my sole obsession: forcing the gates of the world without, inside invading outside, reuniting Eurydice with terrestrial material, building a new vault above her, a new mineral sky, saving her from the hell of that vibrant air, of that sound, that song. I would watch the lava gather in volcanic caverns, the upward pressure on the vertical ducts of the Earth's crust: that was the way.

Came the day of the eruption, a tower of lapilli rose black in the air above a decapitated Vesuvius, the lava poured through the vineyards of the bay, burst the gates of Herculaneum, crushed the mule-driver and his beast against a wall, snatched the miser from his money, the slave from his chopping block; a dog trapped in his collar pulled the chain from the ground and sought refuge in the barn. I was there in the midst: I pressed forward with the lava, the flaming avalanche broke up in tongues, rivers, snakes, and at the foremost tip I was there running forward to find Eurydice. I knew – something told me – that she was still a prisoner of the unknown singer: when I heard the music of that instrument and the timbre of that voice, I would have found her too.

I rushed on, transported by the lava flow through secluded gardens towards marble temples. I heard the song and a chord; two voices alternated; I recognized Eurydice's – but how changed! – following the stranger's. Greek characters on the undercurve of an arch spelt: *Orpheos*. I broke down the door, flooded over the threshold. For just an instant I saw her, next to the harp. The place was closed and vaulted, made specially, you would have thought, so that the music could gather there, as though in a shell. A heavy curtain, of leather I had the impression, or rather padded like a quilt, closed off a window, so as to isolate their music from the world around. As soon as I went in, Eurydice wrenched the curtain aside, throwing open the window; outside was the bay dazzling with reflected light and the city and the streets. The midday sun invaded the room, the sun and the sounds: a strumming of guitars rose from every side and the throbbing roar of scores of loudspeakers, together with the jagged backfiring of car engines and the honking of horns. The armour of noise stretched out across the Earth's crust: the cortex which circumscribes your surface lives, with its antennas bristling on the roofs, turning to sound the waves that travel unseen and unheard through space, with its radios stuck to your ears, constantly filling them with the acoustic glue without which you don't know whether you're dead or alive, its jukeboxes with their store of incessantly revolving sounds and the never-ending siren of the ambulance picking up the wounded of your never-ending massacres.

The lava stopped against this wall of sound. Lacerated by the barbs of that fence of crashing vibrations, I made one more move forward to the point where for a moment I had seen Eurydice, but she was gone, and gone likewise her abductor: the song by which and on which they lived was submerged by the intruding avalanche of noise, and I could no longer distinguish either her or her song.

I withdrew, climbing reluctantly back along the lava flow, up the slopes of the volcano, I returned to live in silence, to bury myself.

Now, you who live without, tell me if by chance you happen to catch Eurydice's song in that thick paste of sounds that surrounds you, the song that holds her prisoner and is in turn prisoner of the non-song that massacres all songs, and if you should recognize Eurydice's voice with its distant echo of the silent music of the elements, tell me, give me news of her, you extraterrestrials, temporary victors, so that I can resume my plans to bring Eurydice to the centre of terrestrial life, to restore the realm of the gods of within, of the gods who inhabit the dense compactness of things, now that the gods of without, the gods of the Olympian heights and the rarefied air have given you all they could give, and clearly it isn't enough.

The Memoirs of Casanova

1

Throughout my stay at ——— I had two steady lovers: Cate and Ilda. Cate came to see me every morning, Ilda in the afternoon; in the evening I went out socializing and people were amazed to see me always on my own. Cate was well-built, Ilda was slim; going from one to the other renewed desire, which tends as much to variation as to repetition.

Once Cate had left I hid every trace of her; likewise with Ilda; and I think I always managed to stop either of them finding out about the other, both at the time and perhaps afterwards too.

Of course I would sometimes slip up and say things to one of them that could only mean something if said to the other: 'I found these fuchsias at the florist today, your favourite flower,' or 'Don't forget to take your necklace again,' thus provoking amazement, anger, suspicion. But these banal improprieties only occurred, if I well remember, at the beginning of the double affair. Very soon I learnt to separate the two relationships completely; each relationship took its course, had its continuity of conversations and habits, and never interfered with the other.

At the beginning I thought (I was, as you will have appreciated, very young, and looking for experience) that amatory arts would be transferable from one woman to the other: both knew a great deal more than me and I thought that the secrets I learnt from Ilda I would then be able to teach to Cate, and vice versa.

I was wrong: all I did was to muddle things that are only valuable when spontaneous and direct. Each woman was a world unto herself, or rather each was a sky where I must trace the positions of stars, planets, orbits, eclipses, inclinations and conjunctions, solstice and equinox. Each firmament had its own movement, in line with its own mechanism and rhythm. I couldn't expect to apply notions of astronomy I'd learnt watching Cate's sky, to Ilda's.

But I must confess that freedom of choice between two lines of behaviour was no longer an option: with Cate I had been trained to act one way and with Ilda another; I was conditioned in every way by the partner I was with, to the extent that even my instinctive preferences and tics would change. Two personalities alternated inside me; and I wouldn't have been able to say which me was really me.

What I've said holds good as much for the spirit as the body: the words spoken to the one couldn't be repeated to the other, and I very soon realized I would have to vary my way of thinking too.

When I feel the urge to recount and evoke one of the many twists and turns of my adventurous life, I usually resort to the well-tried versions I've developed for social occasions, with whole sentences and more repeated word for word, the effects calculated right down to the digressions and pauses. But certain escapades that never failed to win the appreciation of groups of people who didn't know me, or who weren't involved, had to be considerably adapted if I was to tell them to Cate or Ilda alone. Certain expressions that were common currency with Cate, sounded wrong when I was with Ilda; the quips Ilda picked up at once and returned with interest, I would have had to explain to Cate with every 'i' dotted and 't' crossed, though she appreciated other jokes that left Ilda cold; sometimes it was the conclusion to be drawn from a story that changed from Ilda to Cate, so that I took to giving my stories different endings. In this way I was gradually constructing two different versions of my life.

Every day I would tell Cate and Ilda what I had seen and heard the evening before wandering round the haunts and hangouts in town: gossip, shows, celebrities, fashionable clothes, eccentricities. In my early days of undifferentiated insensibility, I would repeat word for word to Ilda in the afternoon whatever I'd said in the morning to Cate: I thought this would save me the imaginative effort one is constantly having to make to keep people interested. I soon realized that the same story either interested one and not the other, or, if it interested both, then the details they asked for were different and likewise different were the comments and judgements they expressed.

What I had to do then was to produce two quite different stories from the same material: and this wouldn't have been particularly problematic; except that each evening I also had to live through things in two different ways in line with the stories I'd be telling the following morning; I'd look at everything and everybody from Cate's point of view and from Ilda's point of view, and I'd judge them in line with their two different criteria; in conversation I'd come up with two retorts to the same quip from someone else, one that Ilda would like, the other that Cate would like; every retort generated counter-retorts that I had to reply to once again in two ways. I wasn't aware of this split personality operating when I was in the company of one or the other of them, but mostly when they weren't there.

My mind had become the two women's battlefield. Cate and Ilda, who didn't know of each other outside my head, were constantly clashing and fighting for territory inside me, hitting out at each other, tearing each other to shreds. The sole purpose of my existence was to be host to the bitter struggle between two rivals neither of whom knew anything about it.

That was the real reason that persuaded me to leave —— in a hurry, never to return.

2

I was attracted to Irma because she reminded me of Dirce. I sat next to her: she just had to turn her body a little towards me and put a hand over her face (I would whisper to her; she would laugh) and the illusion of being close to Dirce was striking. The illusion awoke memories, the memories desires. To transmit them to Irma somehow, I gripped her hand. Her touch and the way she started revealed her to me for what she was, different. This sensation was stronger than the other, but without cancelling it out, and, in itself, agreeable. I realized that I would be able to derive a double plea-sure from Irma: that of pursuing through her the lost Dirce, and that of allowing myself to be surprised by an unfamiliar presence.

Every desire traces its curve within us, a line that climbs, wavers, sometimes dissolves. The line the absent woman evoked in me might, a second before it began to decline, intersect with the line of my curiosity in the present woman, and transmit its upward thrust to this still all undiscovered trajectory. The plan was worth a try: I redoubled my attentiveness in Irma's regard, until I persuaded her to come to my room at night.

She came in. She let her cloak slip off. She was wearing a light white muslin blouse that the wind (it being spring the win-dow was open) ruffled. That was when I realized that a different and unexpected mechanism was taking charge of my sensations and thoughts. It was Irma who was taking up the whole field of my attention, Irma as a unique and unrepeatable person, skin and voice and eyes, while the resemblances to Dirce that occasionally surfaced in my mind were no more than a disturbance, so much so that I was eager to be rid of them.

Hence my meeting with Irma became a battle with the shade of Dirce who kept on sneaking in between us, and every time I felt I was about to capture the indefinable essence of Irma, every time I felt I had established an intimacy between us that excluded every other presence or thought, back came Dirce, or the past experience that Dirce embodied for me, to stamp her impression on what I was experiencing that very moment and prevent me from feeling it as new. At this point Dirce, her memory, the mark she had made on me, brought me nothing but annoyance, con-straint, boredom.

Dawn was coming in through the shutter slats in blades of pearl-grey light, when I realized beyond any doubt that my night with Irma was not the one now about to end, but another night like this one, a night still to come when I would seek the memory of Irma in another woman, and suffer first when I found her again and when I lost her again, and then when I couldn't free myself from her.

3

I rediscovered Tullia twenty years on. Chance, which in the past had brought us together only to separate us just when we realized we liked each other, now finally allowed us to pick up the thread of our relationship at the point where it had broken off. 'You haven't changed at all,' we both told each other. Were we lying? Not entirely: 'I haven't changed,' was what both she and I wished to have the other understand.

This time the relationship developed as both expected. At first it was Tullia's mature beauty which engaged all my attention, and only later did I tell myself not to forget the young Tullia, seeking to recover the continuity between the two. Hence, playing a game that came to us spontaneously when we talked, we would pretend that our separation had lasted twenty-four hours and not twenty years, and that our memories were of things that had happened only the day before. It was lovely, but it wasn't true. If I thought of myself as I was then with her as she was then, I was confronted with two strangers; they aroused warmth, affection, plenty of it, tenderness too, but what I was able to imagine in their regard had nothing to do with what Tullia and I were now.

Of course we still regretted how all too brief our first encounter had been. Was it the natural regret for lost youth? But my present satisfaction I felt gave me no cause for regret; and Tullia too, now I was getting to know her, was a woman too taken up with the present to abandon herself to nostalgia. Regret for what we hadn't been able to have then? Maybe a little, but not entirely: because (again with this exclusive enthusiasm for what the present was giving us) I felt (perhaps wrongly) that if our desire had been satisfied at once it might have removed something from our happiness today. If anything the regret had to do with what those two poor youngsters, those 'others', had lost, and was added to the sum of all the losses the world suffers in every instant never to retrieve. From the height of our sudden richness, we deigned to cast a compassionate eye on those excluded: hardly a disinterested feeling, since it allowed us to savour our privilege the better.

Two opposing conclusions can be drawn from my relationship with Tullia. One might say that having found each other again cancelled out the separation of twenty years before, erased the loss we suffered; and one might say on the contrary that it rendered that loss decisive, desperate. Those two (Tullia and I as we were then) had lost each other for ever, never to meet again, and in vain would they have called on the Tullia and I of today for help, since we (the selfishness of happy lovers is boundless) had entirely forgotten them.

4

Of other women I remember a gesture, a repeated expression, an inflexion, that were intimately bound up with the essence of the person and distinguished them like a signature. Not so with Sofia. Or rather, I remember a great deal about Sofia, too much perhaps: eyelids, calves, a belt, a perfume, many preferences and obsessions, the songs she knew, an obscure confession, some dreams; all things my memory still keeps in its store and links with her but which are doomed to be lost because I can't find the thread that binds them together and I don't know which of them contains the real Sofia. Between each detail lies a gap; and

taken one by one, they might just as well be attributed to someone else as to her. As for our lovemaking (we met in secret for
months), I remember that it was different every time, and although this should be a positive quality for someone like myself
who fears the blunting effect of habit, it now turns out to be a
fault, since I can't remember what prompted me to go to her
rather than anyone else each time I went. In short, I don't remember anything at all.

Perhaps all I wanted to understand about her at the beginning was whether I liked her or not: that was why the first time
I saw her I bombarded her with questions, some of them indiscreet. Instead of fending these off, which she could well have
done, in reply to every question she overwhelmed me with all
kinds of clarifications, revelations and allusions, at once fragmentary and digressive, while I, in my struggle to keep up with her
and hold on to what she was telling me, got more and more lost.
Result: it was as if she hadn't answered me at all.

To establish communication in a different language I risked
a caress. In response Sofia's movements were entirely aimed at
containing and putting off my assault, if not exactly rejecting it,
with the result that the moment one part of her body slipped
away from my hand, my fingers would slither on to another, her
evasion thus leading me to carry out an exploration of her skin
at once fragmentary yet extensive. In short, the information gathered through touch was no less abundant than that recorded
by hearing, albeit equally incoherent.

Nothing remained but to complete our acquaintance on
every level and as soon as possible. But was it one unique woman
this person who undressed before me, removing both the visible
and invisible clothes the ways of the world impose on us, or was
it many women in one? And which of these was it that attracted
me, which that put me off? There was never an occasion when
I didn't discover something I wasn't expecting in Sofia, and less
and less would I have been able to answer that first question I
had asked myself: did I or didn't I like her?

Today, going over it in my memory, another doubt occurs: is it that when a woman hides nothing of herself I am incapable of understanding her; or is it that Sofia in revealing herself so abundantly was deploying a sophisticated strategy for not letting me capture her? And I tell myself: of all of them, she was the one who got away, as if I had never had her. But did I really have her? And then I ask myself: and who did I really have? And then again: have who? what? what does it mean?

5

I met Fulvia at the right moment: as chance would have it I was the first man in her young life. Unfortunately this lucky encounter was destined to be brief; circumstances obliged me to leave town; my ship was already in harbour; the next morning it was due to set sail.

We were both aware that we would not see each other again, and equally aware that this was part of the established and ineluctable order of things; hence the sadness we felt, though to differing degrees, was governed, once again to differing degrees, by reason. Fulvia already sensed the emptiness she would feel when our new and barely begun familiarity was broken off, but also the freedom this would open up for her and the many opportunities it would provide; I on the other hand had a habit of placing the events of my life in a pattern where the present receives light and shade from the future, a future whose trajectory in this case I could already imagine right up to its decline; what I foresaw for Fulvia was the full flowering of an amorous vocation which I had helped to awaken.

Hence in those last dallyings before our farewell I couldn't help seeing myself as merely the first of the long series of lovers Fulvia was doubtless going to have, and to reassess what had happened between us in the light of her future experiences. I realized that every last detail of a passion that Fulvia had surren-

234

dered herself to with total abandon would be remembered and judged by the woman she would become in just a few years' time. As things stood now, Fulvia accepted everything about me without judging: but the day was not far off when she would be able to compare me with other men; every memory of me would be subjected to parallels, distinctions, judgements. I had before me an as yet inexperienced girl for whom I represented all that could be known, but all the same I felt I was being watched by the Fulvia of tomorrow, demanding and disenchanted.

My first reaction was one of fear of comparison. Fulvia's future men, I thought, would be capable of making her fall totally in love with them, as she had not been with me. Sooner or later Fulvia would deem me unworthy of the fortune that had befallen me; it would be disappointment and sarcasm that kept alive her memory of me: I envied my nameless successors, I sensed that they were already lying in wait, ready to snatch Fulvia away, I hated them, and already I hated her too because Fate had already destined her for them . . .

To escape this pain, I reversed the train of my thoughts, passing from self-detraction to self-praise. It wasn't hard: by temperament I am rather inclined to forming a high opinion of myself than a low. Fulvia had had an invaluable stroke of luck meeting me first; but taking me as a model would expose her to cruel disappointments. Other men she would meet would seem crude, feeble, dull and dumb, after myself. In her innocence she no doubt imagined my good qualities to be fairly common attributes amongst my sex; I must warn her that seeking from others what she had found in me could only lead to disillusionment. I shivered in horror at the thought that after such a happy beginning Fulvia might fall into unworthy hands, who would harm her, maim her, debase her. I hated all of them; and I ended up hating her too because destiny was to snatch her from me condemning her to a degraded future.

One way or another, the passion that had me in its grip was, I suspect, the one I have always heard described as 'jealousy', a mental disturbance from which I had imagined circumstances had rendered me immune. Having established that I was jealous, all I could do was behave like a jealous man. I lost my temper with Fulvia, telling her I couldn't stand her being so calm just before we were about to part; I accused her of hardly being able to wait to betray me; I was unkind to her, cruel. But she (no doubt out of inexperience) seemed to find this change in my mood natural and wasn't unduly upset. Very sensibly she advised me not to waste the little time we had left together on pointless recriminations.

Then I knelt at her feet, I begged her to pardon me, not to inveigh too bitterly against me when she had found a companion worthy of her; I hoped for no greater indulgence than to be forgotten. She treated me as though I were mad; she wouldn't let me speak of what had happened between us in anything but the most flattering terms; otherwise, she said, it spoiled the effect.

This served to reassure me as to my image, but then I found myself commiserating with Fulvia over her future destiny: other men were worthless; I should warn her that the fullness she'd known with me wouldn't happen again with anyone else. She answered that she too felt sorry for me, because our happiness came from our being together, once apart we would both lose it; but to preserve it for some time longer we should both immerse ourselves in it totally without imagining we could define it from without.

The conclusion I came to from without, waving my handkerchief to her from the ship as the anchor was raised, was this: the experience that had entirely occupied Fulvia all the time she was with me was not the discovery of myself and not even the discovery of love or of men, but of herself; even in my absence this discovery, once begun, would never cease; I had only been an instrument.

Henry Ford

SPOKESMAN: Mr Ford, I have been entrusted with the task of putting a number ... The committee of which I am a member has the pleasure of informing you ... Obliged as we are to erect a monument to that celebrity of our century who ... The choice of your name, unanimously ... For having exercised the greatest influence on the history of mankind ... on the very image of man ... Having considered your achievements and thought ... Who if not Henry Ford has changed the world, made it completely different from what it was before him? Who more than Henry Ford has given form to our way of life? So, we would like the monument to have your approval ... We would like you to tell us how you would prefer to be portrayed, against what background ...

HENRY FORD: As you see me now ... Amongst birds ... I had five hundred aviaries like this ... I called them bird hotels; the biggest was the housemartin house, with seventy-six apartments; winter and summer if they came to me birds would always find food, shelter and water to drink. I had baskets hung from the trees on wires and filled with bird seed all winter long, and drinking bowls with electric elements so that the water wouldn't freeze. I had artificial nests of various kinds put up in the trees: the wrens prefer swinging nests that sway in the wind; that way there's no danger the sparrows will set up there, since they only like very stable nests. In summer I had the cherries left on the trees and the strawberries on their bushes so that the birds would find their natural food. Every species of bird in the USA passed by my house. And I imported birds from other countries: buntings, chaffinches, robin redbreasts, starlings, bullfinches, jays, linnets . . . about five hundred species in all.

SPOKESMAN: But, Mr Ford, I wanted to talk . . .

HENRY FORD: (*suddenly rigid, extremely alert, furious*) Why do you imagine birds are just something graceful to enjoy for their feathers and warblings? Birds are necessary for strictly economic reasons! They destroy damaging insects! Did you know that the only time I mobilized the Ford organization to solicit intervention from the United States government was for the protection of migratory birds. An excellent law had been drawn up for establishing reserves, but it risked getting bogged down in Congress where they could never find the time to pass it. Of course: birds don't vote! So I asked every one of Ford's six thousand agents, spread all over the USA, to send a telegram to their representatives in Congress. That was when Washington began to take the problem seriously . . . The law was approved. You must understand that I never wanted to use the Ford Motor Company for political ends: each of us has a right to his own opinions and the company mustn't interfere with them. On that occasion the end justified the means, I think, and it was the only exception.

SPOKESMAN: But Mr Ford, enlighten me please: you are the man who changed the image of our planet through industrial organization, motorization . . . What have little birdies got to do with that?

HENRY FORD: What? You're another one who thinks that the big factories have wiped out trees, flowers, birds, greenery? Quite the contrary! It's only when we learn how to exploit cars and industry as effectively as possible that we will have the time to enjoy nature! My position is very simple: the more time and energy we waste, the less is left to enjoy life. I don't consider the cars that bear my name as mere cars: I hope they will serve to demonstrate the effectiveness of my philosophy . . .

SPOKESMAN: You mean that you invented and manufactured and sold automobiles so that people could get away from the factories of Detroit and go and hear the birds singing in the woods?

HENRY FORD: One of the people I most admired was a man who dedicated his life to watching and describing birds, John Burroughs. He was a sworn enemy of the automobile and all technical progress! But I managed to make him change his mind ... The happiest memories of my life go back to the weeks spent together on a vacation I organized with Burroughs himself, and my other mentors and closest friends, the great Edison, and Firestone, the tyre man ... We travelled in a caravan of cars, across the Adirondack Mountains, and the Alleghenys, sleeping under canvas, gazing at the sunsets, the dawns over waterfalls ...

SPOKESMAN: But don't you think that an image like this ... in relation to what people know about you ... Fordism ... is, how can I put it?, misleading ... doesn't it shirk everything essential?

HENRY FORD: No, no, this is what is essential. American history is a history of journeys between boundless horizons, a history of means of transportation: the horse, the wagons of the pioneers, the railroads ... But only the automobile has given Americans America. Only with the automobile have they become masters of the length and breadth of the country, each individual master of his own means of transport, master of his time, in the midst of this immensity of space ...

SPOKESMAN: I must confess that the idea we had for your monument ... was a little different ... a backdrop of factories ... of assembly lines ... Henry Ford, the creator of the modern factory, of mass production ... The first automobile for the common man: the famous Model T ...

HENRY FORD: If it's an epigraph you're after, sculpt out the text of the announcement I used to launch the Model T on the market, in 1908. Not that I ever needed any advertising for my cars, mind! I always maintained that advertising was pointless, a good product doesn't need it, it is its own advertisement! But that leaflet expressed the *ideas* I wanted to get across. It's in advertising as education that I believe! Read it, read it.

> 'I shall build an automobile for the masses. It will be large enough for a family, but small enough to satisfy the needs of the individual. It will be built with the best materials and by the best men available on the market, following the simplest designs that modern engineering can devise. But it will be priced so low that no man with a decent salary shall be unable to possess it and enjoy together with his family the blessing of a few hours' pleasure in God's great open spaces.'

SPOKESMAN: The Model T . . . For almost twenty years the factories of Detroit produced this car and no other . . . You spoke of the needs of individuals . . . But you're quoted as making this joke: 'Every client can have his car in his favourite colour, so long as it's black.' Did you really say this, Mr Ford?

HENRY FORD: Sure, I said it and I wrote it too. How do you think I managed to get my prices down, to put my cars within the reach of everyone's pocket? Do you think I could have done that if I'd introduced new models every year, like ladies' bonnets? Fashion is one of the forms of waste I most detest. My idea was a car whose every component could be replaced, so that it need never grow old. It was the only way I could transform the car from being a luxury item, a prestige accessory, to an essential product everyone must have, one whose worth lies in its utility . . .

SPOKESMAN: That marked a big change in industrial practices. From then on the efforts of world industry have aimed to satisfy the common consumer, and to increase the demand for consumer goods. That is precisely why industry has tended to design products with built-in obsolescence, things to be

240

thrown out as soon as possible, so that other products can be sold ... The system you introduced had consequences which run contrary to your basic ideas: things are produced that soon wear out, or go out of fashion, so as to leave room for other products that are no better than the first but seem newer, products whose fortunes depend entirely on advertising.

HENRY FORD: That wasn't what I wanted. Change only makes sense before you have reached that *unique optimum* method of production that must exist for every product, the way that will guarantee the maximum economy with the highest yield. There is one method and only one method for making everything in the best possible way. Once you've got there, why change?

SPOKESMAN: So your idea is for a world where all cars are the same?

HENRY FORD: No two things are the same in nature. And the idea that all men are the same and equal is mistaken and disastrous. I've never worshipped equality, but I didn't make a monster out of it either. Even if we do all we can to manufacture identical cars, made of identical components, so much so that any component can be taken from one car and mounted on another, the sameness is no more than apparent. Once you've put it on the road, every Ford handles a little differently from other Fords, and after he's tried a car a good driver will be able to distinguish it from all the others, all he has to do is sit at the wheel, turn the ignition key ...

SPOKESMAN: But this world you've helped create ... weren't you ever afraid that it might be terribly uniform, monotonous?

HENRY FORD: It's poverty that's monotonous. It's the waste of energy and lives. The people who stood in line outside our hiring office were Italians, Greeks, Poles, Ukrainians, emigrants from all the provinces of the Russian and Austro-Hungarian empires, crowds of them, speaking incomprehensible languages and dialects. They were nobodies, without trade or home. I made honourable men of them, I gave them all a

241

useful job, a salary that made them independent, I turned them into men capable of running their own lives. I made them learn English and the values of our moral code: this was the only condition I imposed; if they didn't like it they were free to go. But I never turned away those who were willing to learn. They became American citizens, they and their families, on a par with those born to families here for generations. I don't care what a man has been: I don't ask him about his past, nor where he's come from, nor what he's achieved. I don't care if he's been to Harvard and I don't care if he's been to Sing Sing! I only want to know what he can do, what he can become!

SPOKESMAN: Right . . . become by conforming to a model . . .

HENRY FORD: I know what you're trying to say. I have always taken human diversity as my starting point. Physical strength, speed of movement, capacity to react to new situations are all qualities that vary from one individual to the next. My idea was this: to organize the work in my factories so that those who were unskilled or disabled could yield as much as the most skilled worker. I had each department's tasks classified according to whether they demanded unusual vigour, or normal strength and stature, or whether they might be carried out by people whose speed and physical capacities were below the average. It turned out that there were 2,637 jobs that could be entrusted to workers with only one leg (*mimes mechanical operations pretending to have only one leg*), 670 that could go to people with no legs (*mimes as above*), 715 for those with only one arm (*mimes as above*), 2 for those with no arms (*mimes as above*) and 10 jobs that could be done by the blind. A blind man given the job of counting bolts in the warehouse proved capable of doing the work of three workers with good eyes (*mimes*). Is this what you call conforming? I'm telling you I did everything I could to help each man overcome his handicap. Even the sick could work and earn their keep in my hospitals. In their beds. Screwing nuts on small bolts. It helped keep up morale too. They got better faster.

SPOKESMAN: But work on the assembly line ... Being forced to concentrate your attention on repetitive movements, follow a rhythm that never changes, imposed by machines ... What could be more mortifying for the creative spirit ... for the most elementary freedom of having control over the movements of your own body, over the expense of your own energy in line with your own rhythm, your own breathing ... Always to perform only one operation, one movement, always made in the same way ... Isn't it a terrifying prospect?

HENRY FORD: For me, yes. Terrifying. For me it would be inconceivable always to do the same thing all day every day. But not everyone is like me. The great majority of men have no desire to do creative work, to have to think, decide. They simply want a job that allows them to apply the minimum amount of mental and physical strength. And for this great majority, mechanical repetition, participation in a task that has already been organized down to the last detail, guarantees perfect inner calm. Of course, they mustn't be restless types. Are you restless? Me, yes, extremely. Well then, I won't use you for a routine job. But most of the jobs in a big factory are routine and as such suitable to the great majority of the workforce.

SPOKESMAN: They are like that because you wanted them to be like that ... both jobs and people ...

HENRY FORD: We managed to organize the work in the way that was easiest for those who had to do it, and most profitable. I say we the 'creative' ones, if you want to call us that, we the restless ones, we who can't relax until we have found the best way of doing things ... You know where I got the idea of the conveyor that brings the component to the worker without him having to move toward the component? In the meat-canning factories of Chicago, watching the quartered cattle hung on trolleys moving along elevated rails, to be sprinkled with salt, cut up, pulped, minced ... The quartered cattle passing by, dangling ... the cloud of salt grains ... the knife blades sawing back and forth ... and I saw the chassis of the Model

T running along at hand height while the workers tightened the bolts . . .

SPOKESMAN: So creativity is reserved to the few . . . those who design . . . who take decisions . . .

HENRY FORD: No! It is extended! How many artists, real artists, were there in the past? Today we are the artists, we who experiment with production and the men who produce! In the past creative tasks were restricted to putting together colours or notes or words on a painting, a score, a page . . . And for whom in the end? For a handful of world weary idlers who hang around the galleries and concert halls! We are the real artists, we who invent the work that millions of people count on!

SPOKESMAN: But professional skill has disappeared from manual work!

HENRY FORD: Oh enough! You lot are always harping on the same note. Quite the contrary. Professional skill has triumphed, in automobile manufacture and the organization of labour, and this way it's been put at the service of those who are not skilled who can now achieve the same yields as the more talented! You know how many parts go to make up a Ford? Including screws and bolts, about five thousand: big parts, medium-sized parts, small parts and some no bigger than the cogs in a clock. Workers used to have to walk across the shop floor to look for each part, walk to take them to the part to be assembled, walk to look for a spanner, a screwdriver, a welding torch . . . The day was frittered away with this back and forth . . . Then they always ended up banging into each other, tripping over themselves, crowding each other, bunching . . . Was this the human, creative way to work you people like so much? I wanted to organize things so that workers didn't have to run back and forth through the workshops. Was that an inhuman idea? I wanted to organize things so that workers didn't have to lift and carry weights. Was that an inhuman idea? I arranged men and tools in the order of the jobs to be done, I used trolleys on rails or hanging cables, so that arm movements were kept to a minimum. Save ten thousand people just ten steps a day and you've saved sixty miles of pointless movements and ill-spent energy.

SPOKESMAN: To sum up: you wish to save your workers unnecessary movements in the building of automobiles which allow us all to live in continual movement...

HENRY FORD: It's time-saving, my dear fellow, in both cases. There is no contradiction! The first advertisement I used to persuade Americans to buy themselves a car was based on the old proverb 'Time is money!' It's the same at work: for each operation the worker must have the right time: not a second too little and not a second too much! And the worker's entire day must be based on the same principles: he must live near the factory so as not to lose time travelling. That's why I came to the conclusion that medium-size factories were better than enormous ones...and meant you could avoid big urban conurbations, slums, dirt, delinquency, vice...

SPOKESMAN: And yet Detroit... The masses who gathered in the Mid West to look for work in Ford factories...

HENRY FORD: Right, I was the only one able to offer high, ever increasing salaries, in a period when no other factory owners would even consider it... It was hard work arguing for my idea and imposing it on the whole American economy: the idea that it's higher salaries, not higher profits that get the market moving. And to give higher salaries you have to save on the system of production. That is the only saving that's really worth making: saving not to accumulate but to increase salaries, that is purchasing power, that is abundance. The secret of abundance lies in an equilibrium between prices and quality. And it's only on abundance that you can build, not on shortages: I was the first to understand that. If a capitalist works in the hope that one day he'll be able to live off the revenue, he's a bad capitalist. I never felt I possessed anything myself, but that I was managing my property by putting the best means of production at the service of others.

SPOKESMAN: But the unions saw things differently. And for years you didn't want to have anything to do with unions ... As late as 1937 you were paying teams of bouncers and professional boxers to stop strikes by force ...

HENRY FORD: There were some troublemakers who wanted to stir up conflicts between Ford and the workers, conflicts for which there could be *no logical reason.* I had worked out everything in such a way that the workers' interests and the company's interests were the same thing! These people came up with arguments that had nothing to do with my principles, nor with the principles that arise from the laws of nature. There is a work morality, a morality of service that cannot be overturned, because it is a law of nature. Nature says: work! prosperity and happiness can only be achieved through honest toil!

SPOKESMAN: But what people called Fordism, or at least your more popular ideas about society – stable jobs, safe salaries, a certain level of affluence – generated new aspirations in the workers' minds. Were you aware of that, Mr Ford? Out of a shapeless, unstable mass, you helped to create a workforce with something to defend, a workforce with dignity and with an awareness of its own value, and hence a group that demanded security, guarantees, contractual power, the right to decide its own destiny. It was what they call an irreversible process, that your paternalism could no longer either contain or control ...

HENRY FORD: I always look to the future, but in order to simplify things, not complicate them. Yet all those engaged in planning the future, proposing reforms, seem to want nothing better than to complicate things over and over. They're all the same: reformers, theorists, politicians, even presidents: Wilson, Roosevelt ... Again and again I found myself fighting a lone battle against a pointlessly complicated world: politics, finance, wars ...

SPOKESMAN: You're not going to deny that wars brought certain advantages to your business ...

HENRY FORD: Those advantages weren't part of my plans. I've always been a pacifist, no one can ever deny that. I was always against American intervention, in the First World War and in the Second. In 1915 I organized the Peace Ship, I crossed the Atlantic to Norway together with influential people from the Church, the universities and the newspapers to ask the European powers to break off hostilities. They didn't listen to me. Then my own country joined the war too. Even the Ford Company started working for the war. So I announced that I wouldn't touch a cent of the profits on war contracts.

SPOKESMAN: You promised to return those profits to the State, but it doesn't seem you ever did that...

HENRY FORD: After the war I had to face an extremely critical financial situation. The banks...

SPOKESMAN: The banks were always another of your *bêtes noires*...

HENRY FORD: The financial system is another pointless complication which hinders manufacturing rather than helping it. As I see it money should always come after work, as the result of work, not before. As long as I steered clear of the financial markets everything went well: I came through the Crash of 1929 because my shares weren't quoted on the stock exchange. My goal in my work is simplicity...

SPOKESMAN: But you played a very important role in setting up this economic system you say you don't approve of. Don't you think that rather than being inspired by simplicity, your considerations are somewhat simplistic?

HENRY FORD: When it comes to business I always relied on simple American ideas. Wall Street is another world to me... a foreign world... oriental...

SPOKESMAN: Just a minute, Mr Ford... No doubt you have every reason to be annoyed with Wall Street... That's one thing, but to identify the financial world and all your enemies with people of a particular origin, a particular religion... to write anti-Semitic articles in your papers... to collect them in a book... to support that fanatic who was soon to seize power in Germany, these...

HENRY FORD: My ideas were misunderstood ... I had nothing to do with the obscenities that were to happen in Europe ... I was speaking for the good of America and for their good too, these people who are different from us, and who, if they wanted to take part in our community, should have appreciated what the real American principles were ... those principles I am proud to have run my company on.

SPOKESMAN: You achieved an enormous amount in the area of manufacturing, Mr Ford ... And you theorized a great deal too ... But while things always behaved as you forecast and planned, men didn't, there was always something in the human being that escaped you, that fell short of your expectations ... Is that right?

HENRY FORD: My ambition wasn't just to make things. Iron, laminates, steel, they're not enough. Things aren't an end in themselves. What I was thinking of was a model of humanity. I didn't just manufacture goods. I wanted to manufacture men!

SPOKESMAN: Could you explain a bit more clearly what you mean by that, Mr Ford? May I sit down? Could I light a cigarette? Would you like one?

HENRY FORD: Nooooo! You can't smoke here! Cigarettes are a vice and an aberration! Cigarettes are prohibited in Ford factories! I dedicated years of energy to the anti-smoking campaign! Even Edison said I was right!

SPOKESMAN: But Edison smoked!

HENRY FORD: Only cigars. I can forgive a cigar or two. Likewise a pipe. They are part of the American tradition. But not cigarettes! Statistics show that the worst criminals are cigarette smokers. Cigarettes lead straight to the gutter! I published a book against cigarettes!

SPOKESMAN: Don't you think that, as well as cigarettes, you might also have concerned yourself with the effects of rhythms of work on health? Or of the pollution your factories generate? Or of the stench of the exhaust emissions your cars produce!

HENRY FORD: My factories are always clean, well-lit and well-ventilated. And I can demonstrate that when it came to hygiene no one took as much care as I did. But now I'm talking about the moral aspect, the mind. For my plan I needed sober, hard-working, good-living men, with happy family lives, with clean and orderly homes!

SPOKESMAN: Is that why you set up a group of inspectors to enquire into the private lives of your employees? To stick their noses into the love affairs and sex lives of other men and women?

HENRY FORD: An employee who lives in an appropriate way will work in an appropriate way. I chose my personnel on the basis not just of their performance at work, but their morality at home too. And if I preferred to employ married men, good fathers and home-makers rather than libertines, drunkards and gamblers, there were reasons of efficiency for doing so. As far as women are concerned, I am happy to give them factory employment if they have to support their children, but if they have a husband in work then their place is in the home!

SPOKESMAN: Yet your first opponents were the pious puritans who fought against the spread of the motor car because they saw it as a danger to the family! Preachers and moralists thundered against it as something lovers could use to meet far from their parents' watchful eyes; something that encouraged families to gad about on Sundays instead of going to church; something people would mortgage their houses and dig into their sacred savings to buy; they said the car prompted an otherwise thrifty people to desire long trips and vacations; the car generated envy amongst the poor and stirred up revolutions . . .

HENRY FORD: The reactionaries are like the Bolsheviks: they can't see reality, they don't know what people need for the elementary functions of human life. I always acted in line with an idea too, I had my model. But my ideas are always applicable.

SPOKESMAN: Of course, the Bolsheviks . . . What do you think of the fact that right from the beginning Soviet communism took Fordism as its model? Lenin and Stalin admired your organization of production and to a certain extent became disciples of your theories. They too wanted the whole of society to organize itself along the lines of industrial productivity, they too wanted to have their factories and workers operate as in Detroit, they too wanted to produce a disciplined and puritanical workforce ...

HENRY FORD: But they were unable to give their workers what I gave mine. Their austerity, like that of the reactionaries, prolonged shortages; my austerity brought abundance. But I'm not interested in what they did: my idea was an American idea, developed in relation to America, animated by the spirit of pioneers who weren't afraid of hard work and were able to adapt to the new, who were frugal and austere but wanted to enjoy the things of this world ...

SPOKESMAN: But the America of the pioneers is gone. Wiped out by Henry Ford's Detroit ...

HENRY FORD: I come from that old America. My father had a farm, in Michigan. I began to experiment with my inventions on the farm, financed by my father; I wanted to build practical transport vehicles for agriculture. The car was born in the country. I kept my love for the America of my childhood and my parents. As soon as I realized it was disappearing, I started buying and collecting old farm tools, ploughs, millwheels, carriages, buggies, sleds, furniture from the old wooden houses that were going to ruin ...

SPOKESMAN: So, just as ecology originates in the culture that produced pollution, so antique dealing originates from the same culture that imposed the new things that have replaced the old ...

HENRY FORD: I bought a traditional old tavern in Sudbury, Massachusetts, together with its swing sign and veranda ... I even had them rebuild the unsurfaced track the wagon trails used when they headed West ...

SPOKESMAN: Is it true that in order to bring back the atmosphere of the time of horses and stagecoaches around that old tavern, you had the highway diverted, the very highway your Ford cars were roaring along at top speed?

HENRY FORD: There's room for everything in this America of ours, don't you think? The American countryside mustn't be allowed to disappear. I was always opposed to the exodus of farmers from the country. I designed a hydroelectric station on the Tennessee to supply low cost energy to farmers. I would have given them electrical appliances, fertilizers, and they would have stayed away from the city. But neither government nor farmers would hear of it. They never understand simple ideas: there are three elementary functions in human life: farming, manufacturing and transportation. Every problem hangs on the way we grow things, the way we produce things, the way we transport things, and I always proposed the simplest solutions. The farmers' work was pointlessly complicated. Only five per cent of their energy was being spent to good use.

SPOKESMAN: So you don't feel nostalgic for that life?

HENRY FORD: If you think I miss things from the past, then you haven't understood me at all. I don't care one bit about the past! I don't believe in the experience of history! Really, filling people's heads with culture from the past is the most pointless thing you can do.

SPOKESMAN: But the past means experience... In the life of peoples and individuals...

HENRY FORD: Even individual experience serves no other purpose than to perpetuate memories of failures. The 'experts' in the factory only know how to tell you that you can't do this, that that has already been tried but doesn't work... If I had listened to the experts, I would never have achieved any of what I did achieve, I would have been daunted from day one, I would never have managed to put together an internal combustion engine. At the time the experts thought electricity was the solution to everything, that engines should be electric too. They were all fascinated by Edison, rightly so, and so was I. And I went to ask him if he thought I was crazy, as people

251

were saying, because I'd set my stubborn mind to getting an engine rolling that went 'brum brum'. Then, the man himself, Edison, the great Edison, said to me: 'Young man, I'll tell you what I think. I've worked with electricity all my life. Well, electrical cars will never be able to range very far from their supply stations. No good imagining they can carry batteries of accumulators around with them: they're too heavy. And steam cars aren't ideal either: they'll always need a boiler and fire and what it takes to fuel it. But the automobile you've found is self-sufficient: no fire, no boiler, no smoke, no steam; it carries its power house around with it. That's what we were waiting for, young man. You're on the right track! Keep at it, don't lose heart! If you manage to invent a lightweight engine that fuels itself, without the need to charge itself up like a battery, you'll have a great future!'

That's what the great Edison said to me. The king of electricity was the only one who realized that I was doing something electricity could never do. No, being an expert doesn't count, what you've done doesn't count. It's what you can do and what you want to do that counts! The ideas you have for the future!

SPOKESMAN: Today your future is already the past . . . and it conditions the present for everyone . . . Tell me, when you look around today, do you see the future you wanted? I mean the future you saw when you started, when you were a young country boy in Michigan, shutting yourself away in your father's farm shed, trying out different cylinders and pistons and transmission belts and differential gears . . . Tell me, Mr Ford, do you remember what you wanted then?

HENRY FORD: Yes, I wanted lightness, a light engine for a light vehicle, like the small gig I kept trying to fix up with a steam boiler . . . I've always looked for lightness, reducing the waste of materials and effort . . . I spent my days shut up in the garage workshop . . . From outside I caught the smell of hay . . . the whistle of the thrush from the old elm near the pond . . . a

252

butterfly came in through the window, drawn to the glow of the boiler, it beat its wings around it, then the thump of the piston sent it flying away, silent, light . . .

(Images of slow heavy traffic in a big city, of trucks in a jam on the highway, of work at a steel mill press, work at an assembly line, of smoke from smoke stacks, etc., are superimposed over the figure of Henry Ford as he speaks these last lines.)

The Last Channel

My thumb presses down independently of any act of will: moment by moment, but at irregular intervals, I feel the need to push, to press, to set off an impulse sudden as a bullet; if this is what they meant when they granted me partial insanity, they were right. But they are wrong if they imagine there was no plan, no clearly thought-out intention behind what I did. Only now, in the padded and enamelled calm of this small hospital room, can I deny the incongruous behaviour I had to hear attributed to me at the trial, as much by the defence as the prosecution. With this report which I hope to send to the appeal court magistrates, though my defence lawyers are absolutely determined to prevent me, I intend to re-establish the truth, the only truth, my own, if anyone is capable of understanding it.

The doctors are in the dark too, groping about, but at least they were positive about my desire to write something down and gave me this typewriter and this ream of paper: they think this development indicates an improvement due to my being shut up in a room without a television and they attribute the disappearance of the spasm that used to contract my hand to my being deprived of the small object I was holding when I was arrested and that I managed (the convulsions I threatened every time they grabbed it from me were not simulated) to keep with me throughout my detention, interrogation and trial. (How, if not by demonstrating that the *corpus delicti* had become a part of my *corpus*, could I have explained what I had done and – though I didn't manage to convince them – why I had done it?)

The first mistake they made in their diagnosis was to suppose that my attention span is so short that I cannot follow a coherent succession of images for more than a few minutes, that my mind can only capture fragments of stories and arguments without a beginning or an end, in short that the connecting thread that holds the fabric of the world together had snapped in my head. It's not true, and the proof they brought forward to support their thesis – the way I sit motionless in front of the TV for hours and hours without following a programme, obliged as I am by a compulsive tic to switch from one channel to another – can perfectly well be used to demonstrate the contrary. I am convinced that there is a sense in the happenings of this world, that a coherent story, explicable in all its series of cause and effect, is going on somewhere at this very moment, and is not beyond our capacity to verify, and that this story contains the key for judging and understanding everything else. It is this conviction that keeps me nailed to my chair staring at the video with glazed eyes while the frenetic clicks of the remote control conjure up and dismiss interviews with ministers, lovers' embraces, deodorant ads, rock concerts, people arrested hiding their faces, space rocket launches, Wild West gunfights, dancers' pirouettes, boxing matches, quiz shows, Samurai duels. If I don't stop to watch any of these programmes it's because they're not the programme I'm looking for, I know it exists, and I'm sure it's not one of these, and that they only transmit these programmes to deceive and discourage people like myself who are convinced that it's the *other* programme that matters. That's why I keep switching from one channel to another: not because my mind is no longer capable of even the very brief concentration required to follow a film or a dialogue or a horse race. On the contrary: my attention is already entirely projected towards something I absolutely must not miss, something unique that is happening at this very moment while my screen is still cluttered with superfluous and interchangeable images, something that must already have begun so of course I've missed the beginning and if I don't hurry up I risk losing the end as well. My finger leaps across the keys of the remote control discarding husks of empty appearance like the superimposed peelings of a multicoloured onion.

Meanwhile the *real* programme is out there in the ether on a frequency I don't know, perhaps it will be lost in space without my being able to intercept it: there is an unknown station transmitting a story that has to do with me, *my* story, the only story that can explain to me who I am, where I come from and where I'm going. Right now the only relationship I can establish with my story is a negative relationship: that of rejecting other stories, discarding all the deceitful images they offer me. This pushing of buttons is the bridge I am building towards that other bridge that fans out into the void and that my harpoons still haven't been able to hook: two incomplete bridges of electromagnetic impulses that fail to meet and are lost in the dustclouds of a fragmented world.

It was when I realized this that I stopped waving the remote control at the screen and started pointing it out of the window, at the city, its lights, its neon signs, the façades of the skyscrapers, the roof spires, the scaffolding of the cranes with their long iron beaks, the clouds. Then I went out in the streets with the remote control hidden under the flap of my coat, pointing it like a weapon. At the trial they said I hated the city, that I wanted to make it disappear, that I was driven by a destructive impulse. It's not true. I love, I have always loved our city, its two rivers, the occasional small squares transformed by their trees into oases of shade, the harrowing wail of its ambulance sirens, the wind that rakes the Avenues, the crumpled newspapers that flit just above ground like tired hens. I know that our city could be the happiest in the world, I know that it is the happiest, not here on the wavelength where I find myself, but on another frequency, it's there the city I've lived in all my life finally becomes my habitat. That's the channel I was trying to tune into when I pointed the remote control at the sparkling windows of the jewellers', at the stately façades of the banks, at the awnings and rotating doors of the big hotels: prompting my gestures was the desire to save all stories in one story that would be mine too: not the threatening and obsessive malice I have been accused of.

They were all in the dark, lost: police, magistrates, psychiatric experts, lawyers, journalists. 'Conditioned by the compulsive need to keep changing channel, a TV addict goes crazy and tries to change the world with his remote control': that was the outline that served with only very few variations to define my case. But the psychological tests always ruled out the idea that I had a vocation for destruction; even my response to programmes presently transmitted is not far off average levels of acceptance. Maybe by changing channel I wasn't trying to disrupt all the other channels but looking for something that any programme could communicate if only it were not corroded within by the worm that perverts everything that surrounds my existence.

So they thought up another theory, capable of bringing me back to my right mind again, they say; or rather, they claim that I convinced myself of this theory on my own and that this constituted the unconscious brake that stopped me committing the criminal acts they thought me ready to commit. This is the theory according to which for all my changing channels the programme is always the same or might as well be; whether they're transmitting a film or news or ads there is only one message whatever the station since everything and everybody are part of the one system; and likewise outside the screen, the system invades everything leaving space only for apparent changes; so that whether I go wild with my remote control or whether I keep my hands in my pocket makes no difference, because I'll never be able to get out of the system. I don't know whether those who put forward these ideas believe in them or whether they only say them in an attempt to draw me into the discussion; in any event they never had any hold on me because they cannot shake my conviction as to the essence of things. As I see it what counts in the world are not likenesses but differences: differences that may be big or then again small, or minute, perhaps even imperceptible, but what matters is precisely to tease them out and compare them. I know myself that in going from channel to channel you get the impression that it's all the same old story; and likewise I know that life is governed by necessities that prevent it from varying more than a certain amount: but it is in that small difference that the secret lies, the spark that sets in motion the machine of consequences, as a result of which the differences become considerable, large, huge, even infinite. I look at the things around me, all awry, and I think how the tiniest trifle would have been enough – a mistake not made at a certain moment, a yes instead of a no – to have generated entirely different consequences, albeit leaving the general shape of circumstances intact. Things so simple and natural that I was always expecting them to reveal themselves at any moment: thinking this and pressing the buttons on the remote control was one and the same thing.

With Volumnia I thought I'd finally hit on the right channel. Indeed in the early days of our relationship, I gave the remote control a rest. I liked everything about her, the tobacco-coloured *chignon* hairstyle, the almost contralto voice, the knickerbockers and pointed boots, our shared passion for bulldogs and cactuses. Equally congenial, I felt, were her parents, the places where they had invested in real estate and where we spent invigorating vacations, and the insurance company in which Volumnia's father had promised me a creative job with profit-sharing after we were married. All doubts, objections, and conjectures that did not converge in the desired direction I sought to banish from my mind, but when I saw how they kept coming back more and more insistently, I began to wonder whether the small cracks, the misunderstandings, the embarrassments that had so far seemed no more than momentary and marginal eclipses might not be interpreted as ill omens for our future prospects, that is that our happiness might contain within it that sense of contrivance and tedium you find in a bad TV serial. Yet I never lost my conviction that Volumnia and I were made for each other: perhaps on another channel a couple identical to ourselves but to whom destiny had granted just slightly different gifts were about to embark on a life a hundred times more attractive than ours...

It was in this spirit that I lifted my arm that morning, gripped the remote control and pointed it towards the corbeille of white camellias, towards Volumnia's mother's bonnet with its little blue bunches of grapes, the pearl on the father's plastron cravat, the priest's stole, the bride's silver-embroidered veil... This gesture, just when the whole congregation was expecting my 'yes', was misunderstood: most of all by Volumnia who saw it as a rejection, an irreparable offence. But all I meant to say was that there, on that other channel, mine and Volumnia's story was unfolding far away from the jubilant sounds of the organ and the flashlights of the photographers, yet had many things about it that made it more consonant with my truth and hers...

Perhaps on that channel beyond all channels we didn't break up. Volumnia goes on loving me there, while here, in the world I live in I haven't been able to get her to understand my motives: she doesn't want to see me any more. I never recovered from that violent break; it was then I began the life described in the papers as that of a maniac of no fixed abode, wandering through the city armed with his incongruous gadget... And yet my reasoning was clear as never before: I had realized that I must begin to work from the top down: if things were going wrong on all channels, there must be a last channel unlike the others where the leaders, perhaps not so different from these here, but with some small variation in character, in mentality, in matters of conscience, were able to stop the cracks that open in the foundations, the reciprocal distrust, the degeneration of human relationships...

But the police had had their eye on me for some time. When I shoved my way through the people crowding round to see the Heads of State getting out of their cars for the summit, then sneaked into the building through the French windows amidst a swarm of security men, I didn't even manage to lift my arm and point the remote control before they were all on top of me dragging me away, despite my protests that I didn't intend to stop the ceremony, only wanted to see what they were showing on the other channel, for curiosity's sake, just for a few seconds.

Implosion

'Over the last few years, quasars, Seyfert galaxies, B.L. Lacertae objects, or, more generally, active galactic nuclei have been attracting the attention of astronomers because of the huge quantities of energy these bodies emit, at velocities of up to 10,000 kilometres per second. There are good reasons for supposing that the central driving force of the galaxy is a black hole of enormous mass' (L'Astronomia, *no. 36*). *'Active galactic nuclei may be fragments left unexploded by the Big Bang and engaged in a process exactly opposite to that which takes place in black holes, a process, that is, of explosive expansion involving the liberation of enormous quantities of energy ("white holes"). They could be explained as the exit extremities of a connecting link between two points in space-time (Einstein-Rosen's bridges), expelling material devoured by a black hole situated at the entrance extremity. According to this theory, a Seyfert galaxy a hundred million light years away may now be expelling gas sucked in by another part of the universe ten billion years ago. And it is even possible that a quasar ten billion light years away may have assumed the form we see today by taking in material that reaches it from some point in the future, travelling through a black hole which, as far as we are concerned, formed only today'* (Paolo Maffeir, Monsters of the Sky, *pp. 210–15*).

To explode or to implode – *said Qfwfq* – that is the question: whether 'tis nobler in the mind to expand one's energies in space without restraint, or to crush them into a dense inner concentration and, by ingesting, cherish them. To steal away, to vanish; no more; to hold within oneself every gleam, every ray, deny oneself every vent, suffocating in the depths of the soul the conflicts that so idly trouble it, give them their quietus; to hide oneself, to obliterate oneself: perchance to reawaken elsewhere, changed.

Changed . . . In what way changed? And the question, to explode or to implode: would one have to face it again? Absorbed by the vortex of this galaxy, does one pop up again in other times and other firmaments? Here sink away in cold silence, there express oneself in fiery shrieks of another tongue? Here soak up good and evil like a sponge in the shadow, there gush forth like a dazzling jet, to spray and spend and lose oneself. To what end then would the cycle repeat itself? I really don't know, I don't want to know, I don't want to think about it: here, now, my choice is made: I shall implode, as if this centripetal plunge might forever save me from doubt and error, from the time of ephemeral change, from the slippery descent of before and after, bring me to a time of stability, still and smooth, enable me to achieve the one condition that is homogeneous and compact and definitive. You explode, if that's more to your taste, shoot yourselves all around in endless darts, be prodigal, spendthrift, reckless: I shall implode, collapse inside the abyss of myself, towards my buried centre, infinitely.

How long has it been since none of you has been able to imagine the life force except in terms of explosion? You have your reasons, I know. Your model is that of a universe born from a madcap explosion whose first splinters still hurtle unchecked and incandescent at the edge of space, your emblem is the exuberant kindling of supernovae flaunting the insolent youth of stars overloaded with energy; your favourite metaphor is the volcano, to show that even a mature and settled planet is always ready to break its bonds and burst forth. And the furnaces that flare in the farthest bounds of the heavens confirm your cult of universal conflagration; gases and particles almost as swift as light hurl themselves from vortex to centre of spiral galaxies, burst out into the lobes of elliptic galaxies, proclaim that the Big Bang still lives, the great Pan is not dead. No, I'm not deaf to your reasons; I could even join you. Go on! Explode! Burst! Let the new world begin again, repeat its ever renewed beginnings in a thunder of cannonfire, as in Napoleon's times ...Wasn't it that age, by the way, with its elation at the revolutionary might of artillery fire that made us think of the explosion not just as harmful to people and property, but as a sign of birth, of genesis? Isn't it since then that passions, poetry and the ego have been seen as perpetual explosions? But if that's true, then so is its opposite; ever since that August when the mushroom rose over cities reduced to a layer of ash, an age was born in which the explosion is symbol only of absolute negation. But that was something we already knew anyway, from the moment when, rising above the calendar of terrestrial chronicle, we enquired of the destiny of the universe, and the oracles of thermodynamics answered us; every existing form will break up in a blaze of heat; there is no entity can escape the irretrievable disorder of the corpuscles; time is a catastrophe, perpetual and irreversible.

Only a few old stars know how to get out of time; they are the open door to jump from a train headed for annihilation. At the limit of their decrepitude, shrunk to the size of red dwarfs or white dwarfs, panting out the last glimmering gasp of the pulsar, compressed into neutron stars, here they are at last, light lost to the waste of the firmament, no more than the dark deletion of themselves, ready for the unstoppable collapse when everything, even light itself, falls inwards never to emerge again.

Praise be to the stars that implode. A new freedom opens up within them: annulled from space, exonerated from time, existing, at last, for themselves alone and no longer in relation to all the rest, perhaps only they can be sure they really exist. 'Black holes' is a derogatory nickname, dictated by envy: they are quite the opposite of holes, nothing could be fuller and heavier and denser and more compact, with a stubbornness to the way they sustain the gravity they bear within, as if clenching their fists, gritting their teeth, hunching their backs. Only on these terms can one save oneself from dissolving in overreaching extension, in Catherine wheels of effusion, exclamatory extroversion, effervescence and ebullition. Only in this way can one break through to a space-time where the implicit and the unexpressed don't lose their energy, where the pregnancy of meanings is not diluted, where discretion and keeping distance multiply the effectiveness of every action.

Don't distract yourselves fantasizing over the reckless behaviour of hypothetical quasi-stellar objects at the uncertain boundaries of the universe: it is here that you must turn your attention, to the centre of our galaxy, where all our calculations and instruments indicate the presence of a body of enormous mass that nevertheless remains invisible. Webs of radiation and gas, caught there perhaps since the time of the last implosions, show that there in the middle lies one of these so-called holes, spent as an old volcano. All that surrounds it, the wheel of planetary systems and constellations and the branches of the Milky Way, everything in our galaxy rests on the hub of this implosion sunk away into itself. That is my pole, my mirror, my secret home. It need fear no comparison with the farthest galaxies and their apparently explosive nuclei: there too what counts is what cannot be seen. Nothing comes out of there any more either, believe me: those impossibly fast flashes and whirls are just fuel to be crushed in the centripetal mortar, assimilated into the other mode of being, my own.

Sometimes, of course, I do seem to hear a voice from the farthest galaxies: 'It's me, Qfwfq, I am yourself exploding as you implode: I'm splashing out, expressing myself, spreading myself about, communicating, realizing all the potential I have, I really exist, not like you, introverted, reticent, egocentric, fused in an immutable self . . .'

Then I'm overwhelmed by the fear that even beyond the barrier of gravitational collapse time continues to flow: a different time, with no relation to the time left on this side, but speeding similarly headlong on a road with no return. In that case the implosion I've leapt into would be just a lull I've been granted, a respite before the fate I cannot escape.

Something like a dream, or a memory, goes through my mind: Qfwfq is fleeing the catastrophe of time, he finds an escape route through which to elude his destiny, he rushes through the gap, he is sure he has reached safety, from a chink in his refuge he watches how the events he has escaped gather pace, pities, from a distance, those who are overwhelmed, until, yes, he seems to recognize one of them, yes, it's Qfwfq, it's Qfwfq who beneath Qfwfq's very eyes is experiencing that same catastrophe of before or after, Qfwfq who in the moment he perishes sees Qfwfq save himself, but without saving him. 'Qfwfq, save yourself!' cries Qfwfq, but is it the imploding Qfwfq who wants to save the exploding Qfwfq or vice versa? No Qfwfq can save any exploding Qfwfqs from the conflagration, as they in turn can't pull back the other Qfwfqs from their unstoppable implosion. Any way time runs it leads to disaster whether in one direction or its opposite and the intersecting of those directions does not form a network of rails governed by points and exits, but a tangle, a knot . . .

I know I mustn't listen to voices, nor give credit to visions or nightmares. I go on digging my hole, in my mole's burrow.

Nothing and Not Much

Calculations made by the physicist Alan Guth of the Stanford Linear Accelerator Center suggest that the universe was created literally from nothing in an extremely short space of time: a second divided by a billion billion billions. (*from the* Washington Post, *3 June 1984*)

If I tell you I remember it – *began Qfwfq* – you will object that in nothingness, nothing can remember anything, nor be remembered by anything, which is one reason why you won't be able to believe so much as a word of what I am about to tell you. Tough arguments to knock down, I admit. All I can tell you is that, the moment there was something, there being nothing else, that something was the universe, and since it hadn't been there before, there was a before when it wasn't and an afterwards when it was, from that moment on, I'm saying, time began, and with time memory, and with memory someone who remembered, that is to say myself, or that something that later I would understand was myself. Let's get this straight: it's not that I remembered how I was when there was nothing, because there was no time then, and there was no me; but I realized now that, even if I didn't know I was there, still I had a place I could have been, I mean the universe; whereas before, even had I wanted to, I wouldn't have known where to put myself, and that's a pretty big difference, and it was precisely this difference between the before and the after that I remembered. In short, you must recognize that my reasoning is logical too, and what's more doesn't err on the side of the simplistic like your own.

So let me explain. One can't even say for sure that what there was then, really was: the particles, or rather the ingredients with which the particles would later be made, existed in the virtual sense: that kind of existence where if you're there you're there, and if you're not there you can begin to count on being there and then see what happens. We felt this was a fine thing, and indeed it was, because it's only if you begin to exist in the virtual sense, to fluctuate in a field of probability, to borrow and return charges of energy still entirely hypothetical, that sooner or later you may find yourself existing in reality, wrapping around yourself, that is, a scrap, be it ever so small, of space-time, as happened to an ever increasing number of I-don't-know-whats – let's call them neutrinos because it's a nice name, though at the time no one had ever even dreamed of them – bobbing one on top of another in a torrid soup of infinite heat, thick as a glue of infinite density, that swelled up in a time so infinitely brief that it had nothing to do with time at all – since of course time hadn't yet had the time to show what it would later become – and as it swelled it produced space where no one had ever known what space was. Thus the universe, from being an infinitesimal pimple in the smoothness of nothing expanded in a flash to the size of a proton, then an atom, then a pinpoint, then a pinhead, then a teaspoon, then a hat, then an umbrella...

No, I'm going too fast; or too slow, I don't know: because this expansion of the universe was infinitely fast yet started out from a beginning so deeply buried in nothing that to push its way out and peep over the threshold of space and time required a wrench of such violence as not to be measurable in terms of space and time. Let's say that to tell everything that happened in the first second of the history of the universe, I should have to put together an account so long that the whole subsequent duration of the universe with its millions of centuries past and future would not be enough; whereas everything that came afterwards I could polish off in five minutes.

Naturally enough our belonging to a universe without precedent or terms of comparison very soon became a cause of pride, boasting, infatuation. The split-second yawning of unimaginable distances, the profusion of corpuscles squirting all over the place – hadrons, baryons, mesons, a quark or two – the reckless speed of time, taken all together these things gave us a sense of invincibility, of power, of pride, and at the same time of conceit, as if all this was no more than our due. The only comparison we could draw was with the nothing that had come before: and we put the thought behind us, as of something petty and wretched, deserving only of commiseration, or scorn. Every thought we had embraced the whole, disdained the parts; the whole was our element, and it included time too, all time, the future holding thrall over the past in terms both of quantity and fullness. Our destiny lay in more, more and more, and we couldn't think, even fleetingly, of less: from now on we would go from more to even more, from additions to multiplications to exponentials, without ever slowing down or stopping.

That there was an underlying insecurity in this excitement, a craving almost to cancel out the shadow of our so recent origins, is something I have perhaps only recently come to appreciate, in the light of all I have learnt since; unless it was already secretly gnawing away inside me even then. For despite our certainty that the whole was our natural habitat, it was nevertheless true that we had come from nothing, that we had only just raised ourselves up from absolute deprivation, that only a fragile sliver of space-time lay between ourselves and our previous condition of being without substance, extension or duration. I would be seized by fleeting but intense sensations of precariousness, as if this whole that was struggling to develop were unable to hide its intrinsic fragility, the underlying emptiness to which we might well return with the same speed with which we had emerged. Hence my impatience with the universe's indecisiveness in taking on a form, as if I couldn't wait for that vertiginous expansion to stop, so I could discover its limits, for better or worse, but mainly

267

so that its existence should stabilize; and hence too my fear, a fear I could not stifle, that as soon as the expansion let up the contraction phase would begin at once with an equally precipitate return to non-being.

I reacted by leaping to the other extreme: 'Completeness! completeness!' I proclaimed far and wide, 'The future!' I cheered, 'I want immensity!' I insisted, shoving my way through that confused mill of forces, 'Let potential be potent!' I incited, 'Let the act act! Let probabilities be proven!' I already felt that the barrages of particles (or were they only radiations?) included every possible form and force, and the more I looked forward to being surrounded by a universe populated with active presences, the more I felt that those presences were affected by a criminal inertia, an abnegatory abulia.

Some of these presences were, well, let's say they were feminine, I mean they had propulsive charges complementary to my own; one in particular attracted my attention: haughty and reserved, she would establish a field of languid, long-limbed forces around her. To get her to notice me, I redoubled my exhibitions of excitement at the prodigality of the universe, flaunted a nonchalant ease in drawing on cosmic resources, as if they'd always been available to me, and thrust ahead in space and time as though always expecting things to improve. Convinced that Nugkta (I call her by the name I would learn later on) was different from all the others, in the sense of more aware of what it meant to *be*, and to participate in something that *is*, I tried by every means available to distinguish myself from the hesitant mass of those who were slow to get used to this idea. The result was that I made myself tiresome and unpleasant to everybody, without this bringing me any closer to her.

I was getting everything wrong. It didn't take me long to realize that Nugkta didn't appreciate my extravagant efforts at all, on the contrary she took care not to give me any sign of attention, apart from the occasional snort of annoyance. She went on keeping herself to herself, somewhat listlessly, as though crouched with her chin on her knees, protruding elbows hugging long folded legs (don't misunderstand me: I describe the position she would have assumed if one could have spoken then of knees, legs and elbows; or better still, it was the universe that was crouched over itself, and for those in it there was no other position to assume, just that some, for example Nugkta, did it more naturally). Lavishly, I scattered the treasures of the universe at her feet, but the way she accepted them it was as if to say: 'Is that all?' At first, I thought this indifference was affectation, then I realized she wanted to teach me something, to suggest I assume a more controlled attitude. My wild enthusiasm must have made her think me ingenuous, mindless, a greenhorn.

There was nothing for it but to change my attitude, behaviour, style. My relationship with the universe should be the practical, factual approach of one capable of assessing the objective value of the evolution of any given thing, however immense, without letting it go to his head. That was how I hoped to come across to her, more convincing, promising, trustworthy. Did I succeed? Not a bit of it. The more I banked on solidity, on what was feasible, quantifiable, the more I felt I was coming across as a braggart, a con man.

In the end I began to see the light: there was only one thing worthy of admiration as she saw it, only one value, and that was nothingness. It wasn't that she had a low opinion of me, but of the universe. Everything in existence carried some original defect within itself: being, to her mind, was a depressing, vulgar degeneration of non-being.

To say that this discovery upset me would be an understatement: it was an affront to all my beliefs, my craving for completeness, my immense expectations. What greater incompatibility could there be than between myself and someone with a nostalgia for nothingness? Not that she was without her reasons (my weakness for her was such that I struggled to understand them): it was true that there was an absoluteness about the void, a rigour, a presence such as to make everything that claimed

269

to have the requisites for existence seem approximate, limited, shaky; if one starts to draw comparisons between what is and what is not, it is the poorer qualities of the former that strike you, the impurities, the flaws; in short, you can only really feel safe with nothingness. That said, how should I react? Turn my back on the whole, plunge into the void again? It was hardly possible! Once set in motion, the process by which non-being was becoming being couldn't be stopped: the void belonged to a past that was irremediably over now.

One of the many advantages of being was that it allowed us, from the climax of our achieved fullness, to indulge in a moment's regret for the nothingness we had lost, a moment's melancholy contemplation of the negative fullness of the void. In that sense I could go along with Nugkta's inclinations, indeed no one would be more capable than myself of expressing this feeling of yearning with conviction. No sooner thought than done: I rushed towards Nugkta crying: 'Oh, if only we could lose ourselves in the boundless spaces of the void...' (That is, I did something somehow equivalent to crying something of the like.) And how did she react? By turning away in disgust. It took me a while to realize how crude I had been and to learn that one speaks of the void (or better still doesn't speak) with a great deal more discretion.

From then on it was one long series of crises which kept me in a state of constant agitation. How could I have been so mistaken as to seek the completeness of fullness in preference to the perfection of the void? True, the passage from non-being to being had been a considerable novelty, a sensational development, a discovery guaranteed to impress. But one could hardly claim that things had changed for the better. From a state of clarity, faultless, without stain, one had gone to a bungled, cluttered construction crumbling away on every side, held together by pure luck. How could I have been so excited by the so-called marvels of the universe? The scarcity of available materials had in many cases led to monotonous repetitive states, or again in many others to a scatter of untidy, inconsistent improvisations few of which would lead to anything at all. Perhaps it had been a false start: the veneer of what tried to pass itself off as a universe would soon fall away like a mask, and nothingness, the only true completeness possible, would once again impose its invincible absolute.

So began a time when it was only in the chinks of emptiness, the absences, the silences, the gaps, the missing connections, the flaws in time's fabric, that I could find meaning and value. Through those chinks I would sneak glances at the great realm of non-being, recognizing it now as my only true home, a home I regretted having betrayed in a temporary clouding of consciousness, a home Nugkta had brought me to rediscover. Yes, to rediscover: for together with her, my inspiration, I would slither into these narrow passages of nothingness that crossed the compactness of the universe; together we would achieve the obliteration of every dimension, of all time, all substance, all form.

By now the understanding between myself and Nugkta should at last have been clear. What could come between us? Yet every now and then unexpected differences would emerge: it seemed I had become more severe with the world of existence than she; I was amazed to discover in her an attitude of indulgence, complicity I might almost say, with the efforts that dusty vortex was making to keep itself together. (Already there were well-formed electromagnetic fields, nuclei, the first atoms.)

Here it must be said that so long as one considered the universe as the complete expression of total fullness, it could inspire nothing but banality and rhetoric, but if one thought of it as something made from very little, a poor thing scratched together on the edge of nothingness, it excited sympathy and encouragement, or at least a benevolent curiosity as to whatever might come of it. To my surprise I found Nugkta willing to support it, to assist it, this mean, poverty-stricken, sickly universe. Whereas I was tough: 'Give me the void! All glory and honour to nothingness!' I insisted, concerned that this weakness of

271

Nugkta's might distract us from our goal. And how did Nugkta reply? With her usual mocking snorts, exactly as she had at the time of my excessive enthusiasm for the glories of the universe.

Slow as I am, only later would I come to appreciate that once again she was right. The only contact we could have with the void was through this little the void had produced as quintessence of its own emptiness; the only image we had of the void was our own poor universe. All the void we would ever know was there, in the relativity of what is, for even the void had been no more than a relative void, a void secretly shot through with veins and temptations to be something, given that in a moment of crisis at its own nothingness it had been able to give rise to the universe.

Today, after time has churned its way through billions of minutes, billions of years, and the universe is unrecognizable from what it was in those first instants, since space suddenly became transparent so that the galaxies wrap the night in their blazing spirals, and along the orbits of the solar systems millions of worlds bring forth their Himalayas and their oceans according to the cosmic seasons, and the continents throng with masses whether jubilant or suffering or slaughtering each other, turn and turn about with meticulous obstinacy, and empires rise and fall in their marble, porphyry and concrete capitals, and the markets overflow with quartered cattle and frozen peas and displays of brocade and tulle and nylon, and transistors and computers and every kind of gadget pulsate, and everybody in every galaxy is busy observing and measuring everything, from the infinitely small to the infinitely large, there's a secret that only Nugkta and I know: that everything space and time contains is no more than that little that was generated from nothingness, the little that is and that might very well not be, or be even smaller, even more meagre and perishable. And if we prefer not to speak of it, whether for good or for ill, it is because the only thing we could say is this: poor, frail universe, born of nothing, all we are and do resembles you.

272

Editor's Note

The pieces brought together in this volume originally appeared in the publications listed below. Where both manuscript and printed copy are available, preference has been given to the manuscript version.

Fables and Stories 1943–1958

'The Man Who Shouted Teresa', manuscript dated 12 April 1943.

'The Flash', manuscript dated 25 April 1943.

'Making Do', manuscript dated 17 May 1943; published in *La Repubblica*, 17 September 1986.

'Dry River', manuscript dated October 1943.

'Conscience', manuscript dated 1 December 1943.

'Solidarity', manuscript dated 3 December 1943.

'The Black Sheep', manuscript dated 30 July 1944.

'Good for Nothing', 1945–6, original manuscript title; planned as a novel and adapted into a short story. It was published under the title 'What Noah Wasn't Like' in a small review as yet unidentified since we have only the pages with this story.

'Like a Flight of Ducks', *Il Settimanale*, II, 18, 3 May 1947.

'Love Far from Home', proofs with corrections in the author's hand, 1946.

'Wind in a City', proofs with corrections in the author's hand, 1946.

'The Lost Regiment', *L'Unità*, 15 July 1951, definitive version in the collection, *Fourteen Stories*, Mondadori, Milan 1971.

'Enemy Eyes' (manuscript title); *L'Unità*, 2 February 1952, under the title 'The Enemy's Eyes'.

'A General in the Library' (manuscript title); *L'Unità*, 30 October 1953, under the title 'The General in the Library'.

'The Workshop Hen', *I Racconti*, Einaudi, 1954.

'Numbers in the Dark', *I Racconti*, Einaudi, 1958.

'The Queen's Necklace', published under the title 'Fragment of a Novel' in *Everybody's Days*, Edindustria editoriale S.p.A., 1960. The author's note states: 'The following pages are taken from a novel I worked on between 1952 and 1954 but never finished. Through the picaresque adventures of a lost pearl necklace the novel was meant to offer a satire of various levels of society in an industrial city during the years of post-war tension.'

'Becalmed in the Antilles', *Città aperta*, I, 4–5, 25 July 1957; the author's note of 1979 was written in response to a request from Felice Froio.

'The Tribe with Its Eyes on the Sky', manuscript with a signed note by the author, as follows: 'October 1957 – after the Soviet missile, before the satellite. For *Città aperta*, but not published.'

'Nocturnal Soliloquy of a Scottish Nobleman', *L'Espresso*, 25 May 1958; the editor's note accompanying the publication claims, doubtless after consultation with the author: 'In this fable the writer Italo Calvino expresses his assessment of the Italian situation on the eve of the elections. It's a story *à clef*, where the

MacDickinsons, or Episcopalians, represent the Christian Democrats; the MacConnollys or Methodists, the Communists, and the MacFergusons, or Presbyterians, the non-aligned centre parties. The Scottish nobleman is one of the latter.' The text here published is taken from Calvino's typescript with corrections in the author's hand.

'A Beautiful March Day', *Città aperta*, II, 9–10, June–July 1958.

Tales and Dialogues 1968–1984

'World Memory', Club degli Editori, Milan, 1968.

'Beheading the Heads', *Il Caffè*, XIV, 4, 4 August 1969; the author's note says: 'The following pages are sketches for chapters of a book I have been planning for some time, a book that aims to offer a new model for society with a political system based on the ritual execution of the entire governing class at regular intervals. I still haven't decided what shape the book will have. Each of the chapters here presented could be the opening of a different book; hence the numbers given do not indicate any particular order or progression.'

'The Burning of the Abominable House', *Playboy*, Italian edition, 1973.

'The Petrol Pump' (manuscript title); *Corriere della Sera*, 21 December 1974, under the title 'La forza delle cose' (The Force of Circumstances).

'Neanderthal Man', in the collection, *Impossible Interviews*, Bompiani, Milan 1975.

'Montezuma', in the collection, *Impossible Interviews*, Bompiani, Milan 1975.

'Before You Say "Hello" ', *Corriere della Sera*, 27 July 1975.

'Glaciation', text written in response to a request from the Japanese liquor producer, Suntori, first published in Japanese, then in *Corriere della Sera*, 18 November 1975.

'The Call of the Water', written as introduction to *Aqueducts Past and Present*, by Vittorio Gobbi and Sergio Torresella, published by Montubi, Milan, 1976.

'The Mirror, the Target' (manuscript title); *Corriere della Sera*, 14 December 1978, under the title 'There's a Woman behind the Target'.

'The Other Eurydice', September–October 1980.

'The Memoirs of Casanova', stories written to accompany a collection of etchings by Massimo Campigli published by Salomon and Torrini, 1981. The author's note, in the third person, states: 'After *Invisible Cities*, a catalogue of imaginary cities visited by a resurrected Marco Polo, Italo Calvino begins another series of short stories attributed once again to a famous Venetian, in this case Giacomo Casanova. Like the previous book, this too is a "catalogue", but this time of "amours".' Published in *La Repubblica*, 15–16 August 1982.

'Henry Ford', typescript with corrections in the author's hand, dated 30 September 1982. Television screenplay, never produced.

'The Last Channel', *La Repubblica*, 31 January 1984.

'Implosion', 13 August 1984.

'Nothing and Not Much', *Washington Post*, 3 June 1985.

ABOUT THE AUTHOR

ITALO CALVINO (1923-85) was born in Cuba and grew up in San Remo, Italy. He was a member of the partisan movement during the German occupation of northern Italy in World War II. The novel that resulted from that experience, published in English as *The Path to the Nest of Spiders*, won widespread acclaim. His other works of fiction include *The Baron in the Trees, The Castle of Crossed Destinies, Cosmicomics, Difficult Loves, If on a Winter's Night a Traveler, Invisible Cities, Marcovaldo, Mr. Palomar, The Nonexistent Knight & the Cloven Viscount, t zero, Under the Jaguar Sun,* and *The Watcher and Other Stories*. His works of nonfiction include *Six Memos for the Next Millennium* and *The Uses of Literature,* collections of literary essays, and the anthology *Italian Folktales*.